Sick of living in her parent's basement and encountering her ex-girlfriend on a regular basis, former graduate student Veronica Fletcher signs on to manage the stable for Rowan House, Skye's most exclusive resort for women. After arriving at Rowan house Veronica's vow to remain celibate is tested when she meets Millie Reid.

Sexy, sweet, and funny, Millie is the woman of Veronica's dreams. Or is she? When Millie's past threatens their future together, Veronica is faced with a choice she doesn't want to make. The butterfly effect has never been more personal.

COMPLEX

DIMENSIONS

Brenda Murphy

A NineStar Press Publication

Published by NineStar Press
P.O. Box 91792,
Albuquerque, New Mexico, 87199 USA.
www.ninestarpress.com

Complex Dimensions

Printed in the USA
First Edition
September, 2019

Print ISBN: 978-1-951057-47-3

Also available in eBook, ISBN: 978-1-951057-44-2

Warning: This book contains sexually explicit content, which may only be suitable for mature readers, a deceased family member, references to incarceration, racist language, references to past domestic abuse and murder.

To C, Always.

To Allison and Stuart, I miss you both so much. This book was the last one I wrote at Templeton's and it will always remind me of your delightful company and delicious oaty biscuits.

To Dana, for your wonderful assistance with this story. From our first chat through the sticky middle to the final draft you were there. Thank you for everything.

Chapter One

VERONICA FOLLOWED HER mom through the grocery, navigating the phalanx of Saturday afternoon shoppers. Her thoughts wandered as she trailed behind her mother as she maneuvered their overloaded cart around people staring at the overcrowded shelves, children straying from their parents, and the occasional mobility scooter.

"Ronnie, would you go back and pick up another can of tomato paste? I need two for my sauce. I'm so out of step since they rearranged the store. I don't understand why..."

Not ready to listen to her mom go on about the changes in the store layout for what must be the hundredth time since she had been released, Veronica interrupted her. "Relax, Mom, I got it."

She turned and jogged back two aisles and caught sight of a familiar face. Dee stood at the far end of the aisle, her arm draped around the shoulders of Veronica's ex-friend, Paige. A toddler, her round face and dark brown eyes so much like Dee's she could have been a clone, sat in the basket of the cart in front of them. Paige pressed a kiss to Dee's cheek.

Say hello. Don't act invisible. Get over yourself. So, she's here with Paige and their baby. Should be me. Should have been us. She looked away and gathered herself. *Say something. Be a grown-up. Congratulate them. She looks happy.*

Veronica walked down the aisle toward the women, working hard to keep a smile plastered on her face. She lifted her hand in greeting. Dee glanced up and made brief eye contact before a frown crossed her face. She turned her head away from Veronica. Paige looked past Dee and shot Veronica a challenging glare before she pushed their shopping cart briskly away. *Fuck. No mistaking the message. She's moved on. Let it go.* She stopped and shoved her hands in her pockets to keep from balling them into fists. She turned away, walked to the main aisle, and followed the overhead labels until she reached the canned vegetable aisle.

She stood in the center of the aisle and groaned inwardly as she studied the shelves. *Why do they need twelve different kinds of paste? Damn it. Where the hell is the Bella tomato paste? Mom will flip if it's not the right brand.*

A short woman dressed in a bright red T-shirt and jeans stepped up on the bottom shelf of the section. She extended her arm, her fingers straining shy of the can of tomato sauce she was trying to reach.

Veronica stepped closer. "Hey, let me..." The shelf rocked and teetered. The sharp sound of metal scraping made the hairs on Veronica's arm stand up as the shelf tilted toward the woman.

"Watch out!" Veronica grabbed the woman around the waist and tugged her out of the way as the entire section of heavy metal shelving crashed to the floor. Cans of vegetables slid off the shelves and filled the aisle. A dented can of stewed tomatoes rolled past her shoe as cans continued to randomly slide from the twisted metal shelves.

"Are you okay?" Veronica let go of the woman's waist. Other shoppers crowded around them, drawn by the noise.

A store employee arrived. Red faced and wheezing, he pointed to the avalanche of cans. "Is anyone under there?"

"No. I don't think so." Veronica leaned away from the stale smell of cigarettes and sweat wafting from the employee.

The woman stared at Veronica, her eyes wide. "You...I would have been under there. I would have..." Her cheeks grew pink. "Thank you." She ducked her head, pushed through the crowd, and fled.

More store employees showed up and blocked the aisle with warning signs and yellow tape. The crowd filtered away. Veronica stepped back from the chaos.

The dull edge of the can she was still holding dug into her palm. *What if my mom hadn't needed another can of tomato paste? What if Dee had wanted to chat? What if I hadn't noticed the shelf shift? We both would've been under there. A minute. A second. So much can change in a moment. Butterfly effect. Chaos Theory on display.*

"Ronnie?" Her mother's hand squeezed her arm. She turned and stared down the aisle, her lips pressed together in a thin line. "Good Lord, look at that. You'd have been crushed."

Veronica held up the can in her hand and grinned at her mom. "Got the tomato paste."

Her mother quirked her mouth, "All right, joker, let's get the rest of the groceries before anything else falls down."

THE OFFICE WAS cool after the heat of late April in Richmond. The traffic on Broad Street was muffled by floor to ceiling navy-blue curtains. The desk was barren except for a black leather blotter and a single hunter-green file folder precisely centered in the middle of the desktop.

"I appreciate this opportunity, Miss Pomroy." Veronica studied the woman sitting behind the large dark mahogany desk.

She had broad shoulders set off by a sharply tailored suit, and long black hair framed her face. Her dark eyes were arresting. The small scar splitting her lip added to the air of menace surrounding her. Veronica shifted forward in her seat and squared her shoulders.

Ms. Pomroy's eyes fixed on Veronica's face, her gaze somewhere between predatory and appraising.

"Call me Jaya, and my partner wouldn't have referred you if she didn't think you would be a good fit."

"Doctor Kerr's letters were my lifeline the past six years, ma'am." Veronica swallowed on a dry throat. "I don't think I'd have survived without them."

"Sarah believes in you." Jaya cocked her head, and her expression gentled. "Are you sure you don't want an opportunity to finish your dissertation?"

"No. It's been so long, I'd have to design a new project. I'm finished with that part of my life."

"My offer stands to investigate the matter for you."

Veronica chewed her lip. "I can't afford your fees. I'm in debt to my parents as it is." She tucked her hands under her thighs to keep from balling them into fists. "Even if I found out who set me up, what good would it do? That's behind me now."

"I'm sure we could work out some financial arrangement for my fees, if you change your mind." Jaya leaned forward in her seat. "I understand about revenge. And the need to move on."

Veronica sighed. "I'm grateful for your offer. And for everything Doctor Kerr did for me trying to get my fellowship reinstated, but I need this job. I can't go back to the university." *Not when everyone thinks I'm a criminal. Or looks at me with pity. Or wants to talk to me like I've been on vacation instead of in prison. Fuck.* "I want to pay my parents back. They paid my lawyer's fees. Not that it did any good."

"I understand." Jaya tapped the dark green folder centered on the blotter. "Your supervisor from the prison equestrian program was more than complimentary of your skills. And other than the time you spent incarcerated your record is spotless. Not even a speeding ticket." She sat back in her chair and rested her hands on the desk, spreading her fingers wide. Her gaze pinned Veronica in place. "You know what Rowan House is? You're clear?"

Veronica smiled. "Yes. And I'm clear I am not expected to, um"—she flushed—"participate? I mean, unless I want to?"

Jaya raised an eyebrow. "You are expected to run the stable, and care for the horses. Anything else that transpires will be between you and your employers. My role is to evaluate your credentials, perform your background check, and pre-employment screening. Have you read the contract?"

Veronica took a deep breath. "Yes. I'm ready to sign." *As ready as I'll ever be. Don't chicken out now. After six years in prison how bad could it be?*

Jaya opened the folder and extracted a document. She pushed the file across the desk toward Veronica. "The contract is for one year, renewable if all parties agree. All of your travel, work permits, and relocation expenses are covered, as well as medical expenses." She held Veronica's gaze. "The non-disclosure agreement is for the entirety of your lifetime. And it is strictly enforced."

The nuanced threat in her voice sent shivers down Veronica's back. "I understand."

Jaya pulled a thick-barreled fountain pen from the inside pocket of her suit coat and placed it on the desk next to the contract. "Please sign both copies. I'll sign it as an agent of Rowan House. Mistresses Martha, Elaine, and Lucia will sign as well and you will receive a signed copy upon your arrival at the house."

Veronica shifted in her seat. She picked up the black fountain pen. It was heavy and a gleaming sculpted golden dragon decorated the side of it. She uncapped it and paused, weighing her decision. "What if I'm not a good fit? What if I want to break the contract?"

"That will be between you and the owners. I'm simply their agent here. Rowan House is a cooperative agency. You'll have a vote on issues that may arise, and will be able to bring up any concerns you have with the owners. If you complete a year and decide to renew your contract you'll be eligible for profit sharing." Jaya's gaze softened and Veronica found it more disturbing than her hard glare, the expression in her eyes so at odds with her fierce appearance. "You don't have to sign it. If you have any doubts, don't sign it. I'm sure Sarah can help you with returning to the graduate program here, or at another university."

Sign the thing. Nothing here for me. Start over. So what if it's a pleasure house? I'm not expected to do anything other than manage the barn. No one here will hire me. I can't face those idiots at school. Or deal with seeing Dee again. Veronica squared her shoulders. "I'm sure." She signed the document, her hand steady even as her body trembled.

Jaya smiled at her and pulled the contract over and signed it. She tilted her head toward Veronica. "Well done." She held out her hand and Veronica shook it. "I'll forward your signed contract to the owners. As soon as the travel arrangements are in place Millie Reid will message you with the details."

Millie. What an old-fashioned name. She must be a hundred. "Is there anything else I need to do?"

Jaya reached into her desk and pulled out several forms with Veronica's name typed across the top. "Go to this address. They will complete a physical exam and draw blood for screening."

Papers already prepared. She was sure I'd sign. How? I wasn't even sure. Veronica frowned. "I'm not planning on having sex with anyone."

Jaya's eyes were flinty; she raked her gaze over Veronica's body before returning to her eyes. "Everyone who works at Rowan House is screened, every guest as well. Even if you don't plan on anything"—she raised an eyebrow—"things have a way of happening at Rowan House."

Her tone let Veronica know the medical exam and blood tests were nonnegotiable and she wiped her sweaty palms on her pants before she took the forms from Jaya. "I understand."

Like I'm going to find anyone there. Nope. Not even going to think about it. Not with any of the whores that's for sure.

Jaya picked up her phone. "Go now. I'll tell them to expect you. The address is about fifteen minutes from our building. Make sure your passport is in order, and take care of anything you need to take care of here. You'll leave as soon as your test results are complete. It's usually about ten days from the time of the exam."

Veronica clutched the papers in her hand. *It's really happening. This is it. This is what I wanted. Better than staying here and living with my folks.* She forced a smile and left.

"ARE YOU SURE, honey?" Her mom rubbed her thumb over the back of Veronica's hand. "I don't give a damn what your aunt says about you, or us."

"I know." Veronica squeezed her mom's hand. "I know you don't. I want this. It's exhausting dealing with everyone's questions and pity. It's been two years. I'm thirty-two years old and living in your basement. They won't even let me volunteer at the therapeutic riding center. I'll be able to pay you back."

"We don't care about the money." Her mother's piercing dark eyes pinned her in place. "It's as far from her as you can get, isn't it?"

"I need to move on, Mom. It was over with Dee the moment they led me out of the courtroom." Veronica rubbed her mom's hand.

Her mother sucked her teeth. "She walked right past me in the grocery store. Acted like I was invisible. So rude." She sighed and rested her chin on her chest. "I trust you to do what you need to do for you."

Veronica pulled her into a hug. "It's a year, Mom." Her mother was silent, and her unspoken sadness pierced Veronica's soul. "I'm not doing this to hurt you."

Her mother broke their embrace and leaned back on the couch. "Your father is going to lose it."

Veronica sighed and looked up at the ceiling. "I know. Would you tell him?"

Her mother picked up her hand and squeezed it. "He'll take the news better from you."

Veronica slouched on the couch next to her mom. "You said that when I came out."

Her mother quirked her mouth. "I love you, honey, but not that much. You're on your own with your father."

Veronica closed her eyes. *She's right. Damn it. She usually is. He's going to cry. Fuck, I hate when he cries. It'll be like every visitor's day.* She glanced at the clock. *He'll be home soon. Better get it together to tell him.*

She walked outside into the cool late spring evening. The scent of hot asphalt and fresh cut grass hung in the air. She dug the toe of her boot in the loose rocks edging the driveway before she bent down and picked a small smooth stone. She rubbed her finger over the surface. *Solid. Like my folks. Like my sister. Will I ever be solid?*

The hum of tires on pavement made her glance up. Her dad pulled his Mini Cooper into the drive. He met her gaze through the windshield and smiled at her. She shoved the stone into her pocket as she watched him unfold his long thin frame from the car. She'd inherited his height and lank build, dark brown skin, and square jaw. It was like looking in a mirror when she looked at him and yet not.

Veronica shook her hands out and squared her shoulders. "Hey, Dad."

"Hey, baby mine, what's up? It's been a long time since you've hung out in the driveway waiting for me to get home from work." He gripped her shoulders and pulled her close to him in a hug. "Didn't break Mrs. Thompson's window again, did you?" His voice was light as he teased her. She'd spent more than one Saturday doing odd jobs to make the money to pay for her neighbor's window she had thrown a football through at least twice growing up.

"Not this time." Veronica kept her voice even, but her father pulled her closer, and she knew he sensed her hesitancy.

"Well, whatever it is, let's go have a glass of tea first. Everything's better after a glass of tea."

Veronica leaned into him as they walked through the garage into the kitchen. *He's gonna need more than tea for this.*

Chapter Two

VERONICA STOOD AT the rail to watch the gulls dip and dive as they followed the wake of the ferry as it made its way from Mallaig to Armadale. The wind was chill and the sun bright as they approached Skye. Eyes gritty from her overnight flight, she stretched and fought a yawn. Even with a first-class seat she had been unable to sleep on the plane. She had spent the trip by private car to Mallaig staring out of the window, fascinated by her first views of Scotland.

Veronica tucked her hand in her jacket pocket and fingered the smooth stone she had picked up from her parents' driveway before she left. Her father had kept it together until he dropped her off on the sidewalk outside the Richmond airport. She could still smell the lingering scent of his aftershave from his bone-crushing hug goodbye. After patting his back and assuring him she would call when she arrived, she had wiped away the bit of wetness on her cheek where his tears had fallen, shouldered her bag, and watched him drive off.

She yawned, unable to shake her weariness. As the ferry slowed to dock, a thrum of excitement buzzed around the base of her brain. *I can be Veronica again, not "poor Ronnie who got busted and sent to jail", or "Ron the math freak." A fresh start. Without my bitch aunt looking down her nose, and giving my folks hell about me.*

She scrubbed her hand over her head, still getting used to the feel of her low cut. A last-minute decision, a radical departure from her usual style, the flirty glances she'd received from several women on the flight had let her know it was a good look for her. Veronica scanned the crowd as the ferry docked.

A few men in driver's livery held up signs with individual names, and one or two with names of what must be hotels on the island. She frowned when she didn't see her name. The crowd thinned out and she stood alone on the dock. The stone in her pocket was smooth under her fingers as she fidgeted with it. *Fuck. Maybe they forgot me? Maybe I screwed up the directions?*

Her pulse pounded in her ears. She shrugged out of her heavy backpack and dug into the front pocket for the letter with her instructions on it. She focused on her breathing as she worked to stem her rising anger and panic. Her hands trembled as she took her phone from her pocket ready to call the number she had been given if she had any problems during her trip.

"Miss Fletcher? Veronica Fletcher?" A deep voice sounded behind her and she bobbled her phone, managing to catch it before it hit the asphalt.

"Yes?" The owner of the voice was tall. A driving cap set at a jaunty angle shaded her face. Her dark blue uniform was crisp. *Police? Fuck, I haven't done fuck all and the police are here? A cop with a driving cap? What the hell?* "I'm Veronica." She hated the tremble in her voice.

"Sorry to startle you. I apologize for being late. I had a bit of trouble on the way." The woman's eyes were a light brown with gold flecks. Her gaze was intense, framed by her auburn brows.

"You're from Rowan House?" Veronica's panic subsided. *It's a chauffeur's uniform. She's not a cop. I'm safe.*

"Aye." The driver pulled off her cap. "Millie Reid." Her buzz-cut hair, a soft auburn red shot through with gray, shone in the sunlight. Her broad ruddy face pulled into a wide smile. Millie extended her freckled hand and Veronica shook it. Her grip was as strong and as solid as Millie appeared. "You're our new stable manager." She swept her gaze over Veronica's body before she looked back into her eyes. She tilted her head to the side. "You're even more attractive than your photos. I like the low cut, although your locs were fetching."

Veronica flushed, the heat rising to the tips of her ears, and she pulled her hand from Millie's grip. "It was time for a change. I'm pretty sure the horses won't care what I look like."

Millie laughed. "True about the horses. But everyone at the house is appreciative of gorgeous scenery." She picked up Veronica's large backpack and shouldered it.

Gorgeous? After a red-eye with no sleep? I hope she can see well enough to drive. Veronica's face burned. She reached out to reclaim her backpack. "Um. Thank you. I can carry my bag."

Millie waved Veronica off. "I make it a point to handle all luggage for new arrivals. Do you have any other bags?" She glanced around and raised her eyebrows. "This is it?"

"Yes." Veronica pressed her lips together. *Say something. Make it clear.* "I don't think it matters what I look like. I'm here to work as the stable manager, not a whore."

Millie settled her cap back on her head, the light gone out of her eyes, and her jaw clenched.

Oh fuck. Why did I say that? Veronica averted her eyes, unwilling to meet Millie's thunderous gaze. *I'm an idiot. She processed my papers. She knows.*

Millie blew out a breath before she spoke. "I understand what you were hired for. Wasn't trying to offend you." She turned her back to Veronica. "This way."

She walked away from Veronica, never looking back to see if she followed. Veronica stuffed her hands in her jacket pockets and gazed up at the sky. *Great. I pissed her off. Fuck. Great way to start my new job. I need to chill. Apologize?* She raised her shoulders and let them fall before she hurried to catch up to Millie's long strides. Even through the haze of her exhaustion she admired Millie's easy walk. Her hips were narrow, her gait athletic, the movements of someone confident in their power and ability.

Millie walked across the car park toward a black town car. Veronica quickened her pace. She had already stowed Veronica's backpack in the trunk by the time Veronica arrived at the car. Millie opened the back door of the car and stood to the side, her face a cool mask.

Damn. They sent a limo for me. We must be picking up other guests. "I could ride up front, you know, if there are others to pick up."

Millie's face maintained her neutral expression, her voice even. "No. We're not picking up anyone else. Ride in the back. I'm sure you're tired after your trip." She pointed to the door pocket and a bottle of water. "There's water for you. Coffee and snacks in the basket. Do you need to use the facilities before we leave? It's a long ride to the house, and once we leave Armadale there're not many places to stop along the way."

Veronica avoided making eye contact with Millie. "No. I'll be okay." She slid onto the polished black leather seats. Millie closed the door. Veronica braced herself, expecting a harsh door slam after her thoughtless comment. Millie shut it gently with a barely audible click. *I'm an ass. A total ass.* Millie entered the car, started the engine, and raised the partition between the front seat and the cavernous rear of the limousine.

Veronica scooted her hips back into the wide leather seat. A wicker picnic basket sat on the floor of the car. She picked it up and settled it on the seat beside her. Her mouth watered as the tangy scent of citrus filled the air when she opened the lid of the basket. Two muffins and a thermos were nestled together with a white mug in the basket. She opened the thermos and the aroma of coffee made her giddy. She filled the white cup as high as she dared in the moving car. She took a sip. *They know I take my coffee black? Damn.* Steadying the coffee cup on her thigh, she picked up one of the muffins and took a bite. The sharp sweet taste of citrus and chocolate exploded across her palate and she moaned softly around the delicate morsel. Veronica finished the muffin in three bites and started on the second.

Thoughtful. And delicious. And what the hell is wrong with me I said that? The coffee was the perfect balance to the sweet orange and chocolate notes of the muffin. She pulled her pen and journal from her inside jacket pocket and made a few notes about her trip, the ferry ride, and her arrival. She wrote down Millie's name and underlined it. *Old school butch. Crew cut. The only thing missing was a ring of keys. Built. Those shoulders.* Her face flushed again when she remembered how Millie had looked at her. Her bright cocky smile and the sincere tone of her voice when she complimented her came back to her full force. Veronica shifted in the seat, pressing her thighs together as a tendril of desire curled in her belly. *Work. I'm here to work. Nothing else. Not that she'd want me. Probably likes dainty femmes, not ex-cons with no hair.*

Sleepy now she had eaten, she replaced the cup into the basket with the coffee thermos before she set the basket back on the floor of the car. She stretched out on the seat and used her jacket for a pillow. The rocking of the car soothed her, and she flipped to a new page in her journal.

VERONICA JOLTED AWAKE when the car stopped. Her pen was still clutched in her hand; her notebook had fallen on the floor of the car. *Damn, I fell asleep. Did I drool on the seat?* She picked up her notebook and pen and tucked them back into her jacket. She rubbed her hands over her face. She rummaged through her pockets and found her last piece of cinnamon gum, unwrapped it, and popped it into her mouth to get rid of the sour sleep taste in her mouth.

The door opened and Millie was framed by the soft afternoon light behind her. "I'll take your bag to your room. Do you need anything from it?"

Veronica stifled a yawn. "No. I've got everything." She shrugged into her jacket and patted her pockets to make sure she hadn't lost anything while she slept. "All good." She sat there her brain in a fog from the overnight flight and her nap.

Millie tilted her head at Veronica, a half smile on her face. "You going to stay in the car, love? Or do you want to meet the stunning women you'll be answering to?"

Veronica shoved off the seat and left the car. "Sorry. I'm not awake."

Millie reached up and touched her face. She swiped her thumb over Veronica's cheek. "You've an ink mark here. My gran would have spit on her finger first, but I think I've got it."

Her touch was firm but gentle, and Veronica laughed. "My grandma too." Millie's hand lingered a moment before she lowered it. Veronica stared into her eyes, wondering at the flash of heat she saw there before Millie turned away from her.

"Hey. I'm sorry. About earlier. I'm still getting used to—" *Outside? Life beyond prison? The idea of working at a whorehouse? What the fuck to say? "I'm an idiot, please forgive me?"* "Um, everything."

Millie raised her head and met Veronica's gaze. "Okay. But you might want to use the term sex worker next time. Some of the women here are sensitive about people calling them whores." She lowered her brows and her voice. "And Mistress Lucia will most certainly not react well."

"Got it." Veronica held Millie's gaze. "Thank you."

Millie tilted her head to the side. "For what?"

"The advice. Treating me like I'm somebody. The coffee and the muffins. I didn't know what to expect, but I never imagined a limo and a driver being sent to pick me up. The orange-chocolate muffins were incredible."

"You can thank Robin for the muffins." Millie quirked her mouth, her eyes fixed on Veronica's face. "Someday, love, you're going to have to tell me why you think you don't deserve to be treated well, but right now you need to go see the Mistresses."

Chapter Three

"VERONICA, WELCOME." A tall woman with black hair streaked with a touch of gray, flanked by two marginally shorter women, stood on the steps leading up to the house. "I'm Martha MacLeod." She gestured to the other women. "This is my sister Elaine, and Lucia Caruso."

Am I in the land of the giants? Fuck, they're all so tall. And gorgeous. And my bosses. Damn. Think. Say something. Get it together. You've seen hot women before, be cool. "Hi."

Martha took her hand and shook it. Her grip was firm and her gaze steady as she spoke. "I'm happy you decided to join us. Jaya and Sarah gave you the highest marks on their references. We've been too long without a proper barn manager."

The woman she identified as Elaine moved forward. Her bright red hair was pulled back in a tight chignon highlighting the sharp angles of her face. Elaine's dark-green eyes settled on her like a hawk spotting a rabbit. Veronica had to stop herself from pulling her jacket tighter around herself and crossing her arms.

Elaine took Veronica's hand. She gave it a hard squeeze and rubbed her thumb over the back of her knuckles before she released her. She rested her hand on her hip and cocked an eyebrow at Veronica, her lips pulled back into a sharp smile. "Are you hungry?"

Doesn't look like she means food. Damn. Veronica's ears burned as the flush rose in her face. "I...I'm...I had some snacks on the ride. I'm good."

"Easy Elaine, don't frighten her off." The third woman stepped forward and gripped Elaine's shoulders. She gently moved her to the side before she stepped around her. She smiled a gentle smile at Veronica. "I'm Lucia."

Elaine snorted and shot Lucia a glare. "I was asking about dinner." She returned her laser focus to Veronica, and her face twisted into what passed for a smile. "Staff dinner is at six. Don't miss it." Elaine shot another hard glare at Lucia before she walked back into the house.

Lucia stepped forward and clasped Veronica's hand with both of hers. "I'm sorry. Cook—I mean, Elaine—takes some getting used to. I'm sure you're tired from your trip. Millie will get you settled. Take care of yourself. Martha will talk with you in the morning about your duties." Her gentle command was wrapped in the firm kindness of her voice and Veronica found herself lost in the blue-green of her eyes, and the sensation of Lucia's touch. Lucia released her hand and straightened.

Martha smiled at Veronica before she slipped her arm through Lucia's, the subtle inclination of Lucia's body as she leaned into Martha and the way she settled her hand over Martha's arm a quiet demonstration of the palpable love between them. Veronica turned away. She swallowed the bitterness rising in her throat. *What would it be like to have someone look at you like you were the only woman on earth? Someone who wanted only you? Dee. Why'd I think it would be easier to forget her here?*

MILLIE LED THE way up the covered stairs leading to the second story of the barn. She opened the door and passed the key back to Veronica. The entryway to the room held a coat rack and a boot tray along with a small bench. She followed Millie into the room. A double bed with a brass head and footrail was placed at right angles to the wall. A small refrigerator next to the bed served as a nightstand and held a reading lamp. An oak armoire and small dresser took up space under the eve opposite the bed. A narrow bookshelf held an electric kettle and two cups, a French coffee press, and a small red-and-white tin. Veronica prayed it held whatever coffee she had been served in the car. Heavy dark-blue curtains covered the window at the gable end of the room. Underneath the window was a plain cherrywood desk and chair. Centered in the middle of the desk was a thick folder.

Millie pointed to a narrow door. "The washroom and toilet are through there." She placed Veronica's backpack on the floor before she met her gaze. "I need to add your phone to the tracking app we use for the staff."

Veronica pushed away her rising anxiety over surrendering her phone even though she had closed her accounts and deleted all of the social media apps from it before she left home. After her release, her phone had been her connection to others. On social media she could be an avatar, and no one judged her about her past. It had also been easy to stalk her ex-lover, and make herself crazy-sad as she scrolled through the photos of Dee with her baby and the smoking hot butch she had married. Dee had made a family while Veronica served time. *I can do this. Let it go. Be here. Time to stop torturing myself. Start over. Be present. I'll be so busy with the barn I won't even think about her.*

She pulled her phone from her back pocket, unlocked it, and passed the device to Millie. "Do you need my e-reader?" Veronica opened the padded pocket on her pack and removed her reader.

"Anything that can receive a signal." Millie tucked the phone into her jacket pocket and took the reader from Veronica. "I'll get them back to you this evening and give you the password for the Wi-Fi. We don't allow workers or visitors to have phones or recording devices in the main house, stable, or play areas. Because you're staff and will be sleeping out here away from the house you're allowed access to your phone. When you come to the house for meals, leave it in your room, or the office downstairs. After I enter it in our system, I'll add my number and Mistress Martha's to your contacts."

"Thanks."

Millie raised an eyebrow. "What kind of books do you read?"

"Everything as long as it has a happy ending." Veronica lowered her chin to her chest, shy under Millie's direct gaze.

"Everyone deserves a happy ending." Millie's voice was so soft Veronica wasn't sure she had spoken. "The house has a large library, and a bunch of trade paperback books if you run out of things to read." Millie tapped the e-reader against her palm. "One of the submissives from the house will clean your room on Tuesdays and change your sheets. Place your clothes in the purple laundry bag hanging in the armoire and they'll wash them and get them back to you the next day. Staff meals are at half six, noon, and six. If you want something earlier, or anything else related to food in between, you need to speak with the kitchen staff and arrange it. The folder on the desk has a copy of your contract, a map of the house and grounds, and handbook of house rules. Staff meetings are the first Monday of the month. You've missed this month's meeting but if you have anything you want to discuss before next month's meeting make an appointment with Mistress Martha."

"Um, okay. Wow." Veronica swept her gaze around the room. Despite her nap in the car all she wanted was a hot shower and her bed. She failed to stifle her yawn.

Millie squeezed her shoulder. "You look done in. I'll knock you up at half five for staff meal."

Veronica raised her eyebrows. "What?"

Millie laughed and Veronica loved the way her whole body laughed, the mellow round sound filling the small room. "I guess I shouldn't assume you'd understand. Let me translate. I'll wake you in time for dinner." She left and pulled the door closed with a soft click.

Veronica tossed the key on the desk. She sat on the edge of the bed and dug in her pack for her toiletry bag, sleep shorts, and tank top. *Her eyes. Golden brown. Beautiful laugh. She's hot and doesn't even get it. Hell, they're all hot here. What's the matter with me? Not going there. I bet the femmes are lined up three deep for her.* The familiar ache of isolation settled in Veronica's chest.

A SHARP RAP at the door startled Veronica awake. She rolled off the bed and landed on her feet, her heart thumping in her chest. She gripped the headboard to steady herself. *Safe. I'm safe. No one's going to toss my room. I'm safe. Breathe. In out, let it go.* She walked to the door, touching each piece of furniture on her way to reassure herself she was not dreaming. She took another deep breath and blew it out before she opened the door. Her nipples pebbled in the cool air. Millie's swift glance at her chest before she brought her gaze back to Veronica's face reminded her she was still in her thin tank top and boxer-briefs. "Yes?"

Millie held up her phone and her e-reader. "I finished with these." Her fingers brushed over Veronica's hand as she passed off the items, and Veronica shivered. *Chilly. It's not her. Totally not her. Right. Liar. I'm ridiculous. It's been too long. Way too long. Be cool.* "Thanks. I downloaded a new series of books before I got on the plane and was looking forward to reading the second one tonight."

Millie arched a brow. "We're pretty informal at staff dinner but I'm betting you'll be more comfortable with clothes."

The devilish gleam in her eye had Veronica flushing again. "Yeah. Give me a minute." *Ask her in? No. Think.*

The sparkle in Millie's eyes and the half smile on her face suggested she could sense Veronica's indecision about asking her into her room while she changed. "I'll wait here." She pulled the door closed with a click.

Giving me space. Chivalrous. Good woman. Veronica spilled her backpack contents over the bed and found her best pair of jeans and pulled them on over her briefs. One black T-shirt later she was ready to go. She snagged her jacket from the hall tree as she passed and she stepped out on to the landing.

Millie was at the bottom of the steps. She had changed into a pair of faded jeans, and a dark-green V-neck pullover. The short sleeves were tight across her arms, highlighting her thick triceps, sculpted biceps, and the sharply defined muscles of her forearms. The late evening light backlit Millie's features. Veronica studied her profile and the fine line of her jaw. *Broken nose. More than once. Wonder how? Gives her a rakish look.* Millie's tight shirt also displayed the sweeping curves of her breasts and a stunningly deep cleavage.

Millie glanced at her and smiled. Veronica missed a step, stumbled forward, and clutched the rail. *Damn it. Focus. Falling down the steps is not the way to have her under me. Fuck, where did that come from?*

Millie bounded up the steps between them and stood in front of Veronica, a hand on either rail. She peered into Veronica's face. "You okay?" She turned forward and presented her arm. "Hold on to me. These steps are dark. I'll get a light installed."

Damn she's fast. Get it together. Veronica stared at Millie's thick forearm. She cleared her throat. "Yes. Thanks. I guess I'm still not awake." *Liar. What I get for staring. At least she thinks I'm clumsy instead of a creeper.*

Millie captured Veronica's hand and settled it on her arm, not waiting for her response.

She's ripped. Damn. Veronica fought the urge to squeeze Millie's forearm and the firm flesh under her palm. *She's being nice. That's all.*

Millie made sure Veronica navigated the rest of the stairs without incident. When they cleared the last step and were on the graveled drive, Veronica lifted her hand from Millie's arm. "Thanks. I think I'm good now." She avoided Millie's gaze, curled her fingers into her palm, and tried to forget the sensation of Millie's strong arm under her fingers. *She acts like I'm someone special. Does she treat everyone this way? The concern in her voice, like I was special, someone worth protecting.*

"Do we need to see about the horses?" Veronica stopped and inclined her head toward the barn.

"No. Benita and June helped me. They're tucked in for the night."

Veronica glanced at Millie. "Do you do everything here?"

Millie laughed. "No. It only seems like it. All the submissives start in the stable before they move on to other jobs in the house. We expect everyone to be able to do what needs to be done unless they're hired, as you were, for a specific task. Having them work in the stable is a way to assess their temperament."

Veronica frowned. "How?"

"If they get frustrated with the horses, or mistreat them, we end their contract. Martha believes you can tell a lot about a person by the way they treat animals and children."

"She's right."

"Aye. About many things."

Millie's eyes took on a faraway look, a thousand-yard stare Veronica wanted to ask about but didn't.

THE HOUSE WAS warm, and Veronica peeled out of her light jacket. Millie showed her the mudroom and a hook labeled with her name to hang her coat. She took off her boots and placed them on the mud tray next to the door.

She pointed at a white-painted door to the left of the coat hooks. "Washroom is through there. You can leave a pair of indoor shoes here, under your hook. Floor's cold in the winter." Millie pulled off her shoes and tugged on a pair of loafers. "Hell, it's cold in the summer too." She grinned up at Veronica.

Veronica followed Millie into a large dining room. A long walnut plank table was set for ten. Two chairs at either end and two long benches provided seating. Millie sat and pointed to the bench opposite her. "We don't have assigned places but leave the ends open. Roxy and Danica are left-handed and hate sitting on the benches."

Veronica took a seat directly across from Millie. A curvy woman in a bright white chef's jacket, open at the neck, approached Millie. A thin collar of black and red leather twisted together graced her neck. A small silver tag with engraving Veronica could not read was centered in the hollow of her throat. She leaned down and kissed Millie on the lips. Veronica studied her fingernails, not wanting to intrude on their display of affection.

"Veronica, this is Myfanwy."

Veronica rose up from the bench to shake Myfanwy's hand. "My pleasure. Thank you for the muffins. They were the closest thing to heaven I've tasted in a long, long time."

Myfanwy's hand was soft and her grip firm, her eyes a warm brown. She met Veronica's gaze. "Oh, I like your style, but Robin is the one who made those muffins." She rested her hand on Millie's shoulder. "I hope you're hungry, I got a little carried away with dinner tonight. I read through your application, Veronica, but I always like to check in person. You don't have any allergies?"

"No. And I'll eat whatever you're serving. I'm not a huge fan of lima beans, but other than that, I'm open to anything."

Myfanwy opened her mouth to speak but was interrupted by another voice.

"Are you going to serve the soup, or should I?" A thin woman with a mop of curly blonde hair and large blue eyes pushed through the swinging door leading to the kitchen. She bustled into the room and placed a large platter of sliced bread in the center of the table. She glanced at Veronica, blushed, and backed away. "Sorry. I didn't mean to interrupt."

Myfanwy inclined her head toward Veronica. "Robin, come meet Veronica, the new stable manager. She's in love with your muffins. I'll get the soup."

"Hello," Robin mumbled as she bobbed her head at Veronica, avoiding eye contact before she scurried from the room, not waiting for Veronica to reply.

What the hell? Am I so scary? Veronica twisted the edge of her napkin in her hands.

Millie reached across the table and touched the back of Veronica's hand, drawing her attention. "Robin's a bit skittish. She's been through it." She held Veronica's gaze. Her expression said more than her words could about Robin's fearful exit. Distracted by Millie's eyes, Veronica studied her face, enjoying the moment far more than she should. *Those gold flecks in her eyes, like tigereye gems. So unique. And beguiling. Her eyes are exquisite. And her lush mouth.* Millie's mouth pulled into a cocky grin as if she could read Veronica's mind.

"Hey, Millie, she doesn't seem like your type. Give the rest of us a chance."

Veronica eyed the bleached-blonde woman who entered and sat in the chair at the head of the table. She wore a pale-blue diaphanous peignoir, and a faded brown leather collar with a worn brass tag.

"Roxy, Veronica, Veronica, Roxy. Chief troublemaker, and submissive to the queen."

Roxy laughed. "Elaine would like that you referred to her as such." She smiled at Veronica and extended her hand. "And I'm a free agent."

"Nice to meet you." Veronica shook her hand and forced herself to look into Roxy's eyes instead of her voluptuous body on display under the sheer material of her gown.

The rest of the house staff arrived and arranged themselves on the benches, most of them welcoming, in some cases flirty, all of them wearing collars with brass tags and a few of them not much else.

I'll never remember all their names. A trickle of sweat ran down between Veronica's shoulder blades, and she focused on her meal. No matter how much she had told herself she would be fine in a house full of women whose purpose was to serve other women in whatever capacity they wanted, she was overwhelmed. And charmed. Every woman who entered made a point to shake her hand and welcome her with genuine smiles. *They're people. Like me. Even if they're half dressed.* She flushed when she thought of her whore comment to Millie. *Ugh. I can't believe I used that word. How many times have I used it like a weapon?* Guilt spread over her like a heavy blanket. *So ignorant. Never again.*

The women chatted with one another, occasionally switching to Spanish or Italian as they laughed and talked. Veronica was happy she had paid attention in Spanish class but didn't reveal she could understand them, preferring to listen to their discussions rather than participate. Myfanwy had joined them, sitting next to Millie on the bench opposite Veronica. She listened as Millie spoke quietly to Myfanwy in a language Veronica had never heard and could not even begin to imagine what it was. Casual touches and intimate eye contact passed between Millie and Myfanwy, and Veronica did her best not to stare. The disc on Myfanwy's collar caught the light, and Veronica made out a script "M" engraved on the disc.

They're lovers. She's hers. Should've known she'd be with someone.

Myfanwy returned to the kitchen. A few minutes later, she pushed through the door with a large tureen of soup. She placed it in the middle of the table and served each of them. The soup was a colorful mix of vegetables, lentils, and spicy sausage. Veronica savored a spoonful of the soup, appreciating the complex mix of spices. *I won't starve here. So good.* She was disappointed when Myfanwy left with the remains of the soup and regretted not asking for seconds. She settled for another slice of the bread and mopped up the dregs of the soup in her bowl.

The small hairs on Veronica's arms stood up, and she sensed someone staring at her. She glanced up and into the darkest brown eyes she had ever seen. The woman's hair was slicked back tight against her head, the smile on her face predatory. She rested her hand on her narrow waist, her large breasts marginally contained by the dark-green corset she wore. "I'm Ashley." The latecomer sat down next to Millie and pushed Myfanwy's place setting to the side.

Oblivious to Millie's sharp glare, she kept her gaze fixed on Veronica's face as she extended her hand. Her blood-red nail polish matched the lipstick she was wearing. She licked her lower lip before she spoke. "Welcome. Has anyone given you a tour of the house?"

Veronica reached across the table and shook her hand briefly. "No. I..."

Millie spoke over Veronica, her voice hard-edged and direct. "She's just arrived. And if she's interested in a tour, I'll assign someone."

Roxy cleared her throat loudly. "Stay in your lane, Ashley. As for tours"—Roxy's eyes held a challenge, her tone icy—"you'll have to get in line."

Ashley arched a brow at Roxy. "Don't you have to ask permission?" She turned and quirked her mouth at Millie. "You're such a control freak." She stood up abruptly, snagged a slice of bread from the platter, and flounced from the room.

The room had grown quiet, the sexy fun atmosphere evaporating in Ashley's wake. *Ashley. Won't forget her name. She's got piece of work written all over her. What's that about? And what's up with Millie?* Sensing a power struggle she knew nothing about, Veronica returned her focus to her meal. She spread a thick layer of butter on another slice of bread.

Conversation between the women resumed, a signal the fraught moment had passed. Veronica kept her head down and watched the other women from under her lashes. *A tour. A real tour? Or is it their code for sex? Ashley. So not my type. Maybe I need a "tour." Take the edge off. Who would she assign? Would I have a choice? Sex. With a prostitute. Sex worker. How would it be different from the women I paid for with dinner and drinks? It'd be more honest.* Veronica traced the wood grain of the table with her finger as she sorted through her thoughts.

"Don't let Ashley ruin your meal, Veronica."

Millie's husky voice slid under her skin and sent a shiver down her back. *Not a command. A request. Trying to make me feel better.* Veronica studied Millie's face. *Her eyes. Worried about me. Wants to make sure I'm okay. She's kind. Like Myfanwy. A matched pair.*

"Myfanwy's trifle is not to be missed."

"I'm a fan of desserts." Veronica sipped her water. *And you.*

Chapter Four

"WE'LL MEET IN the barn in the morning. Benita will help you with the mucking. We've been feeding them at seven and then turning them out. Martha will come by at ten to go over her expectations." Millie lowered her chin to her chest. "I'm sure dinner was overwhelming. I'm sorry if Ashley made you uncomfortable. Consent is a priority here."

Why won't she look at me? "I'm okay. Believe me, I've had worse first days." *At least this one didn't feature orange jumpsuits.*

Millie cleared her throat before she spoke. "If you are interested in seeing the rest of the house, I'll arrange it. If you desire the type of tour Ashley suggested with her or one of the other submissives, she'll need to clear it with the Mistresses of the house."

"What?" Veronica failed to keep the shock out of her voice. "Are they slaves?" *Fuck, what have I signed up for?*

Millie frowned. "They are submissives pledged to the house and employees. They have schedules and obligations, duties in the house they are expected to perform. They are well compensated for their availability and talents. That means if we have guests expecting certain women to be available, they need to be. It's part of their contract."

Veronica was too exhausted to keep the anger flaring in her chest under control. "What if I was interested?"

Millie crossed her arms in front of her chest, her gaze hard. "Are you?" She pressed her lips together in a firm line. In the light Veronica made out the fine line of a scar crossing the bridge of Millie's nose.

"I don't know." Veronica shoved her hands in her pockets and leaned on the stair rail. "It's been so long since I've had any action, my clit gets hard when the wind blows."

Millie's face broke into a broad grin before she laughed. The genuine sound of her laugh turned Veronica inside out, fanning the tiny flame of want that had begun on the pier in Armadale.

"And here you are starving, presented with a buffet, and told you can't eat anything."

Veronica scrubbed her hand over her face. "I'm sorry. I'm tired. And a little freaked out."

Millie tilted her head at Veronica. "Get some sleep. If you want something to eat before morning staff meal, Myfanwy or Robin will make you whatever you'd like. And stay out of Elaine's way before she's had her tea."

"Thanks." Veronica walked three steps up to her bedsit. She stopped and turned to watch Millie as she walked away. She moved with grace and a touch of swagger. *Forget it. She's with Myfanwy. Don't get involved with women who are involved.*

VERONICA SAVORED THE last bit of the coffee she had made in the French press. *I would work for this coffee. So good.* She checked the time on her phone before she shoved it into her pocket. She cleaned out the press and washed her cup and dried it. She'd slept better than she expected to, exhaustion solving her sleep issues for once.

Restless to be moving, she tugged on her sky-blue fleece over her shirt and zipped it up. On the landing she patted her pockets. Reassured she had her multitool and her phone, she locked the door and pocketed the key.

The early morning was chill and quiet. A fine mist rose off the rolling fields surrounding the estate. She walked around to the front of the barn and rolled open one door just wide enough to slip through. She waited in the dim light for her eyes to adjust. Ten stalls lined the center aisle. To her left was a door with a brass plate declaring it the tack room and opposite it was another door labeled "office."

She stopped to admire the organization of the grooming area. Labeled boxes and chests of grooming supplies were arranged along a low bench. Built-in covered grain bins with cabinets over them were tucked in next to the office. She walked gingerly past the horses, most still dozing. Some of them raised their heads and turned to watch her with their ears forward as she walked past them. Over each stall hung a brass nameplate. Bruno, Marco, Patrick, Clyde, Jack, Honey, Bella, Luna. *It'll be easier to remember their names than the women I met last night. Clean. Organized. Holy hell the Friesian's mane is going to be so much work.*

At the end of the aisle was another set of double doors. She rolled them back and looked out. Fenced paddocks with gates to three other paddocks were laid out behind the barn. The last stall on her right held hay bales, stacked in tidy rows. The stall on the other side held the mucking gear, barrows, shovels, and pitchforks. Veronica turned around as the large doors behind her rolled open, flooding the barn with light and cool air.

"Good morning." Millie strode down the center of the barn.

Veronica walked back down the aisle to meet her halfway. Millie held out a thermos.

"Myfanwy thought you might need this."

Veronica took the flask. "Thank you. I'm sure I will."

She followed Millie as she walked back to the office. She opened the door and waved Veronica forward. "This is your space."

Veronica entered the room. A large desk, rolling chair, and tall file cabinet took up one side of the cozy office. A credenza behind the desk held a laptop and printer. A worn leather couch, small refrigerator, and a bookshelf lined the other wall. A scuffed captain's chair sat next to the couch.

"All the hard copies of health records for the horses are in the file drawers." She pointed to a green binder on the desk next to a black one. "That's a calendar of the guests we have scheduled for the next six months. There are notes about each guest, along with their riding abilities and desires about their experiences. In addition to the stable and indoor riding arena, there is a fire ring with a turnout area you'll need to keep up with and supply if guests want to use it. The black binder has notes about each horse."

"I've never seen a more organized barn."

Millie smiled. "Martha is meticulous. After our last disaster of a barn manager, Martha took over and organized everything. She expects it will stay this way." Millie's foreboding expression made it clear to Veronica she needed to meet Martha's expectations.

"Hello? Millie?"

"In here, Benita."

Benita, her thick black hair pulled back and dressed this time in jeans and a sweater, smiled at Veronica. "Ready to meet the crew?"

Millie nodded at Benita. "I'll leave you to it. I have a date with Robin's orange rye raisin bread."

"You better hurry. There wasn't much left." Benita sighed dramatically and rested the back of her hand on her forehead and groaned. "Robin's bread makes me weak. I'd do anything for a slice."

Millie laughed and jogged out of the barn. Shaking off her sense of abandonment as Millie left, Veronica shoved her hands in her pockets.

Benita tilted her head at Veronica. "You didn't come for breakfast."

"Not much for breakfast." *Wasn't sure I could handle it without Millie. Or with Millie.*

Veronica followed Benita out of the office. "All of them are well behaved except Luna. She can be pushy about her food." Benita unlocked the feed bin and handed Veronica two plastic tubs, each labeled with a horse's name. The sweet smell of alfalfa pellets and grains filled Veronica's nose. "This is for Bruno and Marco."

They worked together filling each horse's food bucket. Veronica rolled back the door to Luna's stall. The horse planted herself in front of the chest-high mesh stall guard, leaned against it, and stretched her neck as she strained to reach the tub of food in Veronica's hand.

Veronica slipped under the mesh door, backing into the stall. She turned and kept her hand on the mare's shoulder. "You have to wait." The mare pushed into her, threatening Veronica's balance. She spread her legs to steady herself and turned away from the horse. She pressed her back against the horse's shoulder, moving her away from her food bucket. She dumped the food into the bucket and stepped back. Luna bumped into Veronica on her way to her feed bucket. "Easy, girl. I'm not going to take it away." She pushed gently on the mare's side again, moving her out of the way to exit the stall.

Benita was waiting for her. "You did better than me. The first time I fed her I ended up on my ass with the food everywhere."

Veronica grinned. "It was close."

They lined the tubs up on the shelf over the feed bin. "Now we scoop for dinner, then we don't have to do it later." She pointed to the white board on the wall. Each horse's specific diet was listed. "If they are getting anything extra, like medications, it's listed on the board. We store their medications in here." She opened the right-hand cabinet and pointed to small baskets, each labeled with the horse's name. "Bella is on hormones, but she only gets them in the morning. Jack gets medicine for his ulcers with each meal."

Benita led Veronica around the barn, talking to her about the routine, her voice affectionate as she discussed each horse. *Why doesn't she want to be barn manager? It's clear she loves the horses and she's knowledgeable. Ask. Don't ask.*

When the horses were finished eating, they turned them out into two of the fields behind the barn, mares in the left side paddock and geldings to the right.

Once the horses were turned out, they mucked the stalls. *At least this part is simple.* Sweat gathered on the back of her neck and tickled as it ran down her back, and Veronica took her fleece off and hung it in the office. As they cleaned the stalls, Benita answered Veronica's questions about the barn and workflow.

They took a break and shared the coffee Millie had left them. Benita sat on the leather couch resting her cup on her knee. Veronica edged a hip on to the desk. "How come you didn't want to be barn manager?"

Benita pursed her lips. "Money. And vacation time. We get twelve weeks paid vacation. I'm from Brazil. My family lives in Fortaleza. I spend the winter holiday there. Have you been?"

"Not traveled much of anywhere." Veronica sipped her coffee. *Twelve weeks. I get a month. They earn the twelve weeks.*

"It's the only way I can cope with the winter here. If I had to stay through the gray months I would hate it. Besides, I like my work." She arched a brow at Veronica. "I'm pledged to the house"—she slipped her finger under the edge of her shirt and lifted a brown leather collar for Veronica to see—"but I would kill for Mistress Martha and Mistress Lucia. I dream of wearing their collar."

Veronica studied the fierceness in her eyes and the set of Benita's jaw and didn't doubt her words. *What would it be like to have a sub so dedicated? To have a lover who believed in me?* A memory of Dee's arms and legs wrapped around Veronica's body, her eyes bright, the sound of her voice when she declared her love for Veronica warped into her harsh expression when Veronica told her of her lawyer's suggestion she plead guilty. *Why didn't I listen to her? Fuck me, this took a wrong turn down memory lane.*

"I hope it won't come to that." Martha entered the office; her commanding presence filled the small room.

Benita stood up and placed her coffee cup on the table. She lowered her gaze and placed her arms behind her back. "Forgive me, Mistress, if I spoke out of turn."

Martha walked over to Benita and lifted her chin with one finger. "Look at me." Benita lifted her gaze to Martha's face. "Nothing to forgive. I admire your commitment. I need to talk to Veronica. Leave us, please."

"Yes, Mistress." Benita left hurriedly.

Martha turned her gaze to Veronica. "An exquisite submissive, don't you think? If we were interested in expanding our trio, we would collar her."

"She's lovely. I think anyone who collars her will not be disappointed." Veronica met Martha's gaze and lifted her chin. *We? Trio. She and Lucia and who? She respects me, knows I'm a top. She gets me.*

Martha motioned to the captain's chair and Veronica sat down. Martha sat behind the desk. She turned the black binder to face Veronica and opened it. "Each horse has a page detailing their training and personality description and, directly behind it, a form with recent health history. I expect you to learn them and be able to assign a horse for our guests who want to ride. The password for the computer system is listed. You'll need to coordinate with the vet and the blacksmith. Millie entered their numbers into your phone when she set you up on the house network. Anything you need to purchase for the barn work, put in a purchase order. Various submissives will be assigned to tasks to help you with keeping up the barn and fire ring in the wood. We've an indoor ring that will be your responsibility as well. There's always help available. Please don't be resistant to asking for it." She rested her hand on top of the green binder. "Millie will provide you with an updated guest list each week along with detailed personal information. We strive to provide each guest a meticulous, perfectly planned, and executed experience according to their desires." She arched an eyebrow. "Many of our guests think highly of their equestrian skills, but it would be wiser to underestimate what they can handle rather than overestimate."

"I understand." Veronica shifted in her chair as she examined the first page. "Are any of the horses off limits to guests?"

"Elaine does not care for her horse, Luna, to be used for guests. My horse, Bruno, is a warmblood and solid on the trail. For our taller guests he's a perfect fit. He also tends to be chubby, so a little extra work for him is never a bad thing. Marco, the Friesian, is Lucia's horse. He is extremely gentle and well mannered. Neither of us mind if our guests ride them. The rest of the horses were selected for their calm temperaments; all of them are decent on the trail. Bella's a thoroughbred and can be a bit of a handful if she has not been exercised, so lunge her a bit before any of the guests ride her. She benefits from a more experienced rider with a firm attitude."

Martha leaned back in her chair and rested her palms on the desk. "Do you have any other questions?"

Veronica flushed under Martha's gaze. "Could you explain the house rules about contact between the other workers and myself?"

Martha smiled, and all Veronica could think of was a wolf about to devour a small animal. *So like her sister. Damn.*

"Has someone caught your eye?" The slight smirk on her face and light in her eyes suggested Martha had been informed Veronica might ask her the question. *Millie told her. Loyal. No secrets here.* "Ashley? Or perhaps Benita?"

"No." Realizing from the surprised expression on Martha's face how harsh her voice had been, Veronica softened her tone. "No. I don't have anyone in mind." *Liar.* "I want to understand the protocol, that's all."

Martha raised her eyebrow. "Keeping your options open. Very good. Anyone you see with a collar and a number tag is sworn to the house. They are submissives and employees. As submissives, they must ask permission from myself, Lucia, or Elaine to play with anyone outside of business obligations."

Collars. Millie isn't collared. Myfanwy's collar is different. Robin wasn't wearing a collar. Veronica rubbed her sweaty palms on her jeans. "What if they aren't collared?"

Martha lifted an eyebrow, her expression appraising. "Then it is up to them. Only house submissives need to ask. It is a condition of their contracts." Martha pinned Veronica with her gaze. "There are no restrictions on relationships as long as they don't interfere with the services provided to our guests." She pressed her lips together and a slight frown knit her forehead. "You're a very handsome woman, Veronica. I expect you'll receive attention from some of our guests. You are not expected nor required to respond to their advances. If anyone presses you, you must report it to me immediately." The grim set of Martha's mouth made Veronica feel sorry for anyone who violated Rowan House's consent rule. "We have recently instituted a mandatory safe word policy, and it is strictly enforced between workers and guests. Some of our former guests are still getting used to the idea. If you observe any unsafe play, you are required to report it."

Veronica opened her mouth to speak but stopped when Martha raised her hand. "If you decide you would like to scene with a guest, you are free to do so, as long as you follow house rules about consent and safe words, but you will not receive extra compensation unless you'd like to pledge to the house. If you're interested in pledging to the house, a new contract can be drawn up with additional compensation." Martha's tone held no judgment, and she could have been describing a laundry list.

Veronica blew out a breath, her mouth dry. "I don't expect I'll want to interact with the guests in that way, but thank you for explaining my options."

Martha tipped her chin at her. "You mean scene with a guest? Or pledge to the house?"

"Both." Veronica pulled the binders into her lap, holding them like a shield in front of her body. "I'll study these." She dropped her gaze to the toes of her boots.

"Very good. If you have any other questions, my door is always open."

VERONICA PLACED THE binders on the nightstand. She had eaten enough for two people at lunch because she had skipped breakfast. *Not doing that again.* She pulled off her jeans and fleece jacket, folded them, and placed them on the chair before she lay back on her bed. The soft scent of lavender filled her nose as she turned her head into the pillow. *So much to learn. I'll never get everyone's name down. Roxy is funny as hell. Robin acts like I'm going to eat her, not in a good way. And Millie. She and Myfanwy. Elaine's in love with Roxy. Does Roxy get it? Does Elaine?*

She shifted on the bed and flipped the comforter over her body. *Nothing scheduled for this afternoon.* Her left shoulder ached, tight from the morning's work, and she stretched to dispel the stiffness. She massaged the tight scar over her left deltoid. *Could study the binders. Nah, nap then study.*

Chapter Five

"THIS IS AMAZING." Veronica ran her fingers along the cherrywood shelf. Floor to ceiling shelves full of books complete with a rolling ladder covered three walls of the large room. Opposite the shelves three wide windows looked out toward the far mountains. A large overstuffed sofa that begged lying about with a book, a butler's table, and two wingback chairs with matching ottomans completed the library of Veronica's dreams. Millie stood with her hands clasped behind her back. She glanced at Veronica before she shifted her gaze to the carpet. "It's my second favorite room in the house."

Veronica studied the way a blush stole over Millie's face. *Not asking which one is her favorite. What room is it? What could make her blush from her collarbones to her hairline? She's so damn cute when she blushes.*

"I'm sure this will be my favorite. I'd go broke trying to keep my e-reader filled. I've already read through everything I downloaded before I left home and reread some of my favorites."

"Mistress Lucia is an avid reader. She keeps the library stocked. If there's a book you would like in the library, let her know and she'll purchase it. She also insists on strict reshelving." Millie pointed to a wooden chest next to the desk. "Returns go there. Tessa's the librarian; she's as much a hard ass as Mistress Lucia about the shelving. Be sure to return your books here. She'll make sure they get back where they belong."

Her blush deepened. "Sometimes the library is closed." She looked up at the ceiling before she brought her gaze back to Veronica's eyes. "Quite a few of our guests have librarian fantasies. There will be a 'closed' sign hanging from the door handle if it's in use."

Visions of what other activities took place in the library filled Veronica's thoughts, and she chewed her lip as she tried to focus on Millie's words.

Millie pointed to an antique oak card catalog. "That's the catalog. Do you know how to use it?"

Veronica frowned. "What? Of course. I'm older than I look."

Millie laughed. "Sorry. So many of the women who come here are so young they've never seen one. My apologies."

"Do you really have women that young who work here?"

"No one under twenty-one." Millie pursed her lips.

Veronica walked to the leather sofa and sat down. "How does it work?"

Millie traced her fingers over the top of the card catalog. "You can sign a book out for three weeks. If you need it longer you just have to let Tessa know. If you don't bring it back on time, she will find you." A sly expression crossed Millie's face. "Some of the staff don't even read what they check out, hoping Tessa will be in a mood to discipline them for their overdue books."

Veronica huffed out a breath. "Not that. How does it work with the women who work here? Do they apply? How do you find them?"

"I don't. The Mistresses hire the women. Usually they are referred to us from former workers or clients. Or they may have heard of us from other houses."

Veronica forced herself to meet Millie's gaze. "I was referred here." A sudden rush of knowing filled Veronica. "Oh. Oh my." Images of her former advisor and her partner filled her head. "Oh. Wow. They must have... Oh."

Millie sat down next to Veronica. "You didn't know?"

"I read the contract. I knew Miss Pomroy did background checks. I thought she knew about the house that way. Doctor Kerr." Veronica flushed. "I feel so dense."

Millie patted her knee, and then moved her hand up and rested it on Veronica's thigh. "If it makes you feel any better, when Myfanwy recommended I apply for my position here, I was as clueless." Her tone was gentle and laced with kindness.

Veronica stared at Millie's hand on her leg, close to the junction of her thighs. Dangerously close. Her broad palm and thick fingers curled over the top of her leg. The warmth from Millie's palm heated Veronica's skin through her jeans and distracted her from their conversation. *What would it be like to have those hands on me? To have her kneel and wrap her hands around my ankle and beg for my touch? She's too much a top to kneel to me. She's got Myfanwy. Stop. Stop wanting what you can't have and shouldn't want.*

She stood up abruptly, breaking contact with Millie. "I have to get Luna ready for Elaine. I'll come back and find something to read. Thanks." She rushed from the library. *She must think I'm so dense. How could I not get it about Dr. Kerr? And Ms. Pomroy. Damn.*

MILLIE PULLED THE cover off the saddle and placed it on the saddle rack. "Will this do? She had a different saddle she said we could lease if this wasn't right."

Veronica examined the therapeutic riding saddle. "This should be fine. It's got the leg straps and the stabilizing padding in the back." She unfolded the picture she had printed out from the client's email and compared it to the saddle in front of her. "She sent me this today. Sorry I didn't have it for you to take with you. Did they send the safety stirrup converters with it?"

"Aye, they're here." She held up a cloth bag and placed it on the shelf under the saddle rack. "Have you thought about how to coordinate their request?"

Veronica chewed her lip. "Yes. But I'm going to need your help. Will you be able to assist the client with mounting the horse? She's told me she's too unsteady to use the mounting block alone. You're the only one I trust to be able to assist her with the transfer. We'll both need to be there to stabilize her in the saddle until we get the leg straps in place. Once she and her wife arrive at the fire ring we'll both need to be there to assist her off the horse. I'll make sure there is an adequate chair for her to transfer to. Her partner will take care of whatever she needs after we've helped her dismount." She busied herself with replacing the cover over the saddle. "It also means we need to make ourselves scarce while they scene but we need to remain close enough we are available if they need our assistance. When they're ready to ride back to the house, we'll need to lift her back on to the horse."

Millie held her gaze a moment and then glanced away. "Mistress Siobhan and Marilyn have been clients of ours for years. Last year, after Mistress Siobhan's stroke, I thought I'd never see them again. If no one else has said it to you, thank you for working out how to make their request come true and being respectful of them." She turned her gaze back to Veronica.

Millie's praise sent a rush of warmth through Veronica. "I'd want someone to do the same for me. Horses are the best medicine." She shifted her gaze away from Millie's eyes, unsure of what she would see, unwilling to risk exposing herself even more than she already had with her confession. "I struggled with anger and depression. The inmate equestrian program was life changing. Horses saved me."

"And for that I'm eternally grateful." Millie reached out and placed her hand on Veronica's shoulder. The skin exposed by her sleeveless T-shirt blazed under Millie's brief touch. Dropping her hand to her side, Millie turned away. "I've got an errand to run for Cook. See you at dinner?"

"Yeah. See you then."

Veronica watched as Millie strode from the tack room. She touched the place Millie's fingers had rested on her skin and cursed herself for being so caught up in a woman so unavailable.

Chapter Six

"THIS IS YOUR favorite room?" Veronica glanced around the knotty pine-paneled room. A ping-pong table took up one end of the long narrow space. Three card tables were evenly placed around a burnt-orange area rug. With the black-and-white floor tile it was a classic family game room, a monument to the seventies. The shelves held brightly colored boxes of board games.

Millie clasped her hands behind her back. "It reminds me of my gran's house."

Veronica perused the shelves before she turned to face Millie. "What do you like to play?"

Millie met Veronica's gaze. "Um. Well. Lots of things."

Veronica raised her eyebrow, not giving Millie any quarter. "Really?"

"Scrabble." Millie blushed under Veronica's scrutiny and blurted her answer, her normally deep voice high and squeaky. She cleared her throat. "I like Scrabble."

Veronica grinned. "My mom banned Scrabble one summer because my aunt flipped the board when she lost."

Millie's laugh was genuine. "Sounds like your aunt and my cousin have a lot in common. My gran made us stop playing more than once because of the shouting."

"Want to play?" Veronica tilted her head, watching Millie's face for her reaction.

"British or American spelling? Or both?"

Veronica rested her hand on her hip. "How about both?"

"Done." Millie pulled the game box from the shelf and they set the board up.

Alone with Millie in this room, Veronica could imagine they were anywhere but an exclusive brothel on Skye.

Millie held the bag with the letter tiles over her head. "You pick to see who goes first."

Veronica stretched her arm, reached in, and chose a tile. "Y." She laid her tile down on the board. "We had a Crown Royal bag for our tiles. My uncle owned a bar and had so many of the little flannel bags my grandma made him a pair of lounge pants from them."

Millie's snort of laughter made Veronica laugh herself. "You're making that up." She laughed louder. The light in her eyes and the way her face relaxed made Veronica want to make her laugh again.

"Nah. True story. My grandma never let anything go to waste. My aunt forbid him to wear them out of the house so of course he did."

Millie snorted again, and laid her tile down. "E. Looks like you go first."

Veronica chose her tiles and arranged them on her rack. Millie chose hers and did the same. The room was quiet except for the steady hum of a small refrigerator in the corner.

They played quietly, complementing each other when they came up with a high scoring word or made a particularly clever play. Millie was sharp and skilled and Veronica quickly fell behind in points. She tried to tell herself it wasn't because she spent more time studying

Millie than the board, but she'd be lying to herself. The concentration on Millie's face as she worked the board and set down her tiles made Veronica admire her even more.

She made her play and reached for the bag at the same moment Millie did. Their fingers brushed, and an electric current of desire whipped through Veronica. She wanted to know this woman, to be close to her, to share more moments like this. She had never been so relaxed with anyone. She sighed and took the last two letters from the bag, only to realize it was her turn and she had nothing she could use.

Millie looked up and grinned. "You okay?" A tiny smirk twisted her mouth. "Have I stunned you with my Scrabble talents?"

Veronica laughed. "Dude, you have thoroughly spanked me. All I have left is Us and Ns. And nowhere to play them."

Millie grinned. "You're good. The last person I played with I beat by three hundred points."

Veronica leaned back in her chair as a tiny flare of jealousy ignited in her chest. *Ridiculous. I am ridiculous. She's not mine. So what if she played Scrabble with someone else?* "Thank you. We played a bunch growing up. I'm rusty."

"If that's your version of rusty I better be prepared for our next game." She stretched and her shirt pulled tight across her chest. Veronica had to turn away before she embarrassed herself. "I hate to say it, but I've got to go and try to get some sleep. I've an early pickup tomorrow."

Veronica stifled her disappointment. "It's okay. Maybe we can do this again sometime."

Millie met her gaze. "I'd like that. I like being with you."

Veronica's breath caught in her throat. "Me too" was all she trusted herself to say.

They cleaned up the board in silence. Veronica tried to come up with something else to say. *Did she mean like a friend or more? Does she like me? Or* like *like me?* She straightened her shoulders. "Good night."

Millie leaned in and pressed a quick kiss to her cheek. "Good game. Good night." She stepped back, her expression cocky. "Anytime you want me to spank you again let me know." The cheeky grin on her face made Veronica want to kiss it off.

"Yeah." Veronica swallowed hard. "Good game. See ya," she called over her shoulder as she fled the room.

A SINGLE RAP on her door startled Veronica. *Damn. Of course at the good part.* She scooted off the bed and used her finger to keep her place in the book. She hurried to the door and snatched it open.

"Sorry. I disturbed you." Millie's apologetic expression let Veronica know she had failed to keep her annoyance off her face, and her lingering glance at her bare legs reminded Veronica she was once again only dressed in tank top and briefs. *She must think I lay around without pants all the time. Because I do.*

"Um. No." Veronica lowered the book in a feeble effort to hide her lack of pants. *Why is she here? And damn that shirt fits her. Oh man. Be cool.*

"I need a favor. Martha is away and it's chest day. Could you spot me? I mean if you're not busy." Millie toyed with the top of a water bottle she held.

Veronica took in the blush spreading across Millie's face. *Is this a pickup line? Or is she serious about her workout?* "I haven't..." Veronica saw the edge of disappointment and the sadness creeping into Millie's eyes as she took a step back away from Veronica's door. *I hurt her. Damn, she's asking me to help her out. It's not a date. She's been so kind to me. Idiot. Tell her yes.* "It's been a while but I'd be happy to. Give me a minute."

Millie's broad smile was her reward. "I'll wait." She stepped back. "Out here." She turned her back and walked down the steps.

Veronica closed the door. She stuck a bookmark in her book and tossed it on the bed before she tugged on a pair of shorts and laced up her trainers.

ON THE WALK over to a low building behind the main house, Veronica had time to admire Millie's ass and muscular thighs on display in her workout tights. *I'm so gone. Damn. Does she get how beautiful she is?* She forced herself to avert her gaze and didn't notice Millie had stopped. Veronica's breasts and the rest of her came into full contact with Millie's hard body and firm ass as they collided. A rush of heat flowed through her.

"Sorry." She leaned back and stumbled a bit before regaining her balance. She wiped her face with her hand.

Millie grinned at her. "I didn't think anyone else was as impatient to use the gym as me." She turned the key and opened the door to the gym.

Veronica followed her around the fully equipped gym. She rested her hands on her hips and whistled. "Damn. This is amazing."

Millie hung the key on the hook. "We also have a dry sauna, a steam room, and a lap pool if you're interested. Mistress Lucia's idea. Part of the improvements for the staff and guests."

"After seeing the library and this, I guess a tour would've been a good idea." Veronica ran her hand over the rack of dumbbells lining one side of the room.

Millie tilted her head and looked at Veronica. "There's still time." Her voice held a hint of hunger.

Veronica glanced away, striving to douse the spark of desire ignited with Millie's suggestive tone. *Does she mean with her? She's flirting. Maybe she's serious? I couldn't go behind Myfanwy's back. She doesn't act like a cheater. Maybe they have an open relationship?* She sat down on one of the weight benches and rested her arms on her knees and knotted her hands together. *No. Not as a side piece. No matter how much I want her. Maybe with both of them? A ménage? I don't like to share subs. Don't respond. Change the subject.*

"How much do you bench?" Veronica kept her tone even.

Millie pressed her lips in a thin line and turned away from her. "My personal best is eighty-four kilos, but I usually work out my chest with seventy kilos."

"Wow. Do you compete?"

Millie pulled a bench over in front of a rack of dumbbells. She grimaced. "No. I'd be too embarrassed to appear in public in those suits they make you wear."

"I'll be able to assist you, but I couldn't clear the bar if you got stuck." Veronica rolled her shoulders and then stretched them.

"I won't work to failure. I'm going to do some warm-up sets with the dumbbells. Once I'm done with the heavy bench if you want to leave it's okay. The rest is more dumbbell work and machine flys."

"I'll stay." Veronica watched as Millie stretched her long arms over her head, clasping her hands over her elbows. "Do you usually work out alone?"

"Most of the time. Martha spots me when I work heavy on chest, and on leg day." Millie's resigned tone and the hint of melancholy in her voice made Veronica's heart ache. *Lonely. What about Myfanwy? Maybe it's not good between them?*

Millie walked to the rack and picked up a set of ten kilo dumbbells. She stepped back and sat on the bench. Squaring her body, she lay back and pressed the dumbbells up in a straight line with her chest, her face a mask of concentration as she worked. The muscles of Millie's chest bunched and flexed with her movement and displayed a deep cleavage and the hint of riches hidden by her compression top.

What would it be like to slip her shirt down and fill my hands with her breasts, to rub my face over her soft skin? To suck one of her nipples between my lips and feel it harden in my mouth. Millie's nipples peaked with her exertion. *Get a grip. Stop staring. Walk away.*

Veronica clenched and unclenched her hands. She turned away and paced the room, mentally cataloging the exercise equipment while she waited for Millie to finish her set.

Millie sat up and placed the dumbbells on the floor. She met Veronica's gaze in the mirror. "I'm sorry. It's probably boring watching me. I know you get enough exercise with keeping the stable and working with the horses."

"No. Not bored." Veronica met Millie's gaze in the mirrored wall. *Definitely not bored. Wound up? Yes. Get it together.*

Millie stood up and replaced the dumbbells. She returned with fifteen-kilo dumbbells. "I'll need you to spot me with these."

Veronica moved to the top of the bench and kneeled. Millie laid back, the dumbbells even with her chest. Veronica placed her hands on the outside of Millie's elbows. The heat of Millie's skin, damp with sweat, under her fingertips sent a sharp wave of want through her. Fine lines highlighted Millie's face, a smattering of freckles over her cheeks. Veronica admired her deep laugh lines, thick eyelashes, and lush mouth. She wanted to smooth her fingers over her broad cheekbones and kiss her. *Focus. Don't let her get hurt because you're thirsty. She's so handsome. This is killing me. Why'd I say yes? Damn it.*

Millie completed her set, the muscles in her chest larger now with her exertion. She sat up and placed the dumbbells on the floor. She opened her water bottle and took a sip. Her breathing returned to normal and she grinned at Veronica. "Ready?"

"Hell, yeah. You're impressive."

Millie laughed. "Because I can lift heavy things?"

"Not only that." Veronica avoided Millie's gaze. "You take care of people. You're kind to everyone."

Millie stood up and stretched her arms. "Some people would disagree with you." The bitter edge in her voice made Veronica look up. *Who? Someone she cares about. Or cared about.* Millie's back was turned to her, but the set of her shoulders reflected the hopelessness in her voice.

"Help me?" She pointed to the rack holding the Olympic-style weights. They worked together loading plates in tandem to keep the bar balanced on the rack.

Millie lay down on the weight bench and wrapped her hands around the bar. Veronica positioned herself between the upright supports. She set her feet wide on the step-up behind the bench before she placed her hands next to Millie's and helped lift the bar from the supports. She let Millie lower it and then press it up, keeping her hands in a position to help with the barbell if she got into trouble.

Millie worked steadily, her eyes fixed on some vision only she could see, her concentration evident as she pressed the weight off her chest. Sweat poured off Millie's forehead with the strain and her arms trembled. Veronica wrapped her hands around the bar, worried Millie would not be able to rack it on her own. "Last one?"

Millie grunted her answer and lowered the bar again, her knuckles white. Veronica held on lightly, letting Millie handle the weight, assisting her only when she racked the bar. Millie lay on the bench, chest heaving, eyes closed. Veronica walked around to the side of the bench and picked up Millie's water bottle. She stared down at Millie, memorizing her expression. Satisfied exhaustion filled her features. Veronica pushed aside her desire to be the cause of her expression instead of her workout.

Millie opened her eyes, and Veronica stared back, unable to hide her want, dazed by the heat she saw in Millie's eyes. *Kiss her. Do it. Don't think. Kiss her now.* She leaned over her, unable to resist the invitation she saw in Millie's eyes. Millie's hand came up and gently cupped the back of Veronica's neck. She hesitated, her lips a whisper away from Millie's.

The door slammed open and Benita entered followed by Roxy. Millie let go of Veronica's neck and sat up quickly. Veronica stepped back and thrust the water bottle into Millie's hand. A flush rose in her face, and she caught Benita's curious gaze as she shifted her gaze from Millie to Veronica.

"Did I miss the show, Millie?" Roxy's loud voice and incurable flirty attitude filled the space, and the sexual tension between Veronica and Millie melted.

Millie snorted. "You did. But if you show up Tuesday you can watch my ass when I squat."

Veronica forced a laugh, desperate to cover her awkwardness and disappointment. "Now your fan club is here, are we done?"

Millie tilted her head to the side, her expression shuttered. "Sure. Sorry to keep you from your book." She turned away from Veronica, her posture rigid.

Damn. She's pissed off. Because I almost kissed her? Or because I didn't? What is wrong with me? Even if she wanted me to kiss her. I can't fuck this up. I don't want to hurt Myfanwy. Or make things awkward where I work. Fuck me.

Chapter Seven

THE MIDDLE GARAGE bay door was open. Veronica paused outside it to watch as Millie worked. Millie's hand rested on the hood of a classic red MG roadster. She was dressed in short-sleeve gray coveralls and the muscles in her forearms stood out as she unlatched the catch, lifted, and then propped open the bonnet. Her shoulders sagged.

Veronica stepped into the garage. *Say something. Don't be weird. Stop staring.* She took another step, and her wet boots squeaked on the dry floor.

Millie straightened as she wiped her hands on her coveralls. "Did you need help?"

"No. I'm finished until this evening. Not much I can do while it's raining." Veronica walked over and stood next to the car. She shoved her hands into her pockets. "Tune up?"

Veronica's fingers itched with the urge to touch the wrenches and screwdrivers arranged in perfect lines on the crisp white pegboard covering the rear wall of the garage. She surveyed the row of toolboxes resting against the back wall and inhaled the sharp tang of motor oil and dust, the smell of her childhood. Growing up, she had spent countless weekends helping her dad while he took meticulous care of every car they had ever owned, doing his own maintenance and repairs. Memories of sunny afternoons, the soft sounds of classic Motown in the background, working hip to hip as he taught her about engines. At seven, her primary job was handing him tools and sorting screws. By twelve, she had graduated to doing the work under his supervision. When she turned sixteen, with every dime she had earned, she bought a 1972 Mustang Mach One and rebuilt it with his help. When she graduated valedictorian from high school he had paid for the paint job, having it painted a jaunty yellow. She swallowed hard as the awful memory of selling it to pay part of her legal fees surfaced. She blew out a breath and shook her head to rid herself of the kaleidoscope of miserable images cluttering her thoughts and the ache of missing her family. "Need some help?"

Millie grimaced. "I'm fair certain something made its home in the engine over the winter. I've put off finding out." She unscrewed the bolts holding the cover over the dual air filters. She lifted the black cover down and out of the way. Leaves, cat hair, and chewed bits of the air filter stuck out from the edges of the filter compartment and were tucked into the round center of the filters, foul evidence mice had taken up residence as Millie had suspected. She jerked back, dropped the cover on the ground, and stumbled away from the car. Her face was pale and she swore softly under her breath.

She benches one eighty and is scared of mice? Veronica's smile at Millie's reaction faded when she realized Millie was shaking. "Hey, you okay?"

"Do I look like I'm okay?" Millie glared at Veronica before she raised her chin and fixed her gaze on the ceiling. "I hate mice."

Veronica touched Millie's shoulder. "I'm sorry. I know it's not funny."

Millie brought her gaze back to Veronica's face. "It's not. I fucking despise the little bastards. They were everywhere in the house I grew up in. I would hear them in the walls at night. Nothing was safe from them. Nothing."

"You have a vacuum? I'll clean it out."

Millie blushed. "I feel so damn silly."

Veronica squeezed her shoulder. "Hey, no judgment from me. You have to promise if we run into any bats you'll take care of them."

Millie laughed. "They're mice with wings, but it's a deal." She walked to the back of the shop and plucked two black nitrile gloves from a box and passed them to Veronica.

"Sexy." Veronica grinned at Millie as she tugged the gloves on.

Millie guffawed as she rolled the shop bin closer to the car.

Veronica leaned over the engine and pulled two large handfuls of debris from around the air filter housing. She scooped up the remaining bits of the mouse nest and dropped it in the trash bin. She vacuumed around inside the filters before she tugged both of the air filters clear of their mountings and disposed of them. "You have a rag? I want to wipe the mounting seats."

"Here." Millie handed her a red shop towel.

"Who drives this one?" Veronica wiped the mounts down.

"It's mine." Millie rolled the bin back to its place.

"It's beautiful."

Millie rested her hands on her hips. "It didn't look like this when I bought it. I had to strip her down to the frame, rebuild the engine, everything."

The unmistakable pride in her voice sent a rill of pleasure through Veronica. *She likes to work on cars. As if she wasn't sexy enough. I'm so gone.* "My first car was a '72 Mustang I rebuilt. Do you have photos of when you bought it? I love before and after shots."

"I've a whole book. Mistress Lucia photographed it and Myfanwy made a photo book for me." Millie's eyes were bright as she met Veronica's gaze. The delighted expression on her face and the light in her eyes caused Veronica's stomach to tighten and her heart squeeze.

"Will you show me?" Veronica held her gaze.

"I'd love to show you everything." Millie's husky voice made Veronica tremble.

"Yeah?" Veronica kept her gaze fixed on Millie's face, watching the way Millie's eyes darkened.

"The photos, I mean." Millie shoved her hands into the back pockets of her coveralls.

Veronica retrieved the air filter cover from the floor and wiped it down. She started when Millie touched her shoulder.

"On your application you listed hiking as a hobby."

"I like day hikes. I had a lot of time on my hands after my release. I spent as much time outside as I could." Veronica passed the air filter cover back to Millie.

"Would you like to go on a hike sometime?" Millie clutched the filter cover to her chest.

Veronica peeled the nitrile gloves off her hands and disposed of them in the bin. *Be cool. She asked you to hike, not a date or anything. Or is it?* "Sure. When?"

"This Wednesday?" Millie's knuckles were white where she gripped the cover.

Veronica groaned. "I can't. I have to be here for the vet."

"Oh. Okay. Some other time then."

"When?"

"It might be difficult to find another time." Millie's voice was clipped.

"I'm sure Myfanwy's schedule is tough to plan around." Veronica swallowed her disappointment and wiped her hands on the red shop rag.

Millie frowned. "Why would her schedule be an issue?"

Oh. She wants me to go with her. Alone. On a hike. Away from anyone seeing us. Don't freak. Ignore it. Let it go. Veronica forced a smile she didn't feel. "Is there anything else I can help you with? I'm a fair mechanic."

Millie glanced at the clock on the wall of the garage and a fleeting shadow of sadness crossed her face before she smoothed her features. "No. I have to make a run to Portree later."

Veronica glanced around for a place to deposit the shop rag.

"I'll take it." Millie held out her hand.

"Okay. Um, see you at dinner?"

"I won't be back for dinner." Millie's flat voice echoed in Veronica's head.

"HE LOOKS FANTASTIC. You've done a marvelous job with his mane." Lucia rubbed Marco's neck. "What's your secret?"

Veronica adjusted the girth on Marco's saddle. "Gallons of very cheap hair conditioner. It makes it easy to comb and plait."

Lucia smiled at Veronica. "The horses have never looked better. Several of our guests have remarked on how helpful you were." She lifted her chin and pinned Veronica with her eyes. "Are you happy here?"

Veronica shifted her feet, trying to escape the intensity of Lucia's gaze. "Enough. I like the horses. The barn is the best I've ever worked in."

Lucia's gaze softened. "You don't socialize with the rest of the staff and you skip meals. Are you sure you're happy?"

"After being forced to share my life in an open-plan dorm with a shit-ton of people and having no privacy, I'm not much for group activities. I'm okay with being alone."

Lucia's eyes held kindness. "I understand."

Her voice and her expression told Veronica she more than understood. "You do, don't you?" She tilted her head to study the elegant woman in front of her, trying to imagine her in the drab tan jumpsuits she'd had to wear. "You were incarcerated?"

Lucia pursed her lips. "There are many kinds of prisons."

The scuff of boots on the floor interrupted their conversation. Martha strode into the space. She leaned in and pressed a kiss to Lucia's cheek. Lucia turned her head and cupped Martha's face and kissed her. The soft needy sounds Martha made sent a flush of heat through Veronica. It was clear from the kiss exactly who was in charge in their relationship. Lucia swept her other hand up and cupped Martha's breast. Veronica stared as Lucia pinched and rolled Martha's nipple through her shirt. Lucia turned them and forced Martha up against the barn wall. She moved her hand languidly down Martha's body. Martha spread her legs, and Lucia cupped her and moved her finger in slow circles.

Veronica trembled, her mouth dry. *Do I look away? Pretend I'm not here? Oh man. They left this out of the orientation packet. Fuck. Don't watch.* Veronica stepped closer to Marco's side, using his body to block her view and give them privacy. She leaned her head against the horse's shoulder, holding on to his saddle to ground herself, willing her body to not respond to the display she had witnessed. She closed her eyes and focused on her breathing. A long few moments and the unmistakable sound of Martha's climax reverberated through the barn.

Grateful for the horse's calm energy and his broad body that offered her a place to hide, Veronica waited. *Now what? What do they expect me to do? Should I say something? Damn, that was intense.*

"Veronica, did Robin bring out the brunch I ordered?" Martha's voice settled over Veronica like a balm. As if it were commonplace for two women to enjoy each other in the early morning, in the middle of a barn, without a care who was watching. *Not in Kansas anymore, Toto. Damn it, now I'm going to be wound up the rest of the day.*

"Umm, yes. I've packed it in Bruno's saddle pack. Marco's ready, and if you give me five minutes Bruno will be too. He's groomed. I still need to tack him up." *Back to normal. Like it's every day one of your bosses mauls the other one in front of you.*

Martha unclipped Marco's crossties. "I'll take care of Marco. We'll wait for you outside."

Lucia and Martha walked out leading Marco, their heads bent so close together they almost touched. The low murmur of their voices and the easy way they were with each other made Veronica ache for love, for desire so strong it was palpable, and intimacy, the sheer delight in knowing and being known.

"EASY, GIRL." VERONICA attached the crossties to Luna's halter. "Let's get you dolled up for your Mistress." She rubbed her shoulder, and the horse settled. The afternoon sun made the barn warm, and Veronica stripped her shirt off to work in her tank top.

Veronica selected the rubber currycomb and circled it over the Arabian's white coat, the loose hair gathering on the surface before falling in a soft cloud to the floor. She assessed the horse as she groomed her. Her build was light but strong, running true to her breed, her bearing regal. Her eyes were intelligent and held a bit of mischief. The horse stamped and shook her head. Veronica stroked her shoulder and made shushing sounds. "I know. You want to run. I'm hurrying." The horse rubbed her head against Veronica once and settled.

Veronica had seen enough of Elaine's imperious nature over the last month to know she and the horse were well matched in temperament. "I bet you're a lamb with her, aren't you? You just need a firm hand."

She shook her head once and blew out a breath. *I'd like to apply a firm hand to Millie. She's so damn hot. And has a lover. She's so weird since she asked me to go hiking and I couldn't go. She's not into me.* Veronica had borrowed a book on *shibari* and spent most of the previous night imagining Millie bound in intricate knots, her thickly muscled body displayed to perfection. She had spent more than one evening in her room, attending to herself, Millie starring in all of her one-handed fantasies as she imagined what it would be like to smooth her hands over Millie's body, to kiss her, to command her obedience, to bind her. The thought of such a powerful strong woman surrendering tripped her trigger every time.

After their near kiss in the gym she had contented herself with stolen moments of observing Millie at staff meals. When Millie came to discuss guest arrangements she avoided Veronica's gaze and kept to the business at hand, timing her visits to the barn so they were never in the same space alone. The change in Millie's behavior solidified Veronica's belief she wanted to be with her behind Myfanwy's back, certain her coolness toward her was because of her failure to respond to their almost kiss in the gym and then doubling down by saying no to her suggestion of a hike.

Veronica sighed. *What was I thinking? Why did I ever think she'd want me? Only she does. Maybe. But as a plaything. Not for real.* She switched to a stiff brush and flicked it over Luna's hide, getting rid of the loose hair left from the currycomb. A wave of despair filled her and she stilled. *What is wrong with me? Here I am, obsessed with another unavailable woman. Robin is so sweet. And Tessa. Why can't I be attracted to them? Hell, Ashley falls over herself trying to be with me.* She leaned her forehead against the horse's shoulder, seeking the soothing contact of her simple affection. "I'm so fucked. Doesn't matter. She's not into me like that. She's got Myfanwy."

"If you're talking about my sister, or Lucia, I warn you I never keep secrets from them." Elaine's husky voice cut through the quiet of the barn.

Veronica stepped back and stumbled into Elaine. Strong hands gripped her shoulders and held her up. Those same hands spun her around and she found herself much too close to Elaine.

"My God, you are exquisite." Elaine's dark green eyes reflected her desire for Veronica as her lips curled into a tight smile.

Veronica stilled as her body responded to Elaine's hands on her, her dual nature, switch that she was, stimulated by Elaine's intense scrutiny. "No. I..." Veronica trembled in Elaine's grip, caught up in the power rolling off her.

Elaine brought her lips close to Veronica's ear. "I'd like to spend some time with you away from the stable. Are you interested?"

The sensation of Elaine's breath on her neck as she spoke into Veronica's ear had her struggling with her desire. *Let go. Let her take care of you. Give in to her. Surrender. Don't think. No. No. No. She's my boss. She's beautiful. Such a Mistress. She'd be so deliciously cruel. Roxy. She loves Roxy. I'd be a plaything. I'd be entertainment. A new conquest. Nothing real. A hookup. I want. So much. So much more than this.*

Veronica placed a trembling hand on Elaine's chest and stepped away, her breath ragged. "No. No, thank you."

Elaine smirked. "I couldn't help overhearing you. If you're waiting for one of the holy trinity you'll be waiting forever."

"Holy trinity?" Veronica gripped the brush with both her hands.

"Martha, Lucia, and Myfanwy. They're pledged to each other."

Veronica sucked in her breath. "What about Millie? I thought..." She flushed with her confession and confusion. "Never mind."

Elaine arched a brow. "What about Millie?"

Veronica dropped her gaze and focused on the toes of her boots.

Elaine stepped close and lifted Veronica's chin with two fingers, her expression sharp. "I know you're a free agent, Veronica, but when I ask a question I expect an answer." The agitation in Elaine's voice pricked Veronica's conscience.

"I'm sorry. I thought Millie and Myfanwy were..." Veronica faltered, not wanting to give voice to what she had thought.

Elaine lowered her hand and stepped back from Veronica. "Hmm, yes. Well, they are close, best friends since university. But Millie—" Elaine's voice took on a softer tone, the change making Veronica cock her head to study the Mistress in front of her. "Millie's not, has not been with anyone since..." Elaine's expression shuttered. "Let's say a long time." Her haughty tone and Mistress mask were firmly back in place.

Veronica studied Elaine's face, curious about her discomfort at discussing Millie's past.

Elaine rested her hands on her hips. "Will you make sure Bella is ready as well for this afternoon? I've a picnic with Roxy planned." Her predatory expression returned. "Are you sure you're not interested? We would love some company."

"What about Roxy? Wouldn't she be jealous?"

"Roxy never minds a third." Elaine pursed her lips. "She's the one who requested I invite you. Being the generous Mistress I am, I agreed."

Veronica grinned at Elaine. "I'd be lying if I said I wasn't flattered. And tempted. Thank you, but I'll pass."

Elaine snorted. "Suit yourself. Good thing Roxy and I have solid egos." She left the stable humming the "Ride of the Valkyries."

Veronica rolled her eyes at Elaine's retreating back and placed the stiff brush back in the grooming box and pulled out the soft brush and began working over Luna's coat. *Millie's not attached. Does she hook up with whatever woman catches her eye? I haven't seen her with anyone, or even look at anyone like she's interested. Elaine's hiding something. She doesn't seem like the type to spare feelings.*

VERONICA SETTLED BACK into the black leather seat of Millie's red roadster and reveled in the wild beauty of the hills and mountains as the car swept past them. When Millie repeated her offer of a hike, Veronica rearranged her schedule and bribed Benita with her share of Robin's shortbread to get her to cover for her. Millie was quiet on the ride, focused as she guided the little car around the single-track road to their destination. They passed by several small crofts, and then the road ended in a rough gravel car park. Millie parked close to a large metal farm gate.

"Coral Beach." Millie turned and grinned at Veronica.

"Where?" Veronica raised an eyebrow. "Y'all have a funny idea of what a beach is if this is it. And that gate is locked."

Millie exited the car and Veronica did the same. "We go through the kissing gate." She pointed at a smaller gate by the side of the large one.

"Huh. A kissing gate."

The way the passage was built it would be easy for someone to hold it closed to the next person and demand a kiss to be let through the gate. *If only.* "So, I'll have to give you a kiss, like a toll?" Veronica grinned at Millie, enjoying the slight flush coloring her cheeks. Now she knew Millie was single, flustering Millie had become her favorite pastime, when she wasn't recovering from being flustered herself.

"Err. No. The gates aren't fixed. The part you pass through kisses the posts. It's built so sheep and cows can't get in or out but people can." Millie shouldered her daypack, studiously avoiding Veronica's eyes.

Not as much a player when we're alone. And I am deep in the friend zone. Veronica sighed quietly and placed her daypack on the ground. Working together, they pulled the roof of the convertible up and secured it. They walked toward the gate without speaking, their boots crunching the gravel of the car park loud in the silence between them. They navigated the gate, no kissing involved, much to Veronica's disappointment. The stony well-worn track was an easy walk. Millie's shoulders were squared, her body was stiff, her usual easy athletic gait absent.

Veronica chewed her lip and tried to think of something to say to break the uncomfortable silence between them. After a few minutes, they came to a shallow wide stream. They crossed it still not speaking. *She's nervous and uncomfortable, and I'm an ass. I shouldn't have said anything. Shouldn't have teased her.*

They approached another kissing gate. Millie's steps slowed and her body tensed even more as she hurried through the gate. *Damn. I ruined what could have been a pleasant hike. What was I thinking? She's not into me like that. She wants a friend. Not looking for anything more.*

The track angled downhill and toward a rocky shore. They followed the shoreline and crossed several small streams. Distracted by the perfection of Millie's ass as she navigated the steep path of stepping-stones on the opposite side of the stream, Veronica lost her footing on a slick stone. Icy cold water filled her boot before she managed to right herself, narrowly avoiding ending up on her ass in the stream.

Millie bounded back across the rocks and offered her a steadying hand. "You okay?"

Veronica took hold of Millie's hand, forcing herself to ignore how much she enjoyed touching her. "Slipped. I'm okay now."

Millie met her gaze and Veronica swallowed hard. The heat and hunger shone in Millie's eyes and Veronica wondered if Millie was interested after all.

"Let me help you." Millie squeezed Veronica's hand. Her normally deep voice was husky.

Veronica trembled, her body responding to Millie's voice and the sensation of her touch. Millie held on as they crossed the stream and didn't let go when they made the trail on the other side. Veronica bit her lip, not daring to say anything that might break the spell. She let herself be led. They crested the rise and a wide shore spread out before them. The water was a tropical blue and a white band spread along the edge of the water. The beach was deserted. A few gulls spun in lazy circles over the shore and then flew out over the sea. The sound of waves washing against the beach and the scent of the ocean made Veronica's heart swell. "I've missed the sound of the ocean. We went all the time when I was growing up. The beach was my happy place."

Millie let go of her hand, and Veronica was immediately bereft. She gestured toward the beach—"Maybe this can be a happy place too"—before she ducked her head and led the way down the path to the shore.

The beach was made of small broken shells and bleached bits of seaweed skeletons. The crisp salt smell of the ocean and the cries of the gulls filled her senses. Millie walked next to her, and on impulse, Veronica took her hand and laced their fingers together. "Thank you. This is what I needed. This place fills my soul."

"I'm happy then." Millie glanced at her, cheeks red. "I like it when you're happy."

Veronica tugged them to a stop so she could peer into Millie's face. Her expression was guarded, hopeful, and it made Veronica's heart ache. She lifted on her toes and pressed a kiss to Millie's cheek. She lowered herself and studied Millie's eyes. Fear had replaced longing. *Too much. Back off. Let her have her space. She feels it too. She's freaked out.*

Millie gave her a tight smile and released her hand and stepped back. "Let me show you my favorite place to have tea." She turned and walked away.

Veronica struggled to focus as she walked behind Millie, distracted by mental images of her hands and mouth on Millie's body, fantasizing about tracing her tongue over her soft curves and hard muscles, pressing her lips against the nape of Millie's neck as she lay beneath her. *How am I ever going to tell her how much I want her? She's freaked out. Why? Is it the work thing? Or she's one of those women who always have to be in control. Maybe she doesn't like being pursued? Or she's not into women who look like me. Maybe it's the race thing.*

Veronica chewed her lip as she walked, studying the ground, so distracted she bumped into Millie. Again. Millie turned and grinned at her. "Anxious to eat?"

Veronica's heart squeezed hard. It was the first flirty thing Millie had said since they had left the house.

Veronica laughed. "Hell yes. It's been a while since breakfast."

"This is the Ghrobain. Best view of the beach."

They dropped their packs and Millie pulled out a green-and-white checkered oilcloth, shook it open, and spread it over the ground. Veronica sat on the cloth, careful to keep her shoes off the side. Millie pulled two thermoses from her pack. She handed one to Veronica. "This is for you. Robin knows you don't fancy tea."

"She's very thoughtful. I like her. We've gotten to know each other a bit."

Millie paused in laying out the small boxes of food and looked at Veronica. "She's a good person. Had a hard life." She leveled her gaze at Veronica. "Are you seeing her?"

"What? No." Veronica realized how harshly she had spoken from the change in Millie's expression. "No. She's not my type." She spoke softly this time.

"Because of her past?" Millie's face was neutral, her voice even. "Because she was a sex worker?"

"No. I didn't know. It's not that." *She's not you.* "I'm not into blondes."

"Blondes. In general?" Millie fiddled with the wrapping on her sandwich. "Do you not date white women?"

"I date who I'm attracted to. I've not dated a white woman, but I'm not opposed to it. Robin's a wonderful person, but I don't feel a spark with her." *Like I feel with you. Say it. Don't say it.* "We're friends."

"Good. That's good." Millie lowered her chin to her chest as she traced a finger over the oilcloth's pattern. "I mean that you aren't judging her because of her past."

Veronica took a sip of coffee. "I'm not in a position to judge anyone."

Millie took a bite of her sandwich and chewed slowly before she swallowed. "Position or not, it doesn't stop some people."

"What about you?" Veronica nibbled on her sandwich. "Do you date women who are aren't white?" *Might as well get it out there.*

"Yes. But not in a very long time." She crumbled the wrapper in her fist. "Hurry up. I want to show you the rest of the beach. If I timed the tide right, we can cross over the causeway to Lampay." She pointed to a tiny island offshore.

Chapter Eight

VERONICA RODE JACK out to the picnic area. After removing his tack, she turned him loose in the small paddock. She moved the tarp covering the cord of firewood on the far side of the turnout shed and restocked the wood in neat rows between two trees near the fire ring. Veronica assessed the seating area before she pulled on a pair of black nitrile gloves and picked up the remainders of the fireside buffet. A pair of white silk panties hung in tatters over one of the wooden bench seats, a leather paddle next to them. She picked up the paddle and placed it into the red plastic bag for toys. After a moment's hesitation, Veronica gingerly picked up the remains of the panties and dropped them into the black plastic bag she had brought for trash.

Two floggers and a strap-on later she had finished cleaning up the aftermath of a client's fantasy come true. Working her way around the site, she tidied up. She moved the wooden seats back into a neat circle, trying not to let her own fantasies get in the way of her work. *Millie's unattached. Skittish as hell. Maybe she's stone? Elaine sure got quiet. What is the story there? Do I want to find out?* The simple nature of her work left plenty of time to think, and Veronica turned events over in her head.

She grimaced as she bent to pick up a crop left on the ground. *I wonder if they treat their own toys like this? What the hell, they could have at least left it off the wet ground. Well, they pay for the privilege. I'll ask her to take me to Portree to drop off Bella's saddle.* She laughed out loud, remembering the bedraggled wet-to-the-skin-guest who didn't take her warning about not letting Bella linger too long in the stream. She'd promptly divested herself of her rider and rolled in the water, saddle and all. The guest was good-natured about it. Veronica had been impressed with her humor, not to mention the way her wet riding clothes hugged her body.

Millie looked like she wanted me to kiss her on the hike. I need to talk to her. Away from everyone so we can talk and not be interrupted, somewhere she can't run away when she gets uncomfortable. When Veronica finished picking up the circle, she raked the ground. She filled the fire bucket and placed it next to the fire ring.

Veronica tied off the plastic trash bag and placed it on top of the fence post. "You'd be happy if we stayed here all day, wouldn't you?" She patted Jack's shoulder. He lifted his head from the hay crib and fixed her with his large dark brown eye. "But we have work to do." She led him away from the hay. After slipping his bridle over his head she buckled it in place and tied his reins to the rail before she saddled him. Veronica used the fence as a makeshift mounting block to step into the saddle. *We need a mounting block out here. And a bin.* She stopped long enough to pick up the bag of toys and trash bag from the top of the fence to carry back to the house. *Millie. That almost kiss. What would have happened? This is silly. I need to know one way or the other. I'll ask her out. Today. When we stack the hay.* "Let's go, boy, before I lose my nerve."

They rode back at a fast walk. Veronica settled into the horse's rhythm. *I can do this. She's not collared. She's a free agent. And so am I.*

WHAT AM I thinking? She doesn't like me like that. Why didn't she kiss me on the hike? Veronica rolled the muck cart out the door. *If she wanted me she'd let me know. She's not into me. But she seems like she is. Fucking queen of mixed messages. Why am I so chicken-shit? She's a grown-up and so am I. I'll ask her. If she says no, she says no.* She dumped the cart into the manure pit. *I'll ask her. Lunch is a good date, no pressure.* She trudged back to the barn with the muck cart. She leaned it against the wall and glanced at the clock. *She'll be here soon. Not like I'm counting the minutes. Much.*

MILLIE STOOD IN the hayloft backlit by the light filtering in from the gable end doors. "Which side do you want me to stack the older hay on?"

Kona, the barn cat, twisted and rubbed against Veronica's leg. Veronica leaned over and scratched the cat's ears before she pointed to the left side. "I want to move the bales from the last delivery to the left side, then I'll know to use it first." The cat meowed her annoyance at their disturbing her most favorite hunting ground and bolted down the loft steps.

They worked side by side, lifting the bails and stacking them neatly. "Orrin said he'd be by after lunch with the hay delivery."

Millie quirked her mouth. "That means after his nap, so he won't be here until close to supper." Her shirt was wet with sweat and her skin glistened, and all Veronica wanted to do was to nibble and kiss the long line of Millie's throat. She imagined the salt taste of the skin there. Millie rested her hands on her hips and tilted her head at Veronica, her expression curious, a half smile on her face, letting Veronica know she had caught her staring.

Ask. Ask her now. "Do you think you could take me to the saddlery in Portree? I need to leave Bella's saddle with them for repair. And then I could take you to lunch?" The words came out in a rush, and Veronica cursed herself for being so nervous. *When did that happen? When did I get so shy? Because she's not a player. And neither am I.*

"Like a date?" Millie raised both eyebrows.

Veronica squared her shoulders and took a deep breath. "Yeah. Yes. A date."

"I can't. I've got to—" Millie tucked her hands in her front pockets.

Veronica stifled her flinch at Millie's refusal and spoke over her, not wanting to hear her excuse, not wanting her to know how disappointed she was. *Friends. She wants to be friends. Or friends with benefits. Not someone to date. She's not into me that way.* "Never mind. It's okay. I know you're busy. I've got another saddle I can use. You could drop it off for me next time you have to make a supply run." Veronica turned her back to Millie and busied herself with straightening the already straight bale of hay in front of her. *Let it go. She's not into you. Get it together.*

Millie's hand on her shoulder made her tremble. "I can't this week because of guest pickups." Her breath tickled the back of Veronica's neck. "I'd love to go on a date with you. Would next week be too long to wait?"

Veronica turned to face her. Millie held her ground, their bodies pressed together, her body fitting neatly into Millie's. Before she could talk herself out of it, Veronica raised her hand and cupped the back of Millie's head and kissed her, a soft brush of her lips. Millie answered the kiss with a low growl, and her broad hands gripped

Veronica's hipbones and pulled her harder against her. Veronica moaned at the firm press of Millie's body, the softness of her breasts contrasting with the hard muscles of her stomach. The scent of hay, salt tang of sweat, and Millie's cologne, a mixture of cedar and sandalwood that always made Veronica think of cold winters snuggled in front of warm fireplaces, surrounded her.

They kissed softly at first, their lips and tongues exploring each other, the kiss building into more as they clung to each other. *She tastes so good. So much I want with her. But not here. We need to slow down.*

Veronica pulled back and looked into Millie's eyes. "No. Not too long to wait." She kissed Millie's throat and the underside of her jaw. "For the saddlery." Millie trembled under her kisses as she scattered them along her throat. She gave her the edge of her teeth, and Millie's pulse beat a rapid tattoo under Veronica's lips. "I'll wait for you." A gentle groan rattled Millie's chest, sending a current of desire whipping through Veronica. She bit back her own moan of want as need raced through her like heat lightning.

Millie's strong hands stroked her back on either side of her spine before they settled on her hips. She rubbed her thumbs up and down Veronica's waist. "You would?" She kissed Veronica again, mouth fierce, and Veronica's body responded with a rush of wet heat soaking her jeans. She wrapped her arms around Veronica and held her close, the intensity of her kiss rendering Veronica senseless. She placed a hand on Millie's chest and eased back from the kiss, their harsh rapid breathing loud in the loft. She leaned her forehead against Millie's chest. "As long as you need. Whenever you're ready."

Millie's phone chimed, and they both groaned. Millie stepped away from her and answered the call. "Yes, Ma'am. I'll have the car around in fifteen minutes. No, Ma'am, not working out. Helping Veronica in the stable." She ended the call and grinned at Veronica. "What are you doing this evening, after the hay delivery?"

Veronica stepped up on a hay bale to give herself a height advantage. Millie leaned forward and nuzzled her breasts through her shirt. Veronica held her close, her hand on the back of Millie's head, fingers rubbing the fine short hairs on the back of her neck. She held her there as she arched into her, forcing her breasts against Millie's face. She shuddered as Millie mouthed a nipple through her shirt.

"Whatever you're doing," she murmured against the top of Millie's head, loving the way her brush cut tickled her cheek.

Millie lifted her head and stared into Veronica's eyes. "Meet me at my apartment? After supper. Please."

The earnest plea in her voice and the way her eyes burned with desire had Veronica fighting not to come on the spot. "Yes."

THAT EVENING'S DINNER was the longest Veronica could ever remember sitting through. Not willing to risk sitting across from Millie, she had chosen to sit next to her. Millie shifted on the bench and the long length of her muscular thigh pressed against Veronica's leg. She willed herself not to tackle Millie and finish what had begun in the loft that afternoon. *I want her so much. I've wanted her since she wiped the ink mark off my cheek.* She pushed her food around with her fork, her stomach in knots. Thoughts of what she wanted to do with Millie, and replays of their kiss in the loft, made her shift and press her legs together in a futile attempt to stem the flow of wet heat between her legs.

"Hello, Veronica, are you in there? Pass the salt." Benita's teasing tone cut through Veronica's haze.

"Oh. Sorry. Sure." Veronica passed the salt to Benita who fixed her with a raised eyebrow as she took the shaker from Veronica's hand.

Millie was engaged in conversation with Myfanwy. *Welsh. Who knew it was so damn sexy?* The melodious tones of her deep voice as she spoke to Myfanwy did things to Veronica, wonderful erotic things. *Her voice. This is killing me. Slow. I need to slow my roll. I want more. More than a one-off. I don't want a friend with benefits. I want more. All of it. What if she's not into power play?* Veronica sipped her water. She'd had women who were vanilla. *She seemed to like it in the barn, but what if she isn't? I wouldn't be satisfied, not in the long term. Not going to rush into a relationship. No more U-hauls for me. Relationship. Is that what this will be? Talk. We're going to talk first. Then it'll be what it will be.*

Veronica caught Ashley alternately glaring at her and then at Millie. She returned her hard expression, making sure she used her most fierce *what-the-hell-is-your-problem* look. Ashley averted her gaze, threw her nupkin down, stood and left the table abruptly. Her sharp exit made a few people glance up. Most ignored her.

Benita raised her eyebrow at Veronica and quirked her mouth. "Some people are poor losers." She shifted her gaze to Millie and then back to Veronica. Benita's words had been said softly, but in an instant Veronica knew whatever idea she had about keeping her interest in Millie quiet was not about to happen. *Not here, where everyone seems to know everything about everyone. Great. Everyone will be in our business.* Veronica grimaced as she remembered navigating the ever-shifting sea of alliances during her incarceration, how hard she had to work to keep to herself, and not become embroiled in short term hookups. They had teased her, nicknaming her "the fighting nun", but she had been tough enough and big enough to defend her choice to remain celibate. *I'm free. I'm safe. I'm okay. No one here will try to force themselves on me.*

"They are. And they need to get over themselves if they want to keep their jobs." Myfanwy's tone was sharp and cut through the conversation at the table. A beat went by as Myfanwy made eye contact with each of the women at the table before she went back to eating.

Veronica was unsure what had happened. She didn't know what went on in the house proper as she had confined her exploration of the house to the library, the game room, and the kitchen. She finished her last bite of potatoes and touched her napkin to her mouth. "Excuse me please, ladies."

"Not staying for pudding?" Myfanwy's tone of mock surprise and wicked grin reinforced Veronica's suspicion she knew exactly why she was so anxious to end her meal.

"I've got some things to attend to, um, in the barn."

Veronica left the dining room rapidly and changed back into boots. She glanced at the clock over the door in the mudroom. *Time for a shower. What to wear?*

VERONICA PATTED HER hair in place. It had grown out from her low cut, and she knew she'd have to start twisting it if she wanted locs again or get it trimmed if she wanted to keep her low cut. *Millie's haircut is always sharp. Myfanwy keeps it trimmed for her. Would she trim mine? I'll ask. Too late for tonight.* She chose a baby-blue short-sleeve button-down and her best pair of jeans to wear. Sorting through her clothes to find an outfit reminded her of the sorry state of her closet. She'd have her mom ship the rest of her clothes. She had come with very little, not wanting to have to worry about transporting a bunch of things home if the job didn't work out. The freedom she had in this little part of Scotland was more than she had ever experienced at home. She was well paid and was well on her way to paying her parents back for what they had laid out for her poor excuse of a lawyer and her fine. She couldn't even imagine not renewing her contract. She texted Millie to make sure she was back at her apartment. After her phone vibrated with her positive response, Veronica checked herself in the mirror one last time before she closed the door to her room and locked it.

THE SIX-CAR garage was on the opposite side of the house from the barn. The gravel crunched under her boots and Veronica's steps were quick. She arrived at the steps up to Millie's apartment out of breath and waited a minute before she climbed the stairs, not wanting to arrive panting. She walked haltingly up the steps. Millie opened the door before she got there. She was wearing a white tank top and black jeans hugged her thick thighs.

Veronica's mouth went dry. "Hi."

"Hi yourself." Millie stepped back and Veronica entered her space. *Kiss her? No.* She stepped back. *She's nervous too.* The entryway led to a spacious layout, an open plan with a small kitchen area. Veronica saw a short hallway with two closed doors. The apartment was decorated in a simple style and bold bright colors, a sharp contrast to the dated elegance of the main house and extravagant compared to Veronica's bedsit, modern but not over the top. As she swept her gaze around the room she noticed a guitar on a stand. "Hey, do you play?"

Millie ran her finger around the top of her glass. "Some of us play open mike nights at a pub in Portree. Benita sings and Tessa plays the fiddle. Would you like a drink? I've a bottle of Talisker if you like single malt, or beer?"

Veronica noticed the glass on the sideboard with a small bit of liquor in it. *She started early. Really nervous.*

"What are you drinking?"

"I'm finishing the last of my Edradour. Sorry, I should have waited." Millie turned back to the bar.

"No problem. Single malts have been above my pay grade forever. I'd like to try the Talisker."

Millie poured out a healthy two fingers of scotch into a squat glass and passed it to Veronica.

Veronica took a sip, the sweet smooth taste and slight burn convincing her all the people who raved about single malts were right. "Delicious."

Millie tapped the empty bottle of Edradour. "When I get another bottle, you have to try it. It's different, a little less peaty, and my favorite."

"It's a date." Veronica sipped her drink, her body responding to the alcohol, a warm relaxation spreading through her. *Need to slow down before I'm drunk. It's been forever.* She placed her drink on the end table next to the couch.

"May I?" Veronica tilted her head at the guitar.

"Certainly." Millie sipped her whisky.

Veronica picked up the guitar, sat down on the couch and cradled it against her body. It was a Dreadnought, a full-size guitar fitted for Millie. Veronica strummed her fingers over the strings. She focused and picked out a tune she remembered from years of guitar lessons, from the time when her mother was convinced Veronica would be a classical guitarist. It had lasted until Veronica took her first algebra class, fell in love with mathematics, and joined the academic challenge team. College and her graduate school fellowship had slammed the door on anything other than her studies and teaching. She picked out a tune from memory, reminded how exquisite it was to create beautiful sounds. She missed a chord and stopped playing.

"It's not tuned for classical music. We play some classic rock favorites, and some rockabilly tunes." Millie sat in the chair across from Veronica. "You studied guitar." It wasn't said as a question, but as an acknowledgment of Veronica's skill.

Veronica stopped and put the guitar back in its holder. "I did. Once upon a time. I'm rusty."

Millie fixed her gaze on her. Veronica struggled with her sense of being exposed. *Another layer peeled back. This is how it goes. Learning about each other. The joy of being known.* "I haven't played in years."

Millie met her gaze. "You should. You enjoy it; it shows on your face. I've not seen you so peaceful and relaxed since you arrived. I can't imagine how beautifully you would play if you practiced."

Veronica flushed. "Thanks for letting me plunk around on your guitar."

"That was more than plunking. It's big for you and not tuned for classical playing and still it sounded amazing. You've a gift. You should share it."

"I'll think about it." Veronica shifted her gaze away from Millie's face. "Your apartment is fantastic. I like the bold colors."

Millie laughed. "Thank you. Myfanwy decorated it."

"She takes good care of you, doesn't she?" Veronica worked hard to keep the wistfulness out of her voice. She had not had a friend, a best friend in years. Her ex-best friend had ghosted while she was incarcerated. Veronica picked at the fabric of her pants, shoving her anger and hurt over her friend's abandonment down into the tight box she kept it in.

Millie tilted her head. "She does. Since Uni. We played rugby together and shared a room for four years."

Veronica raised her eyebrow. "Myfanwy played rugby? She seems so—gentle." She giggled. "I can't imagine her tackling anyone, she's such a lady."

Millie laughed with her. "She steps on a rugby pitch and becomes a beast." She stood and went over to the bookshelf and pulled a large album from the shelf. She sat next to Veronica on the couch and flipped through the pages. She turned the book toward Veronica. On the page was a rugby team shot, Myfanwy and Millie easy to pick out in the group. Below the group photo was an action shot of Myfanwy straight-arming a player, her lips pulled back in a snarl as she avoided a tackle. The photograph gave Veronica an entirely new appreciation of the woman who made the most delicious food she had ever eaten.

"Damn. She was fierce."

"Still is."

Veronica flipped the page. A team shot with women dressed in all-black rugby kits stared back at her. Millie was in the back row, her red hair and build making her easy to pick out. "You played for the Black Ferns?"

Millie took the photo album from Veronica's hands. "For a bit."

"Scotland is a long way from New Zealand. How did you end up there?" Veronica traced her finger over the edge of the photo album.

"I was recruited by a woman I met on holiday in New Zealand." Millie tugged at her shirt collar, her tone flat.

"Recruited?" Veronica raised an eyebrow.

Millie grimaced and glanced down at the page, avoiding Veronica's eyes, her knuckles white where she gripped the photo album. "You know about the Black Ferns?"

Aware of Millie's discomfort, Veronica kept her tone even. "My first college girlfriend played rugby. I learned a lot watching her play. And she was obsessed with the Black Ferns. You must have been outstanding to play with them."

"Better than most, not as good as some." Millie closed the album and placed it reverently on the shelf. "Ancient history."

Veronica had a million questions she wanted to ask but took the clue and let it go.

Millie picked up the guitar and sat in the chair across from the couch and settled the guitar next to her body. Her fingers moved over the strings as she played a song Veronica was unfamiliar with, a ballad she suspected from the ebb and flow of the music.

Veronica was entranced as she watched the change in Millie's features as she played. She focused on her hands, fantasizing about how it would be if Millie's skillful hands were on her. Millie finished playing and placed the guitar back in its stand.

She moved back to the couch and sat next to her, so close the length of their thighs touched. Millie clasped Veronica's hand. "I know you didn't come here to talk about my decor, or guitars, or listen to me play."

Veronica barked out a laugh. "No. But I didn't have an agenda." At Millie's raised eyebrow she continued. "I'm out of practice."

Millie squeezed her hand. "You seemed to remember fine in the loft."

Veronica turned to Millie. She brushed her lips over her mouth. The quiet needy noise from Millie was laced with want. Veronica pulled back and raised her hand to Millie's face. She touched her lips with her fingertips before she shifted her hand and gripped the back of Millie's neck. She held her still while she kissed her way along her neck, leaning over to scatter nips and kisses over her wide shoulders. In one movement, Millie slid an arm around Veronica and pulled her onto her lap. Veronica straddled her hips. Millie's hands cupped her ass and pulled her close as she ground determinedly against Veronica, the pressure on her clit intense and pleasurable.

She palmed Millie's breast, relishing the way her nipple hardened under her hand, her flesh warm and pliant beneath the soft cotton. She squeezed her breast as she rolled her nipple, rewarded by a deep groan from Millie. She rolled her hips against Millie, pushing hard against her body. The change in Millie's breathing signaled her, letting her know she had found the right pace. Millie's hands were a vise on her hips, and her fingertips dug into Veronica's flesh. Veronica took Millie's mouth, unable to get enough of the strong woman under her. She pinched and tugged her nipple in rhythm with the movement of her hips. Moving her lips to the shell of her ear, she whispered. "Do you want to come for me?"

"Yes. So much." Millie panted. "Please."

Veronica rocked hard, hating the clothes between them, so desperate to hear Millie come for her she didn't want to stop to get undressed. She increased her movements and moved her other hand to Millie's other nipple as she rolled and pinched both of them. She leaned back and fixed her gaze on Millie's face. "Come on, babe, give it to me."

Millie's body shook as she came, mouth open, eyes closed, no sound other than her harsh breathing. Veronica lowered her head to the apex between her neck and shoulder and bit down hard. She took the smooth skin and hard muscle between her teeth, rolling it, stopping shy of breaking the skin, forcing a shout and a second orgasm from Millie. She released her teeth and licked and sucked at the mark she had left and nuzzled her neck while Millie's breathing returned to normal. Veronica leaned back to admire the aftermath of their session and the way Millie's face glowed post orgasm. Unable to resist, she kissed her eyelids, the sharp angle of her cheekbone and the scattering of freckles across her cheeks.

Millie opened her eyes and pulled Veronica into a bone-crushing embrace. "You remember fine. I don't remember the last time I came from grinding." She kissed the side of Veronica's neck and Veronica trembled with want. "How about you? What do you need?"

She slipped her hand down between their bodies. Millie thumbed open the top button of Veronica's jeans and pushed her hand inside. Veronica groaned and shuddered as Millie's fingertip brushed her clit, once, twice, and then she exploded in a flash of pleasure. Millie pushed lower and slipped one thick finger inside Veronica and stroked her to another orgasm.

"Oh. Enough. You're going to kill me." Veronica panted and shifted her hips. She rested her head on Millie's shoulder.

Millie jerked her hand from Veronica's pants. "Did I hurt you?"

Her sudden movement made Veronica sit up so she could see Millie's face.

Her brow was knit. "I'm sorry. I didn't mean to be so rough."

The fear and concern in her voice brought Veronica out of her pleasant post-orgasm lassitude. "You didn't hurt me. I'm fine." She kissed Millie gently. "More than fine." Veronica sensed the tension in Millie's body fade as she kissed her way down Millie's neck and then along her jaw before she returned to her mouth. Her body hummed with pleasure. *So much for going slow. I could kiss her for days. So delicious.*

Millie shifted under her. She cupped Veronica's ass in her broad hands and squeezed. *Slow down. Don't rush this. So hard. Do this the right way.* She pulled back to look into Millie's eyes again. She placed her hand on her chest and spread her fingers wide. "I want. So much I want to do with you. I don't want you to think it's because I'm desperate." Veronica wrapped her arms around Millie's shoulders.

Millie's hands stilled. She moved her hands to Veronica's hips and leaned her brow against Veronica's chin. "I don't think that. If you had only wanted a hookup you would have taken Ashley up on her offers, or any of the others who were angling to get to spend time with you in the stable, sure they could woo you away from your monk-like existence."

Veronica sat back. "What?"

Millie smirked. "You didn't notice the constant stream of new barn helpers? You made shoveling manure appealing. There's a waitlist to be your helper. And a contest to see whose charms you would succumb to first."

"A contest? Oh for fuck's sake." Veronica moved her arms in an attempt to lever her body up and off Millie's lap. "What? Why?"

Millie held tight to Veronica. "Have you looked in the mirror? You're gorgeous. Why wouldn't they try to get your attention?"

Veronica placed both hands on Millie's chest. "Let me go. Now."

Millie's voice softened and her tone became serious as she relaxed her grip on Veronica. "Why, Veronica? Why have you shut them down and ignored them?" She dusted her fingertips over Veronica's cheek.

This is it. Time to fess up. Say it. Tell her. Be honest. "They're not my kind of women."

Millie drew her hand away from Veronica's face. "Is it because of their profession? Because they're sex workers?" Her voice held censure.

"No. Because I... Because I want more. Someone mine. I'm not into sharing." Veronica picked up Millie's hand and kissed her knuckles. "And because I want more with you."

Millie tilted her head and studied Veronica. "More?" She pressed a gentle kiss against Veronica's jaw. "More of this?" Her seductive delivery had Veronica wanting to kiss her again and not stop until they were both naked. And yet not. She was going to do this right this time.

"Yes. But not only that. I want all of you. Not just sex. I want you, Millie. I want to know you."

Millie inhaled sharply. She broke their embrace, set Veronica off her lap, and stood. "Okay." She paced the room, scrubbing her hand through her hair. She stopped and picked up her glass and gulped the rest of her drink. "Well. Okay, that's different."

Veronica watched as a wariness filled Millie's face. "I didn't mean to make you uncomfortable." *She's not looking for more. Just wanted a hookup. To win the fucking contest? Damn it that's what Benita meant. Fuck. I shouldn't have said anything. She's freaked out. It was a game.* She stood and jammed her hands in her pockets. "I'm not cool with being a prize. I get it. You were trying to win."

Millie stopped pacing and turned to Veronica. "You think I was trying to win the bloody contest? Is that what you think of me?" Her mouth drew down at the corners, her eyes dark.

Veronica studied the pattern on the linoleum avoiding Millie's eyes and sighed. "I don't know what I think. I'm sorry if I gave a different impression in the barn. This was a mis..."

"Don't you dare say it was a mistake." Millie was in front of her now. She cupped Veronica's face with both hands and forced her to meet her gaze. *Hunger. Need. Desire. She wants me. But not like I want her. Damn. Do it. Give in. Something is better than nothing. No. Not going to be a prize in some stupid contest. Fuck, this hurts.*

Millie's voice was rough. "Please. Don't say it was a mistake. I wanted you to kiss me. I wanted you because of you, not because of some idiotic bet. I wanted tonight."

Veronica wanted to kiss her, to spend the rest of the night kissing her, to take what Millie was offering, to say the hell with it, but she couldn't ignore the ache in her heart, the part of her that wanted to matter to someone beyond a one-night stand. She placed both hands on Millie's chest, fingers spread wide. "I can't do this if sex is all it is. Sorry." Millie stepped back, and Veronica moved toward the door.

Veronica reached for the doorknob. Stopped and turned back to Millie. "Thanks for the drink. I enjoyed talking with you. And listening to you play." She flushed. "And the other." She stared into Millie's eyes. "Will you let me tag along some night when you guys play?"

"We have a gig next in two weeks. I'll text you the details." Millie's voice was flat and her expression shuttered.

Not interested in anything other than my body. Friends with benefits. Damn it. I thought she was different. Fuck me. Ugh, this is awkward. Why did I ever kiss her? Or think she was different? Or wanted more with me? Fuck me. The easy time between them ended. Veronica rested her palm on the doorknob. "I've got an early morning. So, um, I'll say good night. Thanks again."

Millie cradled her glass in her hands. "A pleasure having you. I don't have many visitors to my apartment."

"Why?" Veronica dug her fingers into her palm, not certain she wanted to hear the answer, but angry and hurt enough to ask if she was one of many. "Do you go to their rooms in the house?"

A flash of anger crossed Millie's face before she smoothed her expression. "Not in a very long time." Millie turned back to the bar and poured herself another drink. "See you."

Veronica let herself out. *Like everyone else. Only interested in my body. I'm not even a person to her. I'm some exotic prize to be won.* She dashed her hand across her face to wipe away the thoughts of Millie with the other women in the house. *Should've known. Should've guessed. She's all that. But not with me. Unless it's to win a contest. Fuck that. This was a quick hookup to win a bet. It wasn't anything. Damn, I wanted it to be.*

Chapter Nine

VERONICA KICKED THE covers off her legs and turned to her side. She turned on the light, picked up her book, and began reading, hoping the police procedural mystery would distract her from the bonfire of humiliation and anger in her chest. In her thoughts she sorted through her interactions with Millie, trying to pick apart why she had let her guard down and believed Millie was different. Two months of thinking Millie was special, someone who saw past her appearance. No matter how she added up the sum total of their interactions, the end result was always the same. Veronica had been some notch to carve, a prize, a goal. Something to brag about the next time the other women of the house sat around the dining table.

"Not going to breakfast that's for sure." She spoke out loud. And then grimaced at the hollow pathetic sound of her voice. She groaned and stuck her bookmark back into her book before she marched to the small mirror over her sink. She studied her reflection briefly before bushing her teeth. *Look at me. Wallowing. Feeling sorry for myself. I'm stronger than this. Fuck her. So what? It's not the first time I've been used. So fucking what? Get over it. I'm not in jail for something I didn't do. I'm safe. I'm in control. This place is so big I can avoid her if I want to.* She finished brushing her teeth. She soaked a washcloth in cool water and wiped her face and the back of her neck. *Sleep. It'll be better in the morning. I've got a job I like.*

Books to read. Time to think. Three hots and a cot. What else do I need?

PHONE. MY PHONE. Who the hell is calling me this late? Anxiety kicked in as she imagined some horrible reason her family was calling her in the middle of the night. She scrambled out of her bed and stubbed her toe on the way to her desk. "Fuck." She squinted at the screen. *What the hell?* She thumbed the phone on. "Do you know what time it is?" She didn't bother to stifle her angry tone.

Millie's voice rumbled through the phone. "Yes. Half three."

Drunk. She drunk dialed me. From across the yard. "Are you drunk?"

"Aye. Guttered."

"And you felt compelled to wake me at three thirty in the morning to tell me?" Veronica blew out a breath.

"Are you mad at me?"

"No. Yes. I'm pissed off. I don't like being used. That was fucked up."

"It wasn't about the idiotic contest. Not for me. I wasn't in it. I swear." Millie's tone was earnest. "It wasn't for the contest. Please believe me."

Is she lying? She's trying to make it right. Even if she's drunk. Veronica pursed her lips. "I believe you."

"Thank you. Did you mean it? About the other?" Millie's voice was a whisper, and Veronica had to strain to hear her.

"Mean what? I said I believe you."

"No. When we... After we... Did you mean what you said? You want to know me? Like really know me?" Millie's words were slurred but clear enough for Veronica to hear the fear laced through them.

"Yes. I don't say things I don't mean." Veronica twisted the hem of her sleep shirt in her hand. Millie mumbled something Veronica couldn't understand. She heard what sounded like a lamp breaking and cursing. "Are you okay? Do you need me to come over?" More mumbling and cursing came through the phone. "Millie! Hey! Answer me," Veronica shouted into the phone while reaching for her jeans, ready to cross the yard to make sure Millie was okay.

"Sorry. I'm here."

"Did you fall?"

"No. Knocked the lamp over, dropped my phone."

"Millie, don't drink anymore. Please. Go to bed. We'll talk in the morning. I meant it. I want more with you. You. Not only your body. All of you. Go to sleep, okay?"

"'Kay. Night. You really mean it?"

"Yes. We'll talk in the morning. Go to sleep. Good night."

Veronica placed her phone back on the desk. She groaned when she thought of the early morning ride she had to prepare two horses for, in addition to the other barn work. She slipped under her covers, willing herself to sleep and failing. *It's going to be a long day. She's interested in more. Will she be when she's sober? She was tore up. Is she an alcoholic? Or was she freaked out? I've never seen her drink at supper. Maybe she doesn't like wine.* Veronica lay in bed, mulling over her conversation with Millie. She waited until she knew Myfanwy would be baking the day's bread before she dressed and walked over to the kitchen. *Coffee. I need coffee and answers. Myfanwy. Myfanwy's her best friend.*

MYFANWY GLANCED UP from where she was bent over sliding the day's unbaked loaves into the oven when Veronica opened the kitchen door. "You're early. I've not got the coffee going, but there's tea in the pot."

Veronica shifted her gaze to her hands, avoiding Myfanwy's eyes. "Thank you. I'll wait for the coffee."

Myfanwy made a small sound in acknowledgment of Veronica's words. The kitchen was quiet, and Veronica sat in silence unsure how to proceed, not even knowing what she wanted to ask or if Myfanwy would tell her. A large cooling rack held two dozen muffins. Veronica's stomach rumbled. She knotted her fingers together to keep them from trembling. The silence in the kitchen was uncomfortable. *Say something. Ask her. She's her best friend. Say something.*

Myfanwy kept her back to Veronica as she measured and ground the beans for the coffee press. The smell of the fresh ground beans filled the kitchen and Veronica's mouth watered.

The electric kettle clicked off and Myfanwy poured the water over the grounds and placed the top on the coffee press. "You want something to eat?"

"I don't want to be any trouble. I can wait for staff breakfast."

"Then why're you here? Out of coffee in your room?" The directness of Myfanwy's gaze as she placed a coffee cup in front of Veronica made her squirm.

Veronica held Myfanwy's gaze. "I wanted to talk to you."

Myfanwy pursed her lips and crossed her arms. "If you're here because you think I've got some magical advice for you or inside information about Millie, you're going to be disappointed." She leaned close, invading

Veronica's space and dropped her voice low. "But know this, if you hurt her, there will not be a place in this house for you to hide." The menace in her voice shocked Veronica, and then she remembered the fierce photo of Myfanwy she had seen in Millie's room.

Veronica shifted back in her chair. "Understood."

Myfanwy straightened up and tugged the hem of her chef's coat. "Good." She tapped Veronica on the shoulder. "If you wait a few minutes those chocolate orange muffins you like so well will be ready." Her voice was cheery as if she had not threatened Veronica.

"Thank you. I'd like that."

Myfanwy poured Veronica a cup of coffee and placed the French press next to the cup in front of her. She poured herself a cup of tea and sat down across the table from Veronica. "Do you want to tell me what you thought I might be able to tell you?"

Veronica studied Myfanwy's face. "She told me about the contest."

Myfanwy snorted. "Those women are idiots. I told them it wasn't right." She reached across the table and touched Veronica's arm. "I'm sorry I didn't take it up with the Mistresses."

Veronica met Myfanwy's gaze, her sincerity giving her courage to say what she had to say next. "I thought Millie was with me last night because of the contest." The thunderous anger twisting Myfanwy's features made Veronica rush to finish. "But she told me it wasn't about the contest."

"Are you looking for me to confirm her story?" Myfanwy's voice was sharp.

"No. I believe her." Veronica relaxed as Myfanwy's face shifted from angry to cautious.

"But? You must have some reason you wanted to talk to me."

Veronica took a deep breath, fearful of angering Myfanwy again with her next question. "I was angry when I left her. I didn't believe her at first. I left it bad with her. She called me early this morning. She was drunk. Is that a thing with her? Does she drink to excess?"

Myfanwy glanced up at the ceiling before she brought her gaze back to Veronica's face. "She's had struggles in the past."

Veronica read what Myfanwy didn't say in her expression. "I'm not judging her, Myfanwy." She reached out and touched the other woman's hand. "Thank you."

Myfanwy shook off Veronica's touch and stood up. "Muffin?" She busied herself with arranging two muffins on a plate.

Veronica traced the rim of her saucer. "Yes, please." She took a sip of her coffee and closed her eyes to savor the taste. The door to the kitchen slammed open.

"I'm gasping, please tell me there's tea ready." Millie stopped as she caught sight of Veronica. A blush crept from her collarbones and spread to her hairline. Her eyes were watery, and she appeared rough around the edges but better than Veronica expected after her drunken phone call.

"Morning, love. Tea's fresh, help yourself," Myfanwy called over her shoulder.

"Good morning." Veronica pushed the chair next to her away from the table and nodded at it with her head, a silent invitation for Millie to sit with her.

Millie inclined her head toward the chair and then back to Veronica's face. A hint of a smile played about her mouth as she sat down next to Veronica. "A very good morning." Under the table, Millie reached over, clasped Veronica's hand, and laced her fingers through Veronica's and squeezed once before she busied herself pouring her tea.

Chapter Ten

VERONICA PULLED HER backpack from the back of the car. Dark gray mountains loomed in the distance. Clouds wrapped the angled peaks a lighter gray in contrast to the black stone of the mountains.

Millie frowned. "Not sure it's the best day. This might burn off, but I don't know. We should take our rain gear."

"As long as we're together, it doesn't matter if it rains."

Millie stepped close and pulled Veronica into her arms. "I love it when you say things like that."

Veronica leaned her forehead against Millie's broad chest. "I don't want to rush. I want to take it slow."

Millie pressed a soft kiss to her mouth. "As slow as you want to go. I'm not going anywhere."

Veronica kissed her back. Heat flared in her, and she placed a hand on Millie's chest and stepped back. *Lunch. Hiking and lunch. Don't rush this. Get it right this time.*

The sun broke through the clouds and highlighted the rough terrain of the Quiraing. Gray rocks jutted out from the earth at sharp angles. Patchy grass, green and brown, spread out on the right side of the dull red path leading away from the car park. Millie led the way down the track.

"This is amazing. I've seen photos, but they don't do it justice."

"It's like your Grand Canyon. You can see the pictures, but until you're standing on the rim looking down it, it's not the same."

Veronica squinted at Millie. "You've been to the Grand Canyon?" She huffed out a breath. "That was something I promised myself I'd do once I finished my dissertation. It was going to be my reward."

Millie cocked her head toward her. "No reason you still can't go."

Veronica sighed. "Yeah. As soon as I pay my folks back. Maybe in a couple of years."

Millie touched her arm. "You'll get there. I'm sure."

The sheer dark face of a cliff loomed ahead. Veronica shivered. "Is that the formation they call the Prison?"

"Aye. This next part is a scramble over a stream."

"I'll try to stay dry this time." Veronica adjusted the strap on her daypack.

Millie led on, and they crossed the stream. The path crossed between the Prison and the high cliffs and up a bank of scree. Sharp rock columns jutted out of the ground on their left. They traveled on until they came to a wire fence. They crossed a stile and followed the path bordering a sharp cliff face. A long grassy field sloped off to their right as they traveled the steep path until they topped the summit. In front and below them, sheer cliff faces and rocky prominences surrounded a large grassy plateau.

Millie pointed at the plateau. "The Table. They say the locals used it to hide their livestock from marauders. You can't see it from the valley."

Veronica gazed out at the fantastical landscape. "It's gorgeous. How the hell did they get up there?"

"There's a path, but it's rough and a scramble at the top. We could do it if you want, but not today."

Millie led the way over the wet and muddy path. They found a large rocky formation with a view of the landscape, spread their oilcloth over it, and set out their lunch. Millie pointed out geological features as they ate their sandwiches. Veronica's fingers brushed the back of Millie's hand as they both reached for the last of Robin's cardamom shortbread. An electric current of desire rushed through Veronica, and she pulled her hand back. "Go ahead."

Millie picked up the shortbread, broke it in half, and offered it to Veronica. "Share it with me."

Veronica took the morsel from Millie's hand. She reflected as she chewed. This was what she had missed. The dance of getting to know someone. She brushed the crumbs from her fingers before she took a sip of water.

"What was your dissertation about? Your file didn't list the topic." Millie leaned back on her hands.

"You want the long version or the short version?" Veronica knotted her fingers together.

"Whichever version you want to share." Millie held her gaze.

"I always thought I would work with complex dimensions.

Millie tilted her head at Veronica. "I'm trying to remember my maths but it's been years since Uni. Are complex dimensions like the Riemann Sphere? The points to describe shapes, real and imaginary?"

Veronica stifled her urge to kiss Millie. *She gets it. Gets math. Could she be more perfect?*

"Yes, you get the idea, but then, after working with Doctor Kerr, Sarah, I fell in love with strange attractors. I was working with strange attractors like the Lorenz Attractor." Veronica took a sip of her water.

Millie smirked. "Fell in love with the theory or the woman?

Veronica laughed. "Both. Doctor Kerr is hard not to love."

"That she is. So tell me, what is an attractor, and what makes them strange?"

Veronica leaned back on her elbows. "An attractor can be a group of numbers, or just one point, or a group of points to describe a mathematical problem geometrically. In dynamic systems, systems that can change some attractors have fractal structures, and those are called strange attractors."

Millie raised an eyebrow. "Dynamic systems? Like weather systems? Or planetary orbits?"

Veronica grinned, excitement bubbling in her chest as she spoke. "Yes. And the most intriguing part of it is that out of what looks to be random patterns, strange attractors have a fractal structure. A pattern that repeats but is sensitive to initial conditions. It is chaotic, and yet not chaotic because of its structure. The Lorenz Attractor has a butterfly shape." Veronica wet her finger with her water and traced the pattern over the stone.

Millie scooted closer to Veronica. "Is that where butterfly theory comes from? That a flap of a butterfly's wing in one place can cause a tornado somewhere else?"

"No. That has to do with mathematical chaos and weather predictions and how infinitesimal changes can, as they are repeated over time, lead to large changes in the end result. Like if you are off with a small measurement that makes a very large difference in outcome because it compounds over time." Veronica studied the sky. The cloud cover had burned off, and sunlight reflected off the sea. *Like how a broken taillight landed me six years in prison.* "How much longer back to the car?"

"About an hour at our pace." Millie tucked the thermos into her pack.

Veronica reached out and touched her hand. "Can we sit a little longer? I like the view."

Millie stopped and sat next to Veronica. "Of course. I like the view too." She held Veronica's gaze long enough Veronica had to glance away before she forgot herself and said things it was too soon to say.

"I can't get enough of outside." Millie leaned back on her hands.

"Me too." Veronica picked up a pebble and turned it in her hands. "Until I got accepted into the horse rehab program, I lived for the hour a day we got outside. I didn't care if it was raining, snowing, sleeting, whatever, I had to get out and breathe and look at the sky and remind myself of what free was." She tossed the pebble and wiped her hands on her pants.

"Why didn't you want to go back and finish your dissertation?" Millie nudged Veronica's boot with her own.

Veronica knotted her hands together in her lap. "It didn't seem as important as it once was. I wanted to teach, but after my conviction, I'd never have been hired anywhere. And even if I could afford Miss Pomroy's fees for her to find the person who left those drugs in my car, even if she got them to confess or found hard evidence, and I could prove my innocence, be exonerated, the conviction stays on your record."

"That's so unfair. What kind of justice is that?" The outrage in Millie's voice was palpable.

"It's not any kind of justice." Veronica picked at the stitching on her boots.

"Don't you want to clear your name? I know Jaya would work with you, with your financial situation."

Veronica snorted. "I have negative net worth. My folks took a second mortgage on their house and money out of their retirement accounts to pay for my waste of space attorney who was supposed to keep me out of jail. I want to pay them back."

Millie stood abruptly. "But Veronica, it's not right. If I were innocent, I'd want the world to know."

Veronica studied Millie's expression, the anger and frustration in her eyes startling in its fierceness. "Easy, Millie. I'm cool with it. I like what I do. I like this job. The horses don't judge, and most of the people here don't either."

"I don't understand how you can let this go. Why give up and let some ass get away with it?"

"I told you. It wouldn't make any difference. I don't want my parents to suffer when they retire because of me." Veronica rose to her knees and picked up her pack. "It doesn't matter."

"But it does matter. You could..." Millie's voice was rough.

Veronica raised her voice, cutting off Millie's objection. "I don't want to talk about this anymore. It's a beautiful day. I don't want to think about it. Let it go, Millie. Please."

Millie shuffled her feet and kicked a loose stone down the path. "Right, sorry. None of my business if you want to waste your life shoveling horseshit."

"It's more than that. Don't disrespect my job. I do a lot more than that."

Veronica bent and picked up her pack, shouldered it, and stalked ahead. She focused on the scenery, desperate to stave off her sense of failure brought on by Millie's disapproval.

VERONICA LED CLYDE out to the mounting block, therapeutic saddle in place. Mistress Siobhan, dressed in Victorian-style red hunt jacket, white breeches, and knee-high boots engineered to accommodate her leg brace, rested her hand on Millie's forearm. Head high, imperious as a queen, she stood next to the mounting block. Her submissive, Marylyn, dressed in a dark-green cut-away styled Victorian ladies' riding habit, sat regally on Marco. The sidesaddle Veronica had unearthed from the back of the tack closet and spent hours cleaning and polishing gleamed in the sunlight.

Mistress Siobhan handed her cane to Veronica and allowed Millie to help her up the steps and into the saddle. Millie wrapped her arm around the haughty Mistress, tender and respectful, asking her what assistance she needed as she settled in the saddle. Veronica worked rapidly. With deft hands she secured Mistress Siobhan's leg with the straps that would assist her in remaining upright. Millie remained at her side, making sure Mistress Siobhan was balanced and stable.

"Tighten the strap on my leg, Veronica. I've only ridden in the ring. This will be my first time on the trail."

Veronica opened and adjusted the hook and loop closure, tightening it. "Clyde is rock solid, Ma'am. If you find yourself in trouble, drop the reins, and he'll stop. Millie and I will be right behind you. We'll get you settled at the fire ring and take care of the horses. When you're ready, call my phone, and we'll return."

Mistress Siobhan held Veronica's gaze. Her voice was quiet, for Veronica's ears alone. "Thank you for this. So many people act like having a stroke means you never think of sex again. I'm grateful to you. My Marylyn particularly likes to serve me at the fire ring. Do you have the lunge whip and other items I requested available?"

Veronica spoke in the same low tone. "I have the whip arranged next to the chair that is there for you and a valise with the other items you requested. I left a blanket and picnic basket with refreshments near the turnout shed. Your phone is in the basket. Call me when you're ready to return, or if you need assistance."

"Very good." She sat up straighter in the saddle and clasped the reins with her left hand. "Okay, Millie, you can let go of my ass now, if you got your fill." Her mocking tone made Veronica laugh out loud.

Millie backed away from the horse, laughing. "Yes, Mistress."

Veronica and Millie followed the pair at a distance that was safe and gave the couple their privacy on the ride. The familiar ache of wanting what she observed between Siobhan and Marylyn filled Veronica. *Thought I had that with Dee. The kind of love strong enough to bear up to any challenges life hurled at us. How wrong I was. She bailed. Gave up on us. Gave up on me.*

"That's love." Millie's husky voice startled Veronica.

"It is." She kept her eyes fixed on the couple ahead of them. "At the end of the day, no matter what, you want to be with the person who will wipe your ass if you can't do it yourself."

"Aye. And not dress you funny." Millie waited a beat and then laughed.

Millie's infectious laughter made Veronica laugh with her.

WHILE MILLIE ASSISTED Mistress Siobhan and Marilyn at the fire ring, Veronica settled the horses in the paddock. Satisfied the women no longer needed their company, Veronica and Millie hiked to the glen. Large boulders and rocks bordered the small stream running down the middle of the valley. The sunlight glinted off the water as it meandered its way over flat stones and sharp rocks. Veronica swiped a stray drop of sweat off her face. Millie passed her the thermos from her saddle pack, and she took a long drink of cool water.

"Do you fancy a snack? Robin packed us some biscuits and sandwiches."

Veronica smiled at Millie. "Not hungry"—she trailed her fingers down Millie's arm leaving tiny raised hairs in their wake—"for cookies."

Millie closed the flap on her saddle pack. "No?"

Veronica passed the water bottle back to Millie. "Nope."

Millie stowed the water bottle in the pack. "Sandwich, then?"

"Not hungry for anything but you." Veronica tugged her hand and pulled her into a kiss, loving the way Millie relaxed into her.

Millie's hands rested on Veronica's waist, her thumbs rubbing in small circles over Veronica's hipbones. "And after Robin spent so long making us lunch."

"Later." Veronica had wrapped one arm around Millie's broad shoulders, and with the other she played with the soft brush of hair on the back of her head. She scraped her fingernails along her scalp, and Millie moaned into her mouth and pulled her hips tighter to her. Veronica broke their kiss.

Millie leaned her head against Veronica's brow. "Later."

"Take your shirt off for me?" Veronica traced the edge of her nail over Millie's cheek.

"Vest too?" Millie raised her chin in challenge.

"All of it. I want to see you." Veronica cupped her cheek and brushed her thumb over her lips. "Don't you want to please me?" She stepped back. "Show me."

Millie snagged the hem of her shirt and peeled it and her undershirt off in one smooth movement. Veronica flattened her hands over her broad shoulders and swept them down over her breasts. "You are exquisite." Millie's nipples pebbled under her palms. She cupped her breasts and bent her head to lick at her nipples, teasing them, sucking them into tight points. Veronica tugged at the button on Millie's jeans, snapping it open with a pop, and then she slipped her hand inside. Millie hollowed her stomach, giving Veronica room as she pushed farther inside her pants.

Veronica's fingers swept over Millie's clit, slick and hard beneath her touch. She groaned softly. "So wet. For me?"

"All for you." Millie kissed the side of Veronica's neck.

She touched her fingers to her mouth, tasting Millie's sweetness. "I love the way you taste." She turned them so Millie could lean against one of the large stones. "Do you want me to lick you? Take your thick clit in my mouth? Lick you until you come?"

"Yes, please." Panting, Millie moved her hands to the waistband of her jeans and shoved them down around her knees. They bunched over the top of her boots, binding her legs at the ankles. She bent to remove them.

"Stop. Leave them." Veronica leaned into her and pushed her back against the smooth stone and slid her fingers along her wet heat. Millie panted, shivering under her touch as she leaned back supporting herself with her arms.

Veronica rubbed small circles around the base of her clit and stared into Millie's eyes. "Do you like to be fucked?"

The blush starting at Millie's collarbone and spreading across her cheeks made Veronica's pulse speed up. *Oh yeah. No one has ever challenged her, made her surrender.* She slid her finger lower and teased its tip inside. "Like to be taken?"

"Um. I don't know. No one's ever really..." Millie's voice faded out, and she licked her lower lip.

"Never?" Veronica drew the edge of her teeth over Millie's neck and stroked her thumb over her clit as her fingers feathered over her wet center.

"No." Millie's voice was a harsh whisper. "No one's wanted to."

"Will you let me?" Veronica pulled back and peered into Millie's eyes, assessing her reaction. She dropped one hand down to her breast and rolled her nipple between her fingers.

Millie's eyes were wide, her pupils blown. "Aye. Yes. Please, *Ceannard*, please."

She kissed Millie's lips softly before she nibbled her way along her jaw. "What does *Ceannard* mean?" She traced the shell of Millie's ear with her tongue.

"Chief, leader." Millie panted as she struggled against the pants binding her at the ankles.

"Mmm. I like the sound of that, especially when you say it. Ask me for what you want. Ask me to fuck you. Say it." Veronica pinned her in place with her gaze, searching her expression for reassurance. She needed to know this was what Millie truly wanted.

Millie groaned and moved her hands to clasp Veronica's hips. "Please, *Ceannard*, please." Her lip quivered. "Please fuck me. Please." The desperate sound of her voice undid Veronica, and she shivered at the raw need in Millie's voice. She bit and nibbled her way back to her mouth before she kissed her, devouring her mouth, her own need rampant. "Safe word?"

"Time." Millie's shifted her body, settling back against the rock.

Veronica gripped Millie's jaw, enjoying the way the skin blanched under her fingers. "Time."

She sank to her knees and licked a firm stroke over Millie's clit. "I love the way you smell. So wet. But I'm greedy, I want you soaking wet." Veronica teased her tongue over her slick opening. "I want you to give me every drop." Grasping Millie's thighs to hold them open, Veronica stiffened her tongue and licked up and down, burying her face in the wet.

Millie's hand settled on her shoulders. "That's so good."

"Show me your clit." Veronica lifted her head and nipped the inside of Millie's thigh.

Millie placed a hand on either side of her labia and spread them. Her fat clit glistened. Veronica lapped at the tip, teasing the hot bundle of nerves. Millie trembled and panted. "Please. More. Please."

"You want to come for me?" Veronica licked and sucked, swirling her tongue over the tip.

"So much. Please let me. Please, *Ceannard*." Millie's body trembled under Veronica's palms.

"Come for me, babe. I want you to come in my mouth, give it to me." She pursed her lips and sucked her clit hard, rolling her tongue over it.

Millie thrust her hips into Veronica's mouth. Rocking hard, she came with a deep groan, soaking Veronica's chin.

Veronica rose and planted a kiss on Millie's mouth. She cupped the back of her neck and held her still. She leaned back to watch Millie's face as she pressed two fingers inside her. "Is this okay?" She withdrew her fingers and eased them in a fraction more, teasing Millie as she worked her fingers deeper.

Millie lifted her hand and placed it on top of her wrist. She stared into Veronica's eyes as she slowly curled her fingers around Veronica's arm, held her still, and thrust her hips forward, driving Veronica's fingers deep. They stilled, gazes locked.

Millie shifted her hands to grip Veronica's hips. "Ahh, yes." She panted. "Deeper. Please. Oh, yes, so good."

"No." Veronica lifted an eyebrow. "Hands at your side. No touching. Focus on what I'm doing to you." She firmed her mouth and pinned Millie in place with a hard look while she toed off her boots, slipped out of her jeans and briefs. Millie's eyes were glazed, and pleasure suffused her features as she rocked her hips against Veronica's hand. "I like you inside me. More." The soft pants between her words sent a riptide of desire through Veronica.

A raw groan escaped from Veronica as she swept her fingers over Millie's sweet spot. Millie arched into Veronica's touch. She lifted her hand and palmed Veronica's breast.

"No." Veronica lifted an eyebrow. "No touching. Not until I say." Millie hesitated. "Now. Unless you want me to stop?" She paused her strokes. "Should I stop?" She pulled her fingers out and licked them, savoring the taste, never taking her eyes from Millie's face.

Millie trembled and lowered her hands even as her eyes held a challenge. "More."

"Ask nicely." Veronica flicked Millie's nipple.

"Please."

"Please what?" Veronica teased her fingertips over Millie's clit.

"Please, *Ceannard*. Please. Fuck me. Fuck me now. Please. Don't tease me. I can't...I need..." The desperate edge in Millie's voice made Veronica smile.

Veronica pinched Millie's clit and jacked slowly.

"Oh please. I want to come with you inside me. Please."

Veronica cupped her, giving her a squeeze before she pushed three fingers deep. "Impatient woman." She nipped and kissed Millie's neck, working her way to her ear. She ran her tongue over the delicate shell as she swept her fingers in wide circles over Millie's sweet spot, pressing deeper, her palm grinding against her clit. Veronica bit her earlobe sharply before she nuzzled her neck and kissed the space behind her ear. "Slow down, babe, I'll make it good for you."

Millie moaned and trembled. "Please. Please, *Ceannard*. Please. I can't...don't make me wait. Fuck me hard. Please. I want to come for you. Let me come for you."

Veronica lifted her head and held Millie's gaze. "Patience, babe. You'll come when I want you to." She eased her fingers back and lightly rubbed the back of her knuckles over Millie's clit in slow circles. Millie shuddered and thrust her hips forward, seeking contact, her face a mask of pleasure. "You're killing me, *Ceannard*. Faster. Please." Millie panted.

"Like this?" She punctuated her words with kisses along Millie's shoulder. Veronica slid into her liquid heat and stilled. "Or do you want me to fuck you?"

"Fuck me, please." Millie ground out. "Please, *Ceannard*, fuck me. I want to come for you."

"No." Veronica sucked her lower lip between her teeth, nipped it, drank in Millie's hiss of pain, and then licked away the copper taste with her tongue. Millie could wrest control of the situation anytime she wanted, and Veronica groaned as Millie's body clenched tightly around her fingers. She curled them, hitting the spot that made Millie whimper and shake. Millie's submission drove her own pleasure. Her heart clenched with the knowledge that Millie trusted her enough to surrender her power to Veronica.

"Please. More. Please. Mercy, *Ceannard*. I can't. I want to come for you."

A shiver of pleasure stole through Veronica as Millie pleaded and she swept her thumb over her clit, back and forth, drawing a deep groan from Millie before a long stream of cursing poured from her mouth.

"I can't. Fuckmefuckmefuckme." Louder now. Her pleas urgent, she lifted her hips and met Veronica's thrusts. Her prayers for relief laced with profanity washed over Veronica, the gift of Millie's surrender an aching throb between her legs.

Veronica sped up her pace and thrust deep and hard. She raised her hand and rolled Millie's nipple. "You want to come for me?"

"Aye, *Ceannard.* Please. I'll do whatever you want, please let me come. Please. Yes. Harder. There, right there. Please, *Ceannard.*" Millie begged through gritted teeth, her knuckles white where she gripped the stone.

"Me first. Then you." Veronica straddled Millie's powerful thigh and ground against her, sliding her thick clit against her supple skin, painting her with her desire until pleasure jetted through her body. She closed her eyes against the sensations and lost herself in Millie's body, anxious to give her what she wanted. She fucked her, rolling her body into it, the muscles in her arm straining as she sought to give Millie what she craved, what she longed to give her.

Millie tensed under Veronica's hand. "Please. I can't..." She gasped and panted. Between shuddering breaths, her body tightened and pulsed around Veronica.

She opened her eyes to watch the wonder that was Millie. "Come now. Let me have you. Hold on to me." She kept her rhythm as Millie curled into her and placed her hands on Veronica's shoulders. She held tight, her grip bruising as she came. Wetness surged and flowed over Veronica's hand. Millie rested her head on Veronica's shoulder, and they clung to each other. With gentle shallow thrusts Veronica brought her off again and again, unable to get enough of Millie's deep moans and shudders.

"Oh, enough, *Ceannard.* Please. Enough."

Veronica eased her fingers from Millie, smeared her slick juices over her clit, cupped her one last time and squeezed, smiling at the soft curse and satisfied groan Millie gave as she shuddered through an aftershock of pleasure.

Millie lifted her head and kissed Veronica. "I think you've ruined me."

Veronica laughed. "How?"

Millie blushed. "No one ever…I mean like that. No one ever made me wait before. Or the other." She lowered her chin to her chest, the back of her neck red.

Veronica used her fingers to tip Millie's head up. "Are you okay with it? With power play? With giving over to me?"

Millie's eyes were bright. "I love power play. Not been on this side of it before."

"Is it okay?"

Millie kissed her again, before her mouth pulled into her cheeky grin. "More than okay. Even if you have spoiled me. I might have to become a pillow queen if it's this good." The naughty expression on her face matched the well-fucked look in her eyes and made Veronica giddy.

Chapter Eleven

ROWAN HOUSE WAS only open from March to November, and summer was the busy season, most of their clients not willing to brave Skye in the fall. In the two weeks since they had experimented with power dynamics in the glen as they waited for Mistress Siobhan and Marylyn to complete their adventure, Veronica had come up with a very long list of things she wanted to do to Millie.

Veronica chewed her lip. Millie was busy and very often away from Rowan House shuttling guests, running errands. Twice she had stayed overnight in Portree. Veronica's desires would have to wait until the stream of guests slowed down.

Veronica was just as busy, working long days to keep up with guest outings and the barn. No one came to help with the mucking. *No one wants to shovel manure, or clean tack, or groom horses now the damn bet is over. Jerks.* The week after her date with Millie she had gone back over the list of assistants and marked off the ones who had simply not showed up, and those who suddenly had a conflict in their schedule. Unwilling to work with anyone who had participated in the contest, too embarrassed to even mention it to Martha, Veronica kept to herself and worked fourteen-hour days to keep up.

Benita was scheduled to help her today, but after the series of no-shows, Veronica had learned not to count on anyone turning up. For the past week she had skipped staff breakfast, preferring to eat early before the rest of the house was up. Robin and Myfanwy accepted her into their routine. She thought about the day ahead as she worked her way down the line of stalls.

Not going to feel sorry for myself. So what if no one wants to help me if they don't have a chance of getting in my pants? I miss her. So much. What is in Portree she stays overnight? Images of them in the glen filled Veronica's thoughts, and a trickle of wet into her briefs made her press her legs together. She had fingered herself last night thinking of the way Millie had placed her shirt over the rock for Veronica to sit on, and then kneeled, hands laced behind her back, waiting for permission to feast on her. Millie's strong hands on her thighs and the reverent way she touched her as if she were precious, and the way the muscles in her back flexed as Millie kneeled with her face between Veronica's legs, her skillful tongue pleasuring her, making her cry out when she came. The only prior outdoor sex she'd ever had involved the underside of the bleachers in high school in the dark. Half naked in the sun, she had shouted so loudly when she came she surprised herself. Veronica smiled to herself, and the wet ache between her legs intensified.

In the glen, after they had dressed, Millie had taken hold of her hand, not letting go even while they ate lunch. They had stretched out on the rocks, warmed by the sun, and talked about everything and nothing while waiting for Mistress Siobhan and Marylyn to call them. *Damn, she can kiss. Her hands. Maybe tonight. I have to see her. I've got it bad. So bad. So good. Maybe I should invite her to my room? Would she stay overnight? It'd be so sweet to wake up to her.*

And so it went as she worked, her thoughts spilling over with what she wanted to do with Millie the next time they had uninterrupted time together and questions she wanted to ask filled with desire to know everything about her.

BENITA ARRIVED AT 7:30. She gripped a mucking rake in her hands as she leaned against the stall door. "Hey."

"Hey yourself." Veronica leaned on the handle of her pitchfork. "Thinking you might have another chance? Is there a runners-up category, or did you guys come up with something else to amuse yourselves?"

Benita scuffed the toe of her boot over the floor. "No. And I'm sorry."

Veronica snorted. "Sorry you didn't win?"

Benita raised her head. Her eyes were dark, and her brows lowered. "Sorry I wasn't a better friend. Sorry I didn't tell you about the bet. I thought they'd figure it out and let it go."

"Figure what out?" Veronica turned away from Benita and resumed cleaning the stall. "That I'm stubborn?"

"That you're not a casual person and you only have eyes for one woman here."

Veronica stopped and studied Benita's face. "Were you in on it?"

Benita quirked her mouth. "No. Neither was Tessa or June if you're curious."

Truth. She's telling the truth. "Okay."

Benita smiled at her. "What stalls are left to do?"

"Bruno, Marco, and Bella."

"Got it." She turned to walk away.

"Hey, Benita?"

Benita turned back. She rested her hand on the stall door. "Yeah?"

"Thanks."

"It's what friends do."

They worked steadily and had the stalls cleaned by midmorning and took their break in Veronica's office.

"I'm going to gain twenty pounds if I keep eating all these treats Robin bakes." Benita wiped the crumbs off her mouth. She didn't ask anything about Veronica's relationship with Millie, but Veronica had caught her smiling at her more than once as they sat together.

"What are you smiling at?"

"Nothing."

"Nothing?" Veronica snorted. "Right. Ask what you want to ask. You look like you're going to pop trying to not ask."

"Okay. Why Millie?"

"Why not?"

Benita tilted her head and raked her gaze over Veronica. "I wouldn't have expected a stud like you to go for her. I expected you might go for Tessa, or maybe June."

"Because she's strong? And not femme?"

Benita shrugged. "Well, yeah."

"That's kind of narrow minded, don't you think?"

Benita took another bite of pastry and chewed it slowly before she answered. "Yeah, I guess. I was surprised. I'm not judging."

"Really?" Veronica sighed. "I don't get why people think studs don't go for other studs, or butches, or whatever you want to call gender non-conforming queer women. I'm attracted to who I'm attracted to."

Benita furrowed her brow. "I wasn't trying to piss you off."

"I know." Veronica tipped back her water bottle and took a long drink. "I was kinda surprised she was interested in me."

Benita's eyebrows shot up. "Do you own a mirror? You are hot as hell. And like you said, not every stud wants a femme."

"Like I haven't heard that before? Like you haven't? A lot of people want what's on the outside without giving a damn about what's on the inside. They don't even want to unwrap the package." Veronica shrugged her shoulders and lowered them, trying to relive her tension and squash her anger. *Fucking contest. Like I'm some prize or check box to mark off.* She blew out a breath. "Hey, she said you guys play some open mike nights." Her abrupt change of subject garnered her a raised eyebrow from Benita.

"We have one in two weeks."

"I asked her if I could tag along. Is it okay with you?"

"Sure. It's always good to have a friendly face in the crowd."

Veronica glanced at the clock. "I have to get Bruno and Marco ready for Lucia and Martha. Want to help?"

"I would love to, my friend, but I have to go let June make me beautiful for my afternoon client." Benita scooted to the edge of the couch to stand.

Veronica placed her coffee cup on the desk. "Thanks for coming to help. I've been working my ass off trying to keep up by myself."

"My pleasure. I'll make sure Tessa gets out here to help you too. I like your ass the way it is." Benita waggled her eyebrows at Veronica before she sashayed from the office.

VERONICA CLIPPED A lead shank to an eyebolt mounted on the wall in the stall set aside for play. Located on the far side of the office, Veronica kept it cleaned and stocked for guests who desired a barn setting for their fantasies. She tipped her fingers over the collection of crops and short whips arrayed on the wall of the stall. The floor was covered in clean straw. She moved hay bales around until she had made a platform the size of a double bed and covered it with a tarp and then a thick navy-blue blanket. She moved a small table from the corner of the room next to the makeshift bed and placed a no-harness dildo on a low stool next to a small bottle of lube. She heard the door to the barn slide open and Millie's unmistakable heavy tread as she approached.

"In here," Veronica called out.

Millie stood in the entryway to the stall. She wore a simple black T-shirt stretched tight over her thick body, and the sleeves displayed her strong arms to perfection. Her jeans were worn and hung off her hips in a way that made Veronica hungry.

"You called?" Millie's face pulled into a grin.

"Come in and shut the door." Veronica rested her hands on her hips.

Millie rolled the heavy wooden door shut. The light shone between the bars at the top of the door and cast lined shadows across Millie's body.

"Come here."

Millie came, stood before Veronica, and lowered her head. "You kept me waiting." Veronica tipped Millie's chin up with one finger. She rubbed her thumb over Millie's lower lip.

Millie's tongue edged out, and she licked the tip of Veronica's thumb. "Sorry, *Ceannard.*"

Her top name on Millie's lips ignited the smoldering desire in Veronica. "Take off your shirt and boots."

Millie grasped the ends of her T-shirt and pulled it over her head before she folded it and placed it carefully on the hay bale. She toed off her boots, stripped off her socks, and tucked them inside her boots. She came back and stood in front of Veronica, head bowed, her arms clasped behind her back.

Veronica pointed to the middle of the stall. "Stand there, arms extended."

Millie backed away from her and assumed the position. "Like this, *Ceannard*?"

She obeys without question. Trusts me. "Yes." Veronica took up the leather of the lead and wrapped it once around Millie's palm and closed her fingers over it. She did the same with the other lead. "Hold tight. Don't let go until I tell you to."

The stretched position showed off Millie's hard physique, the lean muscles of her torso, the sculpted curves of her biceps and shoulders, and the flat planes of her stomach. *So exquisite. And mine. Is she? Does she want to be mine? Maybe she has a lover in Portree. We've never talked about being exclusive. Forget it. Don't think about it. Focus. She's here now. Make her want to be yours.*

Veronica trailed her fingers over Millie's nipples and sighed as they hardened under her touch. "Mmm. I like you like this, like an offering displayed for my enjoyment." She dipped her head and raked her teeth over the tip of her nipple, the sharp intake of Millie's breath creating a hard throb between Veronica's legs. She cupped her through her jeans and squeezed hard. "Don't let go of the leads, or I'll stop. Understand?"

Millie groaned under her touch. "Aye, *Ceannard*."

Veronica moved behind Millie and looped her arms around her waist, pressing her breasts against her wide back. She laid her cheek against her smooth pale skin and unbuttoned Millie's jeans. Millie shifted and pressed her legs together.

"Be still." Veronica nipped her. "Stand still or I'll stop." She flattened her hand and slipped it lower into Millie's pants. Her fingers tangled in soft wet curls. "No briefs? Hopeful then? Or is it laundry day?" Veronica nipped her again, smiling at the sharp intake of Millie's breath and the low chuckle that rumbled through her.

"Hopeful, *Ceannard*. I've missed you."

The wistful tone of her voice made Veronica bite her lip and lean her cheek against her broad back. "Me too."

Shaking off the unspoken words between them, Veronica pressed the pads of her fingers against Millie's swollen clit. She drew a groan from her when she pulled her hand free and pressed her fingers to Millie's lips. Millie opened to her and Veronica thrust in and out of her tender mouth, closing her eyes against the sensation of Millie greedily sucking her fingers.

She pulled her hand free and grasped a nipple in each hand. She rolled and tugged them, squeezing them, pulling them into tight buds. Millie panted.

Veronica palmed her breasts and squeezed. "You like this. Can you come this way?"

"I never have, *Ceannard*." Her voice was husky.

"Well, first time for everything." Veronica released her nipples and pushed Millie's jeans down around her ankles before she pulled them free of Millie's body and tossed them to the side.

She kneeled between her legs and brushed the back of her hand over her thighs until she reached the thick lips of Millie's sex. Millie hissed and arched her hips, seeking contact. With one finger Veronica teased back the hood, leaned forward, and touched the tip of her tongue to her fat clit. She dragged her tongue lower and grabbed her ass with both hands, squeezed hard, and pulled her to her mouth. Veronica plunged her tongue deep, seeking Millie's sweet taste. She drove her tongue in and out, taking what she wanted, burying her face in the sweetness of Millie's body.

Millie's legs tensed and her breathing shifted, signaling how close she was to coming. Veronica reveled in her power and pulled back. Millie groaned when Veronica stopped. Veronica gazed at Millie's face. Her jaw was slack and her mouth open, eyes glazed with pleasure. "Oh no. Please don't stop. Please, *Ceannard*."

She left Millie panting and picked up the toy she had prepared from the table. She held out her palms, cradling the twin dildo for Millie to see.

Millie raised her eyebrow. "That's new."

She stroked her fingers over the toy. "No need for a strap." She tapped the shorter end of the toy. "This is your side. Too big?"

"Just right, *Ceannard*." Millie's eager tone sent a fresh wave of desire through Veronica.

"Glad to hear it." She dripped lube over the bulbous end of the shaft before she pressed it into Millie's body, watching as the short phallus disappeared and her body closed around it. Millie's sigh of contentment sizzled in her ears. The other half of the toy stood rampant and bobbed as Millie shifted her feet, setting them wide. Veronica palmed the toy, jacking it with slow strokes as she covered it with lube, watching the blissful expression sweeping Millie's face at the sensation. Wet heat soaked her briefs and she couldn't stifle her own groan of pleasure.

"Oh. That's..." Millie panted, her face red. "Those ridges over my clit, so good."

Veronica kissed her cheek. "Isn't it?" She stopped her motions and Millie sobbed a breath.

"Please, *Ceannard*. Please don't stop. Let me come for you. Jerk me off like this."

"Patience, babe." Veronica sucked Millie's nipple into her mouth. The rough tip of Millie's nipple against her tongue made her squeeze her legs together to relieve the pressure building there. She plucked and teased Millie's other nipple with her fingertips.

"Oh, please. Let me come." Millie's body tensed under her, her muscles straining as she stayed still under Veronica's touch. Veronica held on to Millie's shoulders as she alternated, going back and forth between Millie's nipples, sucking them in turn, gauging her reaction. The heavy shaft between Millie's legs bobbed obscenely as she quivered.

Veronica took her time building Millie's passion, reveling in each shudder of her body. Needful moans and sharp yips punctuated the quiet. *Close but not there. She needs more. She won't ask.*

Veronica lifted her mouth from Millie's breast. "I can feel you. You're close. What do you need?"

Millie's breathing was harsh, her body trembling. "I need more. On my clit. Please, *Ceannard*. I can't. I'm sorry."

Veronica stopped and backed away. Millie's open-mouthed expression and the panic in her eyes made her move back in and press a gentle kiss to her mouth. "It's okay. We're not done, babe. Just taking a break."

"A break?"

Veronica turned her back and took off her jeans and briefs, bending from the waist to give Millie a clear view of her excitement. She turned back to her, the heavy-lidded expression on Millie's face letting her know exactly how effective her display had been.

"Look at me." Veronica lay back on the soft blanket-covered hay bales, bent her knees, and opened her legs wide. Millie's groan shattered the quiet.

Veronica touched her fingers between her legs and drew the wetness up and over her clit. She held herself open with her left hand as she circled her fingers around her clit. "This. This is what I do when I miss you. When I think about having you." She met Millie's desire-filled gaze. "Do you want to taste me? To lick my clit until I come?"

Millie jerked hard on the leather in her hands and the clips rattled against the eyebolts. "Yes, *Ceannard*, yes please. Let me. Let me please."

"Or do you want to fuck? Fuck me with that toy? Do you want to look into my face as I come, to fuck yourself into coming? To come with me?"

Millie pulled hard at the leads wrapped around her hands, her knuckles white, muscles bunching and flexing in her arms. "Please, *Ceannard*. Please let me. All of it please. I'll make it good. Whatever you want. Please."

"Not until you put on a show for me." Veronica held her gaze.

"Anything, *Ceannard*, anything."

"Move your body for me. I want to watch you. Show me how you want to fuck me."

A bright-red blush spread over Millie's face, and Veronica leaned back on one elbow and pushed two fingers inside herself. Millie closed her eyes and set her feet wider and began to move her hips, thrusting slowly into the air.

"That's it, babe. Show me how much you want to fuck me. Show me what you're going to do to me when I give you permission."

She arched into her hand as she watched Millie's hips jerk, knowing the dildo inside her body moved with each thrust and twitch of her hips. Millie's arms were taut. The long lines of her biceps and sharp curves of her forearms gleamed with sweat. Her face was suffused with pleasure as she moved. Veronica's breath caught in her throat. *So beautiful. So powerful. No restraints needed but my voice.* Millie's breath rasped as she worked her hips, striving to do as she had been commanded, to earn the right to fuck Veronica. Millie opened her eyes and their gazes locked and Veronica's own need crested.

"Do you want me?" Veronica spread her legs wider. "Want me now?"

"So much, please, *Ceannard.*" Millie panted. "Please."

"Let go of those straps and come fuck me. Now."

Millie dropped the leathers from her hands and fell on Veronica, covering her with her body. She grabbed her hips with both hands, aligned the tip of the toy, and in one smooth thrust was deep inside. She slipped her arms under Veronica and held tight to her shoulders as her hips thrust wildly. Veronica gasped, her body shaking hard as the sensation of being taken, even as she took, overwhelmed her. She locked her legs around Millie's hips and arched into her, meeting her thrusts with her.

"*Ceannard*, I love being inside you. I can't stop. Please, let me come. Please." Millie's breath was hot on her neck where she rested her head.

Veronica gripped her hair with both hands and pulled her head back.

"Look at me."

Millie lifted her head and met her gaze as she fucked her.

"Now. Give it to me. Now." Veronica dug her short nails into Millie's back.

Millie shouted as she came and sped up her thrusts as she tumbled into an abyss of pleasure, taking Veronica with her. They clung to each other and rode out their pleasure, slowing their movements as they rocked each other, driving each other into one orgasm after another. Millie rolled her hips and Veronica's clit throbbed. Her body clenched and she came again under Millie's driving deep strokes, endless waves of pleasure until Veronica was spent. She patted Millie's back. "Easy, babe."

Millie leaned down and kissed her, taking her time, and Veronica melted under her. Millie began to move her hips again in slow, gentle, tiny movements.

"I don't know if I can go again." Veronica looped her hands around Millie's neck.

"First time for everything." Millie clutched Veronica's shoulders and rolled them over, and now Veronica was on top with Millie's wide hands holding her hips in place.

Veronica's upright position caused the dildo to rub against her in a way that made her grind her hips to feel it again. She rose up and lowered herself. "Damn. Does that feel as good to you?" Veronica placed both her hands flat on Millie's chest and rocked her hips. She trembled as another orgasm built. "Cause now I'm sure I can go again."

"Yes." Millie bared her teeth and panted and arched her hips, thrusting up as she held Veronica in place. "Give it to me, *Ceannard*. Please. Come around me."

Veronica cried out and came again. Millie smoothed her hands over Veronica's thighs. Veronica collapsed on Millie's chest. Millie's arms came up around her and held her tight. She kissed Veronica's temple. "You're the most amazing woman."

Veronica shifted her hips and rose off the toy. She grasped the silicone dildo in her hand, slick from their lovemaking. She jacked it slowly while watching Millie's face. "You want to come again?"

"Yes. Please, *Ceannard*. But I want to feel you inside me. Let me feel you. Please."

Veronica sat up and eased the toy from Millie's body. She was swollen and slick, and three of Veronica's fingers slid in easily as the wet heat welcomed her. Veronica bent over her and took her plump clit in her mouth. She slow fucked her as she suckled her clit, curling her tongue around it and drawing it deep into her mouth, closing her lips around her lushness.

Millie grabbed her head with both hands and held her in place. "Veronica," she whispered as she shuddered through an orgasm and come soaked Veronica's face. Millie relaxed her grip and Veronica kissed her thighs, the tight patch of curls over her clit, and her stomach on her way to Millie's mouth.

Veronica brushed her lips over her mouth, and then kissed her softly.

Millie broke their kiss, her eyes bright. "You. Make me feel—" She kissed Veronica again. "—you make me feel so much."

Veronica gazed into Millie's eyes. *Love. Is that what she wants to say and can't? Or is it I make her feel good?* She cupped Millie's cheek and kissed her again, not knowing what to say herself.

THE OVERHEAD LIGHTS in the gym highlighted the squat rack. It was their routine now, Veronica coming to spot her on days she lifted heavy. Veronica helped Millie stack the plates as they loaded the bar. Taking in Millie's tight ass and well-muscled thighs in her workout tights made Veronica bite her lip to focus on the task in front of them.

Veronica studied Millie's face. She had spent the night in Portree again, not returning until late in the day. Her brows were drawn down, her eyes shuttered. Veronica had asked her about her visit to Portree, and as she had every other time, Millie changed the subject and shut down the conversation. *Does she have another lover? Lovers. Is that what we are? What does she feel? What does she want?* She nibbled her lip as Millie positioned herself under the bar, and Veronica stepped into place behind her.

Millie straightened her legs and rolled the bar forward, releasing it from the safety hooks. She squatted deeply, keeping her back straight and her hips squared under the load and blew out a breath. With a low groan Millie stood, rising quickly from her squat, and paused at the top before descending again. Veronica loved watching her work, watching the way she concentrated. Small beads of sweat gathered along her hairline at the back of her neck, and her thigh muscles bunched and flexed, stretching the fabric of her workout pants. She completed her set and racked the bar. Millie's breath slowed as she recovered.

"Water?" Veronica held out the bottle.

Millie took it and then uncapped it before she took a sip. She handed it back to Veronica. "Let's add ten kilos."

"You sure?" Veronica eyed the amount of weight already on the bar.

"Yeah. You're here. I trust you. You'll help if I get into trouble."

They added the weight plates before the timer sounded, signaling the end of Millie's rest period. She positioned herself under the bar, and Veronica stepped into place behind her and settled her hands on her hips.

Millie took the weight on her shoulders, her body tight under Veronica's fingertips. She sank into position, mirroring Millie's movement, lending her support in maintaining her form. Millie hissed as she straightened, an audible indication of her effort. She completed two more reps. Millie's body trembled and Veronica assessed the strain showing in her face.

"Done?" Veronica tried to keep the worry out of her tone.

"One more." Millie's voice was hoarse. She lowered herself, and Veronica moved her hands to the bar, ready to roll it forward if Millie couldn't finish the repetition. The back of her neck was red, and her whole body shook as she struggled to stand. Her knees drifted out of position, and her back bowed.

Veronica shifted her hand from Millie's hips and gripped the bar loosely. "Let it go. You're going to blow your knees or your back."

"No." Millie's voice was harsh. "I can do it."

Veronica bit her lip, the anger in Millie's words unsettling.

She gripped the bar harder, overpowering Millie's hold on it, and rolled it forward until it settled on the safety rack.

Millie growled and stepped away from the rack, her eyes dark. "I said I could do it. What the hell?"

"You were all kinds of out of form. You'd have popped a disc or torn something in your knees."

"You fucked up my set. I know my body. I could have done it."

Veronica set her mouth in a firm line. "You said you trusted me."

Millie stalked away, turning her back to Veronica, the set of her shoulders sending a clear message.

Not enough. She doesn't trust me. Fuck this. Veronica collected her gear. "I wasn't trying to fuck up your workout. I wanted to keep you safe." She waited a moment. Millie's silence spoke volumes as she kept her back turned, her posture rigid.

What the fuck is up with her? "You want to blow a disk, do it without me." Veronica slammed the door on her way out of the gym.

VERONICA RAN THE figures on the stable spreadsheet again. She frowned at the negative numbers glaring in red at her from the screen. *Where is it? What is out of line? This should balance. Must have entered the figures in the wrong cell.* She took her computer glasses off and rubbed her eyes.

A soft tap on the doorframe made her glance up. Millie walked up to the desk and held up a thermos and plate of cookies, her eyes wary. "You ready for a break? Coffee and Robin's lemon shortbread." She held out the plate like an offering.

Veronica shifted in her seat and studied Millie's face. "Maybe. Are you ready to tell me what the hell crawled up your ass the other night? Why are you so pissed every time you come back from Portree? Want to tell me why you've so carefully avoided me since last week?"

Millie flushed and rested her chin on her chest. Her shoulders sagged. "I'm sorry." She placed the plate of shortbread cookies on the desk and placed the thermos next to it. "I'll go."

"You'd rather leave it like it is than talk?" Veronica huffed out a breath. "I thought you wanted more than a hookup, Millie. You said you did. And then when I ask you anything about yourself or how you feel, you stonewall. Do you have another lover? Is that the problem?"

"No!" Millie shouted. "No. I don't." She scowled at Veronica. "Why would you think that?"

"Because you refuse to tell me anything about why you spend the night in Portree, and you change the subject whenever I bring it up."

Millie shuffled her feet. "Look, I said I was sorry about the other night. I don't know what else you want."

Veronica stood up and rounded the desk. She grabbed Millie's hand. "I want to know why. Why were you so angry at me?"

"I wasn't angry at you." Millie swept her gaze over the ceiling before she brought her gaze back to Veronica's face. "Not much."

Veronica quirked her mouth. "You're a terrible liar. It's okay to be angry. I'm not afraid of your anger, but for fuck's sake tell me why. Why did you risk hurting yourself to accomplish some self-imposed goal? You say you trust me, you trust me with your body, and yet you don't trust me enough to tell me what's eating you alive. Don't think I don't know you're drinking yourself to sleep almost every night."

Millie's throat worked as she swallowed. She held Veronica's gaze. "I, um, I don't know why. Okay? I don't know why I get so angry sometimes. I had a bad day and took it out on you. I'm sorry. I'm not easy to be with. I get it if you don't want to, um, date anymore." Millie stopped speaking with a hard set to her jaw.

Truth. Fear. So much fear. And pain. Veronica cupped the back of her neck as she pulled her close and wrapped her arms around her body. Millie kept her body stiff in her arms. Veronica held her tighter and brought her lips close to her ear. "Don't. Don't give up on me. Us. You can tell me anything. I'm not going to judge you. I want to know you. Warts and all. Trust me. Please."

Millie relaxed against her and rested her forehead on Veronica's shoulder. The soft hum of the refrigerator was loud in the office. Veronica rubbed Millie's back. "Tell me."

Millie drew in a breath. "My gran is dying. She helped raise me and took care of me after..." A shudder rippled through her body. Veronica held her tighter. "She's all I have. My father died of an overdose when I was a baby. My mother wouldn't spit on me if I was on fire. When I got out of the juvenile facility, my gran took me in. She protected me from my mother and helped me get into university. She's dying. She's dying, and she doesn't know who I am, and I can't fix it."

Juvenile? She was in Juvenile? Why? Ask. Don't ask. She'll tell you when she's ready. Veronica stroked her hands over her back. "I'm sorry, babe. So, so sorry."

Millie lifted her head. "I'm always angry when I come back from visiting her now. She doesn't know who I am anymore. She calls me 'that nice young man who visits.'" Her eyes grew dark. "And my mother, my mother who hasn't spoken to me in years, is sniffing around trying to make sure she's in line to get whatever is left from Gran's estate." The bitter edge to her voice shook Veronica.

"Things are bad with your mom?" Veronica chewed her lip.

"She hates me." Millie balled her hands into fists.

"Why?" Veronica fought the urge to step back from Millie, to avoid her anger, sensing it had nothing to do with her.

Millie blew out a breath. "Besides ruining her life by being born? My mother had a boyfriend who beat the living hell out of both of us. When I was fourteen, he started in on my mother one night. Hit her so hard he knocked her out. I thought he killed her. I stabbed him with a kitchen knife. He died."

Millie's voice had taken on a flat tone. Her body trembled under Veronica's hands. "My mother was in a coma for two weeks. When she came out of it, she freaked, told the cops I murdered him, that I attacked her, and he was trying to defend her." A grim expression settled over Millie's face, and she avoided Veronica's eyes. "The evidence didn't support her story, but I had confessed to stabbing him and wanting him to die. Because my gran was able to afford a good solicitor, I was sentenced as a juvenile. I was released when I was eighteen."

The fear in Millie's face broke Veronica's heart. *It was all there in her eyes. How many times has she told her story and had people reject her? How much pain has it caused her?* Veronica rubbed her hand over Millie's shoulder and squeezed it. "I'm not going anywhere."

Doubt was reflected in Millie's face. "You say that now. But later you'll think of it. The next time I get angry. You'll think 'is she going to snap? Am I next?'"

"What?" Veronica raised an eyebrow. "What the fuck? Why would I ever think that of you?" She stepped back and held up her hands. "Anyone who has treated you that way is an ass. I'm not her." She rested her hip on the edge of the desk.

Millie's snorted. "Aye. You're not her. But I'm still me." She shuffled her feet and glanced up at the wall clock. "I've got to go. I have to drive some guests to The Stone Hearth."

"Can I see you later? After dinner?"

Millie shoved her hands in her front pockets. "I won't be back until late." Her expression was shuttered.

She's done. Doesn't trust me. Doesn't believe me. "Okay." Veronica swallowed and looked down at her fisted hands, unwilling to let Millie see her pain at being shut out. "Drive safe."

"Always." Millie leaned forward and pressed a kiss to Veronica's cheek.

Veronica lifted her gaze and watched as Millie left the office. *Gone. She's gone from me. Opened up to me and is too afraid of being hurt.* She poured herself a cup of coffee from the thermos. The shortbread she left untouched, the bitterness of rejection leaving her unable to muster any appetite for the sweet treat.

Chapter Twelve

THE RAIN RATTLED against the windowpane. Veronica turned over and pulled the quilt up higher around her neck. Her stomach rumbled. She closed her eyes, willing herself to go back to sleep. Last night, her mind had replayed her conversation with Millie as an endless loop, the end result always the same. Millie walking away from her, the kiss on her cheek some sort of a fucked-up consolation prize. She scrubbed her hands over her face and stared at the ceiling. *Love. How the hell did I let myself fall in love again? Damn it. I love her. I'm so fucked. How many times did I think about telling her I loved her? How many times did I swallow my words? Glad I never told her. At least I didn't embarrass myself. She can't love me if she can give up like that.*

She had read until her eyes burned, a favorite romance, a classic, and one she had read so many times she could practically recite it by heart. *Is it too much? Why not me? Why can't I find a love like that? I am lousy at picking women. Fuck me.* She pulled her phone off the nightstand and checked the time. *Too early for breakfast and coffee with Myfanwy and Robin. Call Mom? No, she'll know I'm sad and ask why, and then I'll have to explain all of it. Like I even understand.* The closeness of the room overwhelmed her. *I need to get out, think.*

The floor was cold under her bare feet. She washed up and then dressed, grabbed her rain slicker off the peg by the door, and left her room.

THE RAIN HAD slowed by the time Veronica had made her second loop around the grounds. Her body stiff and chilled, she sighed with relief when the lights came on in the kitchen. Her mouth watered at the thought of hot coffee and some of whatever delights Robin was baking for the day.

In the mudroom, Veronica tugged off her boots and hung her slicker up. Myfanwy appeared with a towel in her hand. "Put this under it to catch the water, yeah?"

Veronica took the towel from her and placed it on the floor under her raincoat. The smell of fresh coffee wafted out of the kitchen, and Veronica hurried after Myfanwy.

"Help yourself." Myfanwy tilted her head toward the coffee press. She was preparing a tray with coffee, tea, and an assortment of baked treats. "I'm serving my Mistresses this morning." A hint of a smile played about her mouth and she hummed as she arranged the pastries on a platter.

Veronica studied her as she worked. She sipped her coffee and tried to stifle her jealousy as she witnessed Myfanwy's happiness, knowing she had two women who loved her. *I can't even find one.*

"How did you do it?" Veronica placed her cup of coffee on the table.

"Do what?" Myfanwy wiped the crumbs from the edge of the platter and placed it on the tray with the teapot and the coffee press.

"Find lovers, two lovers." Veronica met Myfanwy's gaze.

The kindness in her eyes made Veronica swallow hard.

"I don't know. It happened. Like things do." She reached over and clasped Veronica's hand. "Be yourself. Give her time. Don't give up. She's happier with you than I've ever seen her." She glanced at the clock and let go of Veronica's hand. She smiled as she picked up the tray. "Perfect. I'll be five minutes late. They'll have to punish me."

She winked at Veronica, picked up the tray, and with a saucy swing of her hips, pushed through the kitchen door.

VERONICA SAT IN the wingback chair, her book balanced on a pillow. The rain beat a steady drum on the floor to ceiling windows and ran in rivulets down the glass. Veronica settled into the quiet and inhaled the sweet smell of books. After turning her down every day for a week, Millie had finally agreed to meet after her late morning errands were completed.

Libraries had long been Veronica's favorite places, but after she and Millie made it their habit to meet in the library whenever it rained to sit quietly and read together, it was her version of what heaven would be. Sometimes they sat next to each other on the couch, thighs touching, shoulders snuggled into each other. Other days, Veronica would lay with her head in Millie's lap, and Millie would read to her. Those were her favorite days, when she would close her eyes and Millie's husky voice would carry her to magical lands as she read epic tales filled with dragons and glorious strong women.

Some days, lulled by Millie's voice, she would fall asleep and Millie would wake her with gentle touches and soft kisses. She squirmed in her seat. Her briefs grew wet as memories of their last library date surfaced. She glanced at the mantel clock. *Two-thirty. Where is she? Maybe the ferry was late. Maybe she's not coming, maybe she's done. I'm so fucked, she has to talk to me. She'll come, she has to. Please let her come.*

The door to the library clicked open. Veronica blew out a breath and stuffed her unbridled excitement back where it belonged as she took in the sight before her, swallowing the greeting she had rehearsed for Millie.

Ashley stepped through the door dressed in black pumps, white capri pants tight enough to show her lack of panties, and a red silk blouse with the top three buttons undone. The black lacy edge of her bra peeked out of the opening of her shirt. "Tessa said you would be here." She frowned at Veronica. "You look like someone kicked your dog. Is it that painful to see me?"

Veronica shifted in the chair and placed her book on the side table, cover down. "I was expecting someone else." She didn't bother to keep the disappointment out of her voice.

Ashley raised an eyebrow. "I was wondering if you could recommend something for me to read." She stepped closer to Veronica's chair.

"Still trying to win the game?" Veronica's anger at Ashley's engineering of the betting pool for her sexual favors bubbled up. She gripped the arms of her chair and glared at Ashley.

"It wasn't a contest. It was a joke." Ashley glanced up and away from Veronica's face.

"It wasn't to me." Veronica balled her hands into fists.

"I'm sorry. Truly sorry." Ashley's tone was far from contrite. "Forgive me?" The practiced little girl pout turned Veronica's stomach.

Veronica blew out a breath. "What do you like to read?" She kept her tone neutral. *What's her game? She's sorry she lost.*

"I like thrillers. What are you reading?"

Veronica flushed. "Nothing exciting. A manual." She reached out to grab the book where it lay on the side table.

Ashley was quicker and snagged the book off the table. She affected a tone of innocence as she read. *"Lover's Knots: An Introduction to Shibari."* She smirked at Veronica. "A manual?"

"Give me the book." Veronica shoved herself out of the chair and took a step toward Ashley.

The insolent expression on her face and flare of desire in Ashley's eyes told her everything she needed to know about her calculated appearance in the library.

"Make me." Ashley held the book out of Veronica's reach with one hand and began to unbutton her shirt with the other.

Veronica lowered her voice and took a step back. "No. And stop."

Ashley unbuttoned the last button and shifted the book between her hands as she shrugged out of her shirt and let it fall. "You sure?" She undid the front clasp of her bra and let it fall open. She pressed her arms together to display her full breasts.

"Not today. Not any day, Ashley. I'm not into you. Not now. Not ever. Now give me the damn book." Veronica turned her back to Ashley and crossed her arms over her chest. "And put your shirt on."

"Take your book." Ashley's voice was closer.

Veronica clenched her jaw and turned around. Ashley had stripped completely. She held the book with both hands in front of her naked body. She inched closer to Veronica.

"What the hell, Ashley? Get away from me." Veronica stepped back and stumbled. She fell back into her chair. Ashley dumped the book on her lap. She leaned over Veronica and placed her hands on the arms of the chair, pinning her in place, pushing her full breasts close to her face. Stunned by Ashley's behavior, Veronica didn't move at first. She raised her hands to shove Ashley away. The violent squeak of door hinges as it opened stung Veronica's ears. With one quick movement Ashley arched her back and shoved her breasts into Veronica's palms.

Horror and anger filled her as the pieces of Ashley's sick plan fell into place. Millie's sharp gasp pricked her ears. Veronica caught a glimpse of her face and the shocked sadness in her eyes over Ashley's shoulder before Millie backed out of the room. The sharp click of the door as it latched shut echoed like a shot in the library. Baring her teeth, she shoved hard, pushing Ashley off her. Ashley landed on her ass. Veronica yanked open the door and sprinted down the hall, desperate to catch Millie. Ashley's spiteful laughter rang in her ears.

MILLIE DIDN'T ANSWER the door of her apartment, and Veronica spent the rest of the afternoon searching for her. Millie's phone went immediately to voice mail and Veronica's texts were unreturned. The rain had continued. Iron-gray clouds scuttled through the evening sky, the bleak weather as ugly as her mood. She gave up and returned to the barn to feed the horses. After sweeping the center aisle, she scooped the grain and pellets for their breakfasts into buckets for the morning. Desperate for distraction, she found a dozen other small tasks to busy herself. By eight she had run out of things to soothe the ache in her heart and cool the anger burning through her.

She grimaced as she imagined what the tableau in the library appeared like from behind. She scrubbed her hand over her face. *Fucked. So fucked. She'll never believe me. Her trust issues are worse than mine. Damn Ashley to hell.* She had skipped dinner, unwilling to face Myfanwy, or anyone else in the house. The tabby barn cat came and twined around Veronica's legs before she jumped up on the feed box. She peered at Veronica, her green eyes curious, and let out a sharp meow.

"What am I going to do?" Veronica scratched the cat's ears. The cat pushed her head against her hand. She picked her up and held her against her chest. The rumble of her soft purrs soothed her. She pressed her cheek to the cat's head, the rough fur tickling her skin. The cat lifted her head and rubbed her mouth against Veronica's face.

A memory burst through Veronica's sadness: a hot June afternoon, the smell of the outfield grass and sweat, and the fine red dust of the softball field that coated her cleats and the hot metal of the bat in her hands. She closed her eyes and saw her mother's face and heard her sharp voice. "I didn't raise a quitter, Veronica Simone. You get back out there. So what if you strike out? Nobody hits a thousand. Even the best hitters only hit three out of ten." Her mom had kissed her on the cheek before she spun her around and firmly shoved her back out on the softball field.

The cat began to squirm in her arms, and she let her go. *Not going to give up. She's going to talk to me. I'm not going to give her up without a fight.*

VERONICA STRODE ACROSS the lot separating the barn from the garage and took the stairs leading to Millie's apartment two at a time. She pounded on the door. The apartment was dark, and there was no answer. She pressed her ear to the door to listen. *Nothing. Not home. I'll wait her out. She'll have to come home sometime.* A sharp ache split her chest as she pondered the possible reasons Millie had not returned to her apartment. *Unless she's found somewhere else to stay. Or someone to make her feel better. Fuck.*

She sat on the top step, ignoring the dampness that seeped into her jeans from the wet stairs. She pulled her jacket tighter around her shoulders and rested her forehead on her knees. *This is a waste of time. She's not going to listen. I have to try. No matter what, I have to try. Let her tell me to my face we're done. She can't avoid me forever.* After the rain had stopped, a cool wind had kicked up, and Veronica shivered. She pulled her phone out of her pocket to check the time. *Ten o'clock. Where is she? Who is she with? Does it matter?*

Veronica stood up and stretched. Tires crunched gravel on the drive, and headlights lit up the front of the small car park. Millie's roadster pulled close to the building, and the bay door opened. The car turned into the garage. Veronica's pulse pounded in her ears and her mouth went dry as she waited. Millie stumbled out of the bay door, one arm slung around Myfanwy's neck, her bulk leaning against the shorter woman.

"Come on, a bit more. Get it together. I can't carry you up the stairs." Myfanwy's voice was harsh. Millie sagged to her knees. Her words were slurred, and Veronica couldn't make them out.

Veronica hurried down the steps. "I can help."

Myfanwy's head snapped up, and she glared at Veronica. "I think you've helped enough."

Veronica firmed her jaw. "It wasn't what it looked like."

Millie groaned and then burped. The sick smell of stale beer filled the air. She attempted to stand and fell back to her knees.

Veronica ignored Myfanwy's snort of disbelief, grabbed Millie's other arm, and draped it over her shoulder. She cupped Millie's jaw gently and turned her head to see into her eyes. "Can you try again, babe?"

Millie's eyes were watery and dull. *Blackout. She's in a blackout. She won't remember any of this.*

"Stand up. We'll help you up the stairs." Veronica grabbed Millie's belt and with Myfanwy's help, she rose to her feet. Arms around Millie's waist, they guided her to the top of the stairs. Myfanwy slipped out from under Millie's arm. She pulled a clump of keys from her pocket, sorted through them until she found the correct one, and opened Millie's door. Veronica assisted Millie through the door.

"Straight back to her bedroom." Veronica and Millie bumped down the narrow hall with Myfanwy trailing behind them. The door to Millie's bedroom was closed. Veronica stopped. She had wanted to cross this threshold so many times after their first date. Myfanwy reached around Veronica and shoved the door open.

"I'm fine. Night." Millie pushed away from Veronica and staggered into the room. She fell face down on the queen-size bed and closed her eyes. Veronica took a step toward the bed.

Myfanwy's arm came down to block her way. "What are you doing?" Her expression was fierce. "Thank you for helping me get her up the stairs. You can leave. What were you doing out there anyway?"

"Waiting. To talk to her. To explain. Ashley set me up. It wasn't what it looked like. I swear. I'm not like..."

"Excuse me if I don't believe you." Myfanwy's gaze burned.

"I don't care if you believe me. I care if Millie believes me." Veronica huffed out a breath. "Besides, she can't sleep like that. It'll be easier if we work together. Let me help you." Ignoring Myfanwy's glare, Veronica ducked under her arm. She kneeled and unlaced Millie's right shoe and then the left one before she pulled them off. She bent over and lined them up next to the closet. Veronica stood up and met Myfanwy's gaze. "I know you haven't known me long but I'm not a liar. If I'd wanted Ashley, I would have said yes the first ten times she offered herself to me. If I'm guilty of anything, it's being too confident and distracted to realize Ashley was setting me up. Please believe me. Let me stay. I want to talk to her. I need to tell her I lo..." *No, not going to share my feelings with Myfanwy.*

Myfanwy studied Veronica's face, her glare lethal. "If I find out later you lied to me, you will be the sorriest person on this earth."

Veronica swallowed hard. "Understood." They worked together and undressed Millie.

"She sleeps nude most of the time. But you'd know." Myfanwy pulled the covers up over Millie's shoulders. She turned on a lamp atop the dresser.

"Um, no. We've never slept together." Veronica's ears burned with the flush that overtook her. "She always leaves to sleep here."

Myfanwy tilted her head. "She said you were taking it slow. I had no idea how slow. Leave the lamp on. She doesn't like the dark."

Veronica pointed to a closed door opposite the closet. "Is that the washroom?"

"Yes. Toilet and shower is through there. I don't expect she'll be in shape to attend breakfast. Come on, I'll show you how to make her tea." Veronica cast one last look at Millie's snoring form and followed Myfanwy out of the room.

MYFANWY LEFT. VERONICA grimaced at the muddy tracks spoiling the pristine apartment. After taking off her coat and hanging it on the hall tree by the door, she toed off her boots and set them by the doormat. Veronica tugged off her damp jeans with muddy hems and draped them over a chair to dry. She shivered as she pulled off her wet socks and laid them over her boots. After locating a sponge and bucket under the sink, she cleaned the mud from the floor. She shivered as she worked on her knees in her briefs and T-shirt.

After cleaning the floor and washing her hands, Veronica returned to check on Millie. She had rolled to her side. The soft hiss of her breath and the occasional snort while she slept were the only sounds in the room.

Worried Millie might vomit, Veronica moved the bathroom trash bin next to the bed. *What am I going to say? She won't believe me. She has to believe me.* She left Millie's room and went back to the living room.

She surveyed the room and found a crocheted blanket rolled up next to the sofa. Veronica curled her long frame into the small couch and lay on her side. She draped the blanket over her and pillowed her head on her hands. Tucked away on the bottom shelf of the squat bookshelf opposite the sofa, a silver-framed photo glinted in the dim light cast from the lamp. A grinning Millie stood next to a buxom woman with light-brown skin and wavy coal-black hair. Her arm was draped over the woman's shoulder, and her broad hand rested on the woman's stomach. *The look on her face. Love. She loved her. Who is she?*

She got up off the couch and pulled the framed photo from the shelf. She cradled it in her hands. Millie was young, her face unlined, her nose straight and unscarred. The woman in the photo gazed up at Millie and her hand rested on Millie's cheek. Her belly was slightly rounded where Millie's hand rested. *Damn. That woman is pregnant. Where's the baby?* She scanned the back of the photo frame for a date or name before she placed it back on the shelf. She rubbed her hand over her chest to rub away the ache.

So what? We all have photos like that. Past loves. She has a child somewhere. So what? She's never looked at me that way. Does she love me? Did she get drunk because she was mad? Or hurt? What the hell am I going to do? I need to talk to her. She can't drink like this. Not because of me. Or any reason. A sharp wave of fear lanced through Veronica. *What if she's violent? What if she's mad enough to hurt me?* She scrubbed her hand over her face. *She'd never hurt me. She's not like that. He was beating her mother. I might have done the same. But what if she was angry? What if she's angry with me? Stop. I need to stop. I'm doing what she said I would do. Ugh, this is hard as fuck. She's got to believe me.*

Chapter Thirteen

VERONICA SPENT A restless hour on the couch awakened frequently by Millie's snoring and intermittent low-key groans. She gave up, wrapped the blanket around her shoulders, and padded down the hall. Millie had kicked the covers off. The nightlight cast a dull yellow glow over the room, and she was sprawled face down across the bed. Veronica fought her desire to cross the room and dust her fingers over her soft skin. She wanted to trace her way over the freckles on her broad back and kiss her neck until she made the soft sighs that set Veronica on fire.

Instead, she crossed the room and pulled the sheet and then the blanket up and over Millie's shoulders. She bent and pressed a delicate kiss to her warm cheek, wondering if it would be the last time she touched her lips to Millie's skin. She cocooned herself in the blanket and sat in the chair opposite the bed, determined to memorize every dip and curve of Millie's form. *What am I going to say? Maybe she doesn't want a relationship because she has a child. But where is the baby? Child. That photo is at least fifteen years old. She has to listen to me. Please let her believe me.*

First light filled the room and turned the black shadows gray. Millie jerked awake and shoved the bedclothes from her body. Veronica stayed quiet as Millie rubbed her eyes. Oblivious to Veronica's presence, she lurched off the bed and walked to the bathroom, her gait stiff. The sound of water splashing and the toilet flushing was loud. *I should have said something. Let her know I was here.*

"Hey, Millie?" She called from the chair and pulled the blanket tighter around herself.

A startled yip sounded from the bathroom, and Millie emerged with a towel in her hand. "What the hell are you doing in my bedroom?" A scowl spoiled her handsome face. "Get out."

"Um. I helped Myfanwy get you up the steps. I wanted to make sure you were okay."

Millie snorted and threw the towel in the direction of the bathroom. "You've seen. Now go." She planted her hands on her hips.

Veronica ignored the hard set of Millie's mouth. "Please talk to me. It wasn't what it looked like. Ashley played me. She wanted you to think there was something going on. Please believe me." She chewed her lip.

"Right." Millie's lip curled in a sneer. "I'm not a fool. Or blind. I saw you with her." She took a step toward Veronica. "Get out. Now."

"Please, Millie. I know what it looked like."

"Do you?" Millie's face was dark red. "Do you know what it was like to walk in and see that? Her tits were in your hands. You could've told me. I wouldn't have cared, but you should've told me. We don't have to be exclusive."

Wouldn't have cared? What the fuck? Oh. She only cares because I didn't tell her? Oh fuck. Not exclusive. Friends. Friends with benefits. Fuck me. She doesn't want what I want. "I've been honest with you." Veronica rose from the chair and took a step toward Millie. "I didn't tell you because there was nothing to tell. I've never lied to you." She straightened her posture. Her knuckles ached from her grip on the edge of the blanket.

Millie stepped back, maintaining the distance between them. "How would I know? Maybe you've been playing me all along. Maybe you get off on sneaking around."

Veronica scrubbed her hand over her face. "You know how the grapevine works here. If I'd been banging Ashley, everyone would have been talking about it. No secrets here. Everyone would have been dying to tell you. Hell, Ashley would have told you herself. Come on, Millie."

Millie's face was stone. She crossed her arms in front of her chest. Her silence hammered Veronica's hopes into dust. Veronica stepped back and wrapped the blanket tighter around her body and turned her back to Millie. *I'm an idiot to think she would listen. Why would she? She doesn't care, not the way I care, doesn't want to be exclusive. Damn, this hurts. I need to go. I'm making a fool of myself.*

She shrugged out of the blanket and folded it carefully before she placed it in the chair. A chill chased over her and the fine hairs on her legs rose on goose flesh, reminding her she only had on briefs. "Sorry I startled you." She balled her hands into fists as hurt morphed into anger at Millie's continued silence. Veronica kept her back turned, not wanting to see the hard set of Millie's jaw. "I thought we had something, Millie."

"Me too." Millie's deep voice was soft.

The ache in her chest swelled, and she gulped down the hard knot in her throat. She strode from the room and closed the door behind her. She lifted her chin and clenched her jaw, willing herself not to run. *Fuck that. Fuck her. I'm so fucked.*

VERONICA SHOVED HER legs into her stiff dirty jeans. She stuffed her socks into her back pocket before she tugged her boots on. She snatched her jacket off the hall tree and opened the door. Head down, Veronica pulled her jacket on as she stormed down the stairs. Her face burned. Anger and hurt twisted a knot in her gut. *Doesn't trust me. Doesn't believe me. Doesn't want to be exclusive. Doesn't care. Just like Dee. Fuck, I sure can pick them. Fuck me. She probably thinks I lied about not being guilty. I can't be with someone who doesn't trust me. Maybe Ashley did me a favor. Something else would've happened, she would've wanted someone else, and then she'd have told me she didn't want to be exclusive and broke my heart.*

Veronica rolled back the barn door. Familiar whickers and whinnies greeted her. She unlocked the grain box and threw back the lid. With trembling hands, she lifted the tubs of grain from the box, made her way down the line of stalls, and distributed the horses' breakfasts. She had done so much work the night before trying to distract herself from her heartache, she had nothing to do this morning.

She walked to her office. From its hook behind her desk, she took down the clipboard with her running list of maintenance tasks and scanned it for things to keep herself busy. She wiped her damp palm on her pants, the stiff fabric reminding her she was dressed in her clothes from yesterday. *Shower. Come back and turn them out. Clean some tack. There's always tack to be cleaned.* As the rush of adrenaline from her fight with Millie wore off, tiredness settled over her and a heavy pain settled in her soul. The ache in her heart intensified, and she pressed her palm to her chest. *Coffee. I need coffee. Call Mom. Need to know someone still loves me.*

ONE SHOWER AND two cups of coffee later Veronica sat on her bed. She nibbled on a protein bar she had stashed. *That's my last one. I'll have to face them at lunch. Ugh.* She entered her mom's number on her phone and sipped her coffee as she waited for her to pick up. Her call went to voice mail, and she hung up without leaving a message. *No use worrying Mom.*

She finished the protein bar, crumpled the wrapper, and sighed. One disastrous afternoon of letting her guard down and her future at Rowan House was over. She chewed her lip as she tried to imagine finding another job she liked as much. Let alone could get hired for. *Maybe the therapeutic stable in Portree? It wouldn't be full time. And where would I live? Would my work visa transfer? Fuck. Six more months here before I have to think about it. What the hell am I going to do? Fucking Ashley cost me my job and a woman I thought I had a future with.* Anger and images of revenge against Ashley filled her thoughts. She rested her head on her desk, stopping short of banging her head on it, knowing the pain wouldn't dull the burning ache in her heart.

A knock at the door startled her. She lifted her head. *No one ever visits me other than Millie, and that sure as hell isn't ever going to happen again. Who the fuck is that? Nothing on the schedule today. Probably Elaine wanting me to get Luna ready for an impromptu ride. Need to turn the horses out anyway.* Veronica ground her teeth and shoved the chair back. Another knock sounded in the room, louder and more insistent. "Give me a minute for fuck's sake." She yelled toward the door, not caring if it might be one of her employers. *The kindest thing they could do for me right now would be to fire me and send me back home.* She snatched the door open, knowing her face reflected her anger and unable to summon the will to care. "What?"

Millie stood on the landing. Veronica blinked. She opened her mouth to speak. Millie stepped into the room and swept Veronica up in her arms. She lifted her off the floor and kissed her. She crushed Veronica to her chest. Her mouth was hot and sweet. *Think. You need to talk.* Veronica placed her hands on Millie's forearms and clutched them, holding on to her.

She was gasping when Millie finally broke their kiss. "What the hell?"

"I'm sorry." She lowered Veronica to the floor, rested her forehead on Veronica's brow, and stroked her hands down Veronica's back "I'm so sorry. I should have listened to you." She pulled back and met Veronica's gaze. "Forgive me? Please."

"What changed your mind?" Veronica kept her gaze fixed on Millie's face.

"What you said. You're right. Ashley would have rubbed it in my face if she had you." Millie's hands rested on Veronica's hips.

Veronica snorted and pushed away from Millie's embrace. She pinned her in place with a glare. "So what? We get back together, and the first person you see you want to be with you go with them?"

"What?" Millie's face pulled into a confused frown. "What the hell are you talking about?"

Veronica embraced her anger like a lost love found. "You said you didn't care. That you didn't want to be exclusive. I don't want that kind of relationship."

"No. I didn't..." Millie ran her hand over her hair and blew out a breath. "I didn't mean it." Millie's anxious expression and the fear in her eyes melted Veronica's resolve.

"Why the fuck did you say it?" Veronica reached up and gripped Millie's chin hard, the skin blanching under her fingers. "I love you. I love you, and I don't want to share you with anyone." Millie trembled under her grip.

Millie gasped. "You do?"

Fuck. Hell of a time to say it. "Yeah. I do." *It's okay if she doesn't feel the same way.* Veronica lied to herself. She kept her gaze steady, watching Millie's face, opening herself, letting her love show in her eyes.

"Why?" Millie grabbed her other hand and squeezed hard.

"Why what?" Veronica raised her eyebrow.

"Why do you love me?" Millie's expression reminded Veronica of a drowning woman. Desperate, unbelieving, fearful.

"For a lot of reasons. I love how caring you are. You're brilliant and sweet and protective. I love your voice, and your body, and your sense of humor. I love how you care for your chosen family, how you care for me. How you remember all the little things I like. I love you, Millie. For everything you are with every bit of my heart. Why'd you run off and drink yourself senseless?"

"I was angry." Millie pressed her lips together.

"Angry?" Veronica released Millie's chin, pulled her hand from Millie's grasp, and fisted her hands on her hips. She raised her eyebrow.

Millie lowered her chin to her chest. "And hurt."

Veronica reached out and touched Millie's cheek, drawing her gaze. "Do you get drunk like when you're in pain? Is it your version of self-medicating?"

"Not always." A flash of anger crossed Millie's face. "So what if I do?"

Veronica pinned her in place with her gaze. "You need to stop. We can't do this if alcohol is the way you deal with anything that hurts you."

Millie snorted. "Are you telling me I have to choose? You or drinking?"

"I'm telling you"—Veronica softened her gaze and she leaned in to kiss Millie—"you need to find some healthier coping mechanisms." She brushed her lips over her mouth before she pressed forward and kissed her softly. She pulled back to observe Millie's expression.

Millie swept Veronica up and off her feet. Veronica had carried her share of women to bed over the years, but she had never been with anyone able to lift her. Her heart squeezed hard. *Cherished. Adored. Desired. Loved?* She clasped her arms around Millie's neck. Millie crushed her to her chest and scattered kisses over her brow and her cheek and then her mouth.

Millie's eyes were dark as she met Veronica's gaze. "I love you, Veronica Fletcher. I need you like air. I wanted to die when I thought you had been with Ashley. I was afraid I had blown it." She kissed Veronica again.

Veronica groaned. The sensation of being loved in return and the way Millie kissed her turned her inside out. She gasped as Millie scattered kisses over her neck. "Wait. Wait. I have to turn the horses out."

"And then?" Millie paused to sweep her tongue over the shell of Veronica's ear. "What are you doing after?" She nipped Veronica's neck and soothed the bite with a sweep of her tongue.

Veronica angled her neck, giving Millie better access. "Letting you show me how much you love me."

Chapter Fourteen

THEY HELD HANDS as they walked across the gravel parking lot, the soft crunch of the crushed stone under their feet loud in Veronica's ears. Her hand was sweaty in Millie's large palm. Millie urged her up the stairs, her fingers resting on the curve of Veronica's ass as she followed close behind her. She reached around her and unlocked the door to her apartment. They pushed through the open door together and clung to each other as they toed off their shoes, scrabbling at each other's clothes. Veronica ripped Millie's T-shirt over her head. She smoothed her palms across the broad expanse of her chest down over her firm curves, cupped her breasts, and thumbed her nipples. *So beautiful. So strong.*

Millie groaned into her touch. "Let me, let me." She tugged Veronica's belt open before she unbuttoned her jeans.

Veronica's breath stuttered. "Yes, yes."

Millie's warm fingers skipped and skidded over Veronica's stiff clit before she pushed inside.

Millie's hands traveled over Veronica's body as she fingered her. She used her body and turned them in the small space. She pulled her hand free before she dropped to her knees. She looked up at Veronica, and the devotion reflected in her eyes split Veronica's heart wide open. *This. This is right. She loves me.* She laid her hand on

Millie's cheek, and Millie turned her face and kissed her palm reverently. Veronica leaned against the door and shoved at her jeans, pushing them to her ankles. Millie grabbed the waistband of Veronica's briefs and yanked them down. Her warm breath tickled Veronica's thigh before she leaned in and flicked her tongue over Veronica's clit.

Her legs trapped by her pants, Veronica was held in place by Millie's strong hands resting on her thighs. Millie's hot wet tongue dipped and slipped over her slick folds.

"That's so good." Veronica groaned as Millie lapped at her. She dug her fingers into Millie's soft brush cut to steady herself against the riot of pleasure filling her. Millie used a finger to gently tease the hood back and touched the tip of her tongue to the hot bundle of nerves there, once, twice so soft, so sweetly. Veronica pulled Millie's mouth tight against her as she bucked and screamed her release.

"Mmm. You taste like every good thing in the world. I can't get enough of you." Millie's voice was soft as she spoke in between small kisses and touches of her tongue, causing a sharp series of aftershocks to crash through Veronica. She stood and cupped Veronica's face and kissed her. Her tongue traced the line of Veronica's lips. Her face and mouth were wet with evidence of Veronica's pleasure.

The taste of herself on Millie's lips sent a fresh rush of desire coursing through Veronica. She struggled against the jeans around her legs. The sensation of being bound ramped up her need. Millie leaned back and stared into Veronica's face as she lowered her hand to trace her way through the tight curls between Veronica's thighs.

Veronica gasped, her body clenching around Millie as she entered her. Sweeping two fingers over the spot that made her buck and arch for more. Veronica struggled and pulled one leg free of her jeans. She lifted it and wrapped it around Millie's hips, urging her closer. She studied Millie's heavy-lidded expression. Dark desire filled her eyes.

Veronica shifted her hips to pull her deeper. "More." A command not a plea, and Millie kept her gaze fixed on Veronica's face as she pulled back and pushed a third finger inside. The sting and burn made Veronica groan as Millie's broad palm rubbed Veronica's clit as she rocked against her. Eyes locked on Veronica's face, Millie slowed her thrusts, drawing out Veronica's pleasure.

Rippling waves of delight spread through her, so much and yet not enough. Need whipped through her body, her nipples ached, and deep moans rattled her chest. Her body tightened around Millie's fingers. Millie stilled and eased a fourth finger in, and Veronica panted around the new sensation. Millie gentled her strokes and Veronica cried out, the slow deep soft thrusts making her desperate for more. She hissed and shuddered as deeper waves of bliss spread out from her core.

Veronica clutched at Millie's shoulders, her nails digging into her silky skin as Millie edged her, giving her enough but not enough. Sweat rolled down Veronica's face and stung her eyes. She relished the sweet torture and clung to Millie. Veronica slowed her breathing and let the sensations fill her, taking her down until she was desperate to go over and needed more.

"Fuck me." Veronica dug her nails in harder, drawing a sharp yip from Millie. "Now."

"Wrap both legs around me." Millie dipped her hips and Veronica raised her other leg. She braced her shoulders against the door. Millie's mouth curved into a feral smile. "Hold on."

Millie set her legs and wrapped her arm around Veronica's hips. Her fingers digging into the soft flesh of Veronica's ass, she lowered her head and mouthed the curve of Veronica's neck as she sped up her strokes, thrusting hard and fast and deep. Veronica's keening wail filled the narrow hallway and she came, digging her short nails so deep she was sure she had drawn blood. Her pleasure crested, one wave building on the next until it pulled her under and there was nothing but Millie's broad body and the sensations between her legs.

She clung to her and kissed her temple, her cheek, her eyelids, anywhere and everywhere her mouth could reach. Millie slowed her movements, easing her down, and Veronica gasped as another gentle orgasm rippled through her when Millie slipped her fingers free and pressed gently on Veronica's clit with her thumb. She gripped Veronica's ass with both hands and lifted her. The press of the soft skin of her stomach was soothing against Veronica's swollen flesh. She rested her head on Millie's shoulder. Millie turned them and strode down the hallway to her bedroom. She lowered Veronica to the bed.

Millie smiled down at her. "You look good in my bed." Her usual cocky grin was back in place. "Stay right there."

Boneless, Veronica nodded her willingness to comply, unable to form words.

Millie returned with two glasses of water. Veronica pushed up on her elbows and then sat up to take one of the glasses. "Thanks." She swallowed, the cool water soothing against her throat. "My throat's a little sore."

Millie smirked. "You screamed a bit."

"A bit? I'm glad we were here instead of my room. I'd have frightened the horses."

Millie's booming laugh echoed off the wall of the bedroom. "Aye, you would have." Her expression became serious. "I didn't hurt you, did I?"

Veronica placed her glass on the side table. "Not at all." She raked her gaze over Millie's shirtless body. "You still have your pants on. Unacceptable."

Millie stood and set her glass aside. She grasped the top button of her jeans and tugged. It popped open. Veronica swallowed hard against the burning need to possess Millie.

"You want me?" Millie lowered the zipper one notch at a time until it was halfway down and stopped.

Veronica fixed her with a level gaze. "Do it. Now. Get naked and get in this bed."

Millie shucked her jeans and jumped onto the bed. "Or what? You going to punish me?" She lifted Veronica's hand and kissed the palm before trailing kisses up her wrist and to her elbow until she was at the apex of her shoulder and neck.

Veronica brought her hand up and wrapped her fingers around Millie's throat lightly. She pushed on Millie's chest with her other hand. Millie lay back on the bed, panting, her pupils blown wide.

"Yes." Veronica straddled Millie, keeping one hand in place around her neck. "Spread your legs. Open yourself to me."

Millie's tongue slid over her lower lip as she spread her legs wide and used her hands to expose her clit. Veronica lifted her body and glanced between her legs. The sight of Millie's hands between her legs, obeying Veronica, made her clit throb.

Veronica shifted until her body made contact with Millie's center, clit to clit. The glorious sensation of the slick slide drew a deep growl from Millie. "Move your hands."

Millie complied and fisted her hands in the sheets. Her eyes were closed, her face suffused with pleasure, and her pulse rapid beneath Veronica's fingertips. *Trust, she trusts me. Wants me. Loves me.* She rolled her hips, caught up in their intimate dance, their flesh as one. "Look at me."

Millie opened her eyes and met Veronica's gaze.

"You want to come for me?"

"Yes, please, *Ceannard*, please."

Veronica flexed her fingers, tightening her grip on Millie's throat. "You want to be mine?"

Millie lifted her chin, signaling her desire, her voice thick. "Only yours, *Ceannard*."

Veronica leaned down and kissed her. She rotated her hips, bringing Millie off, swallowing her shouts as she came. *Mine. She wants to be mine.*

"HEY, THIS CAME for you." Robin held out a thick cream-colored envelope. Veronica tugged off her gloves and wiped her hand on her jeans before she took the letter from Robin. It was addressed in flowing copperplate script. She flipped it over and read her parents' return address on the back. Veronica fought the rising sense of dread that settled in the pit of her stomach.

Robin flopped on the office couch. "So, who's getting married?"

"My sister. Damn it." Veronica tossed the envelope on her desk blotter. "I knew this was coming. She sent me a 'save the date' card, six months ago, but with the job and everything I forgot all about it."

"Is the guy a douche?" Robin's lips thinned.

"He's not a douche, but damn, I don't know what I'm going to do. My parents and my sister expect me at this thing."

"So, what's the problem? You go. It's your sister's wedding. You don't blow something like this off. You said your family is cool with you. What's your problem?"

"My family is fine, but the whole rest of the damn family will be there. Most of them haven't talked to me since I got out. They stare right through me. Fuck. And my aunt will be there. My aunt is the worst. Right after I got out, I went to my little cousin's baptism, and my aunt made a huge scene on the sidewalk outside the church. Said my being there was an affront to God because I was a drug dealer. Which I never was. Her own kids smoke weed. My cousins could light up in front of her, and she'd deny it." Veronica scrubbed her hands over her face. "What am I going to do?"

Robin rested her chin on her hand. "Don't be ridiculous. You go, you don't talk to them. Take somebody with you." Her eyes shone with glee. "Take Millie. Oh, that's so romantic, going as a couple to a wedding. It's the perfect solution. Millie's charming, and they'll be so busy staring at her and trying to figure out what's up with you two, you won't have to worry about anybody being jerks."

Veronica glared at Robin. "I don't want them treating Millie like some sort of sideshow attraction. I wouldn't do that to Millie. This guy my sister's marrying, he's not a douche but his family will be there, and they're total assholes. They'll never be okay with me." She sat heavily on the couch and leaned back on the cushion and studied the ceiling. "I am well and truly fucked. If I don't go, I'll break my sister's heart, and my parents will be pissed as hell."

Robin reached over and rested her hand on Veronica's knee. "My friend, you can't miss your sister's wedding. You only get one family. Don't break her heart." Robin's mouth turned down. "My family hasn't talked to me in years. I don't exist to them and haven't since I was fifteen."

Veronica started at Robin's words. "But you want to visit them, you told me you wanted to visit them."

"I want to visit my chosen family. I want to visit the friends who are more family than my birth family. Don't let one bitch keep you from having a family. Your parents and your sister love you. They stood by you. They believed you when no one else did. Fuck your aunt. Fuck his family. You go and be with your family. That's what's important." Robin's eyes were bright with unshed tears.

Veronica sighed. "I know I should. But I'm not sure it's the right thing." She stared at the envelope on the desk.

Robin stood up and stretched. She reached down and offered her hand to Veronica. "Come on."

Veronica stood and clasped Robin's hand. "Where're we going?"

"Whenever I have a problem, I go to the number one problem solver."

Veronica quirked her mouth. "And who is that?"

"Mistress Lucia is the smartest woman I've ever met. She'll know what to do. She'll help you. Mostly she helps you figure out what you already know." Robin held onto Veronica's hand and led her out of the office.

VERONICA AND ROBIN stood outside the dark wood six-paneled door leading to Mistress Lucia's office. Robin squeezed Veronica's hand. "I'm going to leave you here. Talk with her, she'll help you figure this out." She knocked on the door and left Veronica in the hall.

Mistress Lucia opened the door, tilted her head at Veronica, and raised an eyebrow. "Yes?"

Veronica lost herself in the tall elegance of Mistress Lucia, captivated by her blue-green eyes. "I'm...Robin thought you could, I have a..." She struggled to organize her thoughts.

"Why don't you come in, and we'll talk about it. No need to stand in the hall." Mistress Lucia turned, and Veronica followed her into the office, mesmerized by her cool presence and grace. The walls were covered in large floral photographic prints, a sharp contrast to the dark wood paneling and the large mahogany desk occupying one corner of the room.

Mistress Lucia sat on a Victorian-style fainting couch covered in dark-blue velvet. "Sit. Let's talk."

Aware of her dusty jeans and barn clothing, Veronica brushed off the seat of her pants before she sat in the chair that matched the couch. She knotted her fingers together in her lap. "My sister's getting married."

Mistress Lucia raised an eyebrow. "And you'd like some time off? I don't see why there would be a problem. Were you afraid to ask Mistress Martha? I'll speak to her if you are."

"No. It's not that." Veronica unknotted her fingers and tucked her hands under her thighs to keep them from shaking.

Mistress Lucia shifted her position on the couch as she raised an eyebrow. "I'm not sure I'm understanding your problem."

Veronica took a deep breath and exhaled slowly. "My extended family will be there and my sister's future husband's family. And, and...they don't, well, none of them speak to me since I got out of prison. I don't want my aunt to be an ass and cause all kinds of problems. I don't want to ruin my sister's wedding."

"I know what it is to be unwanted and an unexpected guest, but your sister invited you and your family want you to be there, yes?"

Veronica slumped in her chair. "They do. They do expect me to be there."

"But you're worried your presence will be a distraction?"

"Yes. I went to my cousin's baptism, and my aunt raised a stink about it. She was awful. My mother and father stood by me, but I knew they were embarrassed. And the worst part was it took away from my cousin's special day."

"Understandable." Mistress Lucia got up from the couch and walked to the window and stared out at the grounds. Her hands were clasped behind her back. "How many sisters do you have, Veronica?"

"Just the one."

"And you love your sister? She's been kind to you. She visited you when you were in prison. Did she shun you or stay away because people might not approve of you? Was she worried at all about what other people would think or say to her? Was she ashamed she had a sister who was in prison?"

"No." Veronica shifted in her chair.

"And your parents, did they walk away from you, worried about what other people would think or say? Or did they stand by you?"

"They all stood by me. They came to visit. They believed me when no one else did."

Mistress Lucia turned around and skewered Veronica with her gaze. "And you really have to ask me what you should do?"

Veronica flushed and began to sweat under Mistress Lucia's examination.

She sat on the couch and extended her arm along the back as she studied Veronica's face. Her eyes and her expression softened. "You have your answer, Veronica. You said yourself they didn't give up on you. Why would you give up on them?"

Veronica scrubbed her face with her hands. "Robin said you were good at this."

Mistress Lucia tilted her head and studied Veronica. "Are you planning on going alone to the wedding?"

Sweat trickled down the back of Veronica's neck. "I haven't thought about it. I might ask Millie if she'd go with me."

"Are you concerned about that too?" Mistress Lucia's sharp gaze was back.

"I've never brought anyone like her home."

"Like her? You mean a woman?"

"Oh no, they know I'm queer."

"So, what do you mean 'like her'?" Mistress Lucia's eyes were hard and cold.

"I've never brought home a butch woman. And I've never dated a white woman ever."

Mistress Lucia pressed her lips together in a firm line. "Do you think it would be a problem with your family?"

Veronica frowned. "I don't think so, but I don't know. No one in my family's ever dated anyone white, that I know of."

"My father is white."

Veronica's chest tightened and she shifted in her chair. "Was it hard? Growing up?"

"Yes. His family hated my mother and me for the color of our skin. And my mother's family hated my father for not standing up to his family. I understand your fears. Have you talked to them about Millie?"

"No. Not yet." Veronica quirked her mouth.

"You need to." Mistress Lucia's voice was kind. "I know this is hard for you, and you've had a lot of things not go your way in the past. You need to trust the love your family has already shown for you. If they were going to abandon you, they would've abandoned you the second you were led out of the courtroom in shackles, but they stood by you. Do you think they'd abandon you over a choice in partner? They've shown you how they feel about you. Trust them. Listen to your heart, Veronica."

Chapter Fifteen

"LIE DOWN." VERONICA placed a hand on Millie's chest and pushed her back on the bed. "Roll over on your stomach. Arms out to the side."

Millie moved into position. "Aye, *Ceannard*."

Veronica touched her hip. "Spread your legs, babe."

Millie obeyed. Veronica kneeled between her legs. She poured massage oil into her palm to warm it. With firm strokes she passed her hands over the firm deliciousness that was Millie's ass on her way to the flat planes of Millie's' broad back. Millie hummed her satisfaction as Veronica kneaded her muscles, working her way along both sides of Millie's spine as she scattered light kisses over her freckled skin.

Veronica cupped her ass and began squeezing and massaging her cheeks as she licked and nibbled her way down her spine. She stopped to tongue at the dimple at the base of Millie's spine. Millie groaned and shifted her hips, spreading her legs wider. Veronica teased a finger over her slick center. "Need something?" She flicked a finger over Millie's clit, and her whimper of need sent a wave of desire coursing through Veronica's body.

"Yes, *Ceannard*. I need."

Veronica lay flat over Millie, rubbing against her firm ass, groaning as her clit made contact with Millie's slick firm flesh. "I love your ass."

Veronica shifted her body so she could finger Millie from behind, teasing a finger over her clit and then slipping a finger into her. "You're so wet for me."

"Only for you." Millie raised her hips. "Please, *Ceannard*, more please."

Veronica bit the curve of Millie's neck, sinking her teeth into the delicate skin there as she slid another finger deep. She licked the spot she had bitten. "Want it fast and rough, don't you?"

"Yes. Please, *Ceannard*. I do. Please."

"Mmm. I like that too. But today I want to take my time." She took her fingers from Millie and ignored her sad moans of loss. "No pouting." She kissed Millie's ass and nipped it, drawing a yip and squirm from Millie. "It'll be worth it. Turn over for me. Same as before. Hands out to your sides, legs spread."

Veronica moved to stand at the foot of the bed as Millie complied. She began at Millie's left foot, kissed the top of her foot, and then the inside of her ankle. From there Veronica took her time as she nipped and licked her way up the inside of Millie's leg. Closing her eyes, Veronica lost herself in Millie's soft smooth skin. She drew her tongue along the crease of her thigh. The sharp scent of Millie's desire made her mouth water. She brushed her lips over the wet curls, used her hands to spread Millie wide, and licked with the flat of her tongue. Millie panted and pressed her hips into Veronica's mouth. Veronica shifted and slid her hands under Millie until she was able to cup her ass. Hot and wet, and hers to enjoy. She thrust her tongue deep, lapping at the sweetness Millie's body offered. She took her time, savoring the taste of her along with her soft cries and the deep groans rattling Millie's chest.

Veronica stopped and rested her head on Millie's' thigh. "I love the way you taste."

"Please don't stop, *Ceannard*. Please. I want to come for you." Veronica kissed her thigh and then bit hard. The sharp yip and gasp from Millie's mouth had Veronica grinding her hips against the bed.

"Do you?" Not waiting for Millie's reply she returned to licking her, focusing on her clit. She took it between her lips and sucked, alternating soft and hard. Millie arched under her, seeking more. Veronica thrust two fingers deep and fucked her slowly, curling her fingers over her G-spot, as she sucked her, edging her, drawing out her pleasures. Millie's voice was rough as she begged Veronica to come, begged to be fucked, begged to be allowed to give everything to Veronica.

Millie's body tightened and clenched around her hand. Sensing her need, Veronica lifted her head. "Come for me, babe. Give it to me." She lowered her head and sucked hard and thrust deep, sweeping her fingers over her sweet spot. She was rewarded with a gush of fluid that soaked her chin and ran down her wrist. Millie's shout as she came echoed in the room, and her hands wrenched the sheets loose, her body shaking. Veronica fucked her hard, taking everything she wanted, everything Millie had to give.

Millie rested her hand on the top of Veronica's head and pushed weakly against her. "No more, *Ceannard*, please, I can't."

Veronica stopped and placed a tender kiss on Millie's clit. She slid up to capture her mouth, opened her legs, and mounted Millie's thigh, pressing her aching center to the hard muscle there. She rode her hard, driven by Millie's surrender. Millie clasped her ass, holding her tight. She flexed her thigh, the muscle a hard ridge beneath Veronica's clit.

"Please, *Ceannard*. Come on me. Please."

Veronica arched back as she came hard, coating Millie's leg with her liquid satisfaction. Millie pushed her hand between her legs, gathered the slickness there, and brought it to her mouth. She groaned as she sucked her fingers clean. "Please, *Ceannard*, please. Come in my mouth. Please. Let me lick you."

She urged Veronica up and over her face, her wide hands supporting Veronica.

"Lick me." Veronica opened herself with one hand. She shivered when the cool air hit her hot wet clit as she lowered herself to Millie's eager mouth.

Veronica grabbed for the headboard and gripped it to steady herself as Millie's wicked tongue swept over her clit. It circled the tip hard and fast and she came again, with a sharp cry. Her clit too sensitive for more, she lifted clear of Millie's mouth and collapsed to her side. Millie lifted her arm and Veronica snuggled under it and rested her head on her chest.

Millie wrapped both arms around her and she shifted and lifted her hips. "I'm in a giant wet spot. Did I squirt?"

Veronica leaned up and kissed her, their tastes melding and mixing in their kiss. "Yeah. It was... Wow." She kissed her again. "It makes me want to make you do it again."

"I've not done it before. It was a bit shocking." Millie's voice was soft.

Veronica studied the blush coloring Millie's cheeks. "Hey. It was sexy as hell. I loved it." She scooted over on the bed. "Come on, this side is dry."

Millie shifted, and Veronica rolled on top of her and stretched out over her, their legs tangled together. She shivered.

Millie tugged the duvet over them. "You make me do all kinds of things I've never done before."

Veronica traced her fingers over Millie's collarbone. "Is that a good thing or a bad thing?" She hated the uncertainty she heard in her own voice.

Millie hugged her tight. "It's a good thing, a very good thing."

Veronica touched Millie's face and lifted her head to gaze into her eyes. "You're amazing. I've not been able to be myself with other lovers."

Millie raised her hand and rubbed her thumb over Veronica's cheekbone. "Their loss."

MILLIE SAT UP and switched on the bedside lamp. "Would you stay here tonight? I'll change the sheets." Her infectious grin was back, the one that made Veronica's heart squeeze hard every time she saw it.

She laced their hands together. "I have to be up early. Elaine wants me to have Luna and Bella ready for her and Roxy. Elaine has been crazier than usual about it. She called me three times to remind me. I think she has something special planned for Roxy."

Millie turned their hands over and kissed the back of Veronica's hand. "I don't mind. Please stay."

Veronica feathered her hand over Millie's brush cut. "I'll stay." She glanced at the clock on the dresser. "We missed staff meal. And you made me hungry. You have anything to eat?"

"I've some crisps, and I'm pretty sure there is a tin of soup in the kitchen."

"You know how to woo a woman, don't you?"

Millie laughed and left the bed. "I know you aren't with me for my cooking skills."

Veronica crooked her finger. Millie leaned down and rested her palms on either side of the mattress, framing her. Veronica cupped her cheek and kissed her. "Nah, but I sure as hell like your other skills." She deepened their kiss.

Millie broke their kiss and raised an eyebrow. "You kiss me again and we'll never get to the crisps. Or the soup."

Veronica slid out from under Millie's arms and crossed to the bathroom. "I'll meet you in the kitchen."

She finished in the bathroom. She plucked Millie's shirt off the floor and pulled it over her head. Veronica lifted the collar to her nose and inhaled the faint sent of Millie that clung to the shirt. Her stomach rumbled. She gave up on finding her briefs and followed the delicious scent of beef and potatoes to the kitchen.

MILLIE WORE A black tank top and her faded jeans rode low on her hips as she stirred a small red pot of soup. The smell of potatoes and beef filled the tiny space that served as the kitchen.

"Beef stew?" Veronica peered into the pan.

"Scotch Broth. Barley, potatoes, beef, mutton, peas, carrots, some onion."

"Sounds like my grandma's beef stew, except she doesn't put mutton or barley in hers." Veronica's stomach growled.

Millie pointed at two bowls on the counter. "Hand me those and I'll serve. I lived on this at Uni."

Veronica passed her two bowls and Millie ladled the soup into them. "Spoons?"

"Top drawer. Crisps are in the cupboard."

Veronica collected two spoons and pulled a lurid orange and yellow bag from the cupboard. "Nik-Naks Nice 'n' Spicy. What the hell are these things? Nice and Spicy. What does that mean? Are they really?"

Millie tilted her head at Veronica. "You've been here four months and not had Nik-Naks?"

"I've been a little busy." Veronica rested a hand on her hip, raised an eyebrow, and met Millie's gaze.

Millie shook her head. "Forgive me. I have been remiss in your education." Her put-on posh accent made Veronica laugh.

Millie stuffed two napkins in her back pocket and picked up their bowls and led the way to the couch. She placed the bowls on the table in front of the sofa before she sat down. Veronica tossed the bag of crisps to her. "Should I get us something to drink?"

Millie inclined her head toward the refrigerator. "If you like beer I have some."

Veronica removed two cans from the refrigerator. "Tennent's. That'll do."

She placed the two cans on the table and then passed a spoon to Millie. They ate in companionable silence.

Veronica spooned the thick soup into her mouth. Too hungry to savor it, she finished her serving hastily and placed her empty bowl on the table. "That was good." She wiped her mouth with her napkin before she stuck her hand in the bag of crisps. She pulled one out and eyed it before taking a bite. "Back home we'd call this a chip, and these are not so spicy." She took another crisp, ate it, and chased it with a sip of beer.

Millie pulled the bag toward her and fished a crisp from the bag. "See. Now you know what you've been missing." She ate her crisp in two bites and leaned back on the couch and finished the last of her soup. She placed the bowl on the end table before she turned to Veronica and trailed a finger down her shoulder. "I like you in my shirt."

"That's good because I couldn't find mine."

Millie picked up her beer and tilted the top toward Veronica. "You look like you want to say something."

Veronica glanced up at the ceiling before she brought her gaze back to Millie's eyes. "My sister's wedding is in November."

"And? Are you worried about time off? I'm sure we could cover the stables. Martha would have final say, but I'm sure she'd approve it."

"It's not that. I mean it is, sort of. But I don't want to go."

Millie frowned. "Why? You and your sister are close, right?"

"What I meant was I don't want to go by myself."

Millie pressed her lips together in a firm line. "You have to go."

"I know. I'm going to go. Would you go with me? I'd like you to meet my family." She studied Millie's expression.

A flash of anxiety crossed her face before her expression shuttered. "No. I can't."

"Can't or won't?" Veronica lifted her beer from the table and rolled it between her hands.

"I'm not so good with parents."

"Oh. Um. Okay." Veronica took a quick swallow of her beer to stem the burning sadness in her throat. "Just a thought."

Millie circled the edge of her beer can with her fingertips. "You've made friends here. Maybe someone else would go with you."

Veronica's stomach clenched. *Not enough. Loves me but not enough to meet my family.* "Yeah, sure. I'll figure it out." She tipped her beer back and finished it in one long swallow.

VERONICA GLANCED AT the barn clock. *Shouldn't have had a second cup of coffee with Millie.* She forced her thoughts away from Millie's refusal and the accompanying ache in her chest. She settled the saddle pad over Luna's back.

"Don't bother tacking Bella." Elaine's wicked-sharp voice cut the air. "Roxy will not be joining me today. Or any day."

Veronica stepped around Luna to ask why. Elaine's face was pale, jaw clenched, her shoulders rigid. Her glare was the coldest thing Veronica had ever seen, and she turned away from it. "Uh. Okay."

Elaine huffed out a breath. "I'll wait outside."

Veronica placed the saddle on Luna's back and tightened the girth. Moving steadily, she replaced her halter with the bridle and buckled it in place.

She tucked Elaine's hard hat under her arm and led Luna out to the mounting block.

Elaine was pacing with her hands clasped behind her back. She glanced up when Veronica and Luna appeared. Without a word she stopped and mounted the block, her hands on her hips.

Veronica walked Luna to the block and Elaine mounted her horse. After settling herself into her saddle, she leaned down and adjusted her stirrups before she picked up the reins.

"When should I expect you back?" Veronica released her hold on Luna's bridle.

"When I get here." Elaine's voice dripped acid. "I don't recall having a curfew."

Stung by Elaine's attitude and tone, Veronica silently offered Elaine her hard hat.

Elaine waved it away. "Not today. I'm not in the mood."

Veronica frowned at her. "To be safe?"

"We all have to die of something." Elaine's voice was raw. She dug her heels in, Luna responded, and they charged out of the yard and through the front gate. Luna's hooves clattered on the drive, Elaine bent low over her neck, her flame-red hair trailing loose behind her.

Veronica clutched the hard hat in her hands as she watched Elaine until she rode out of sight. *Where's Roxy? What the hell happened? Should I go after her?*

VERONICA TOED OFF her boots and placed them under the peg for her jacket. The smell of fresh baked bread made her mouth water. She washed her hands in the small lavatory off the mudroom and hurried into the kitchen. "That's the best smell in the world." She grinned at Robin as she took her seat at the table. "Second only to good coffee brewing."

Robin gave her a tight smile that didn't reach her eyes. "Coffee's ready, and I'm glad someone's in a good mood today."

"I saw Elaine off on her ride. I've never seen her like that. What the hell happened?" Veronica poured herself a cup of coffee and helped herself to a thick slice of bread.

Robin shifted her gaze from Veronica's face. "Roxy's leaving."

"What? Why?" Veronica spread butter over the slice of bread on her plate.

"I don't know." Robin traced her finger over the wood grain on the table. "If Elaine asked me to wear her collar..." Robin blushed. "I'm gossiping, and I promised myself I wouldn't."

Veronica touched the back of Robin's hand. "Sorry I asked. You care for her, don't you?"

Robin quirked her mouth. "Does it show?"

"Only a bit, and your secret's safe with me."

"I owe her so much. I don't know what would have happened to me if she hadn't given me a second chance." Robin stood and wiped her hands on her side towel. "I've got to start on the chocolate tarts for dinner. I promised Mistress Lucia I'd make them."

"Will I be in your way here?" Veronica took another sip of coffee.

"No. I'd like the company if you don't mind talking to my back while I work. Myfanwy is otherwise occupied this morning." The wistful tone in Robin's voice was unmistakable.

Veronica smeared her bread with butter. "I don't mind, and I'm half starved."

"I noticed you and Millie missed staff meal last night." Robin glanced over her shoulder at Veronica and smiled, a real smile this time. "I trust it was worth it."

Veronica flushed. "Yes. And no. She won't go to my sister's wedding with me."

"I'm sorry."

"Would you go?" Veronica hated the pathetic sound of her voice.

Robin turned from the butter she had been chopping into small bits. "I can't leave here. It's not safe for me."

"Why?" Veronica placed her coffee cup in its saucer. "What do you mean?" Her skin prickled with goose flesh.

"I was forcibly involved in a scheme to extort money from the house. I confessed to Martha, told her everything I knew. The people behind it were not happy." Her voice grew quiet. "They found the other woman involved, or rather what was left of her, in a barrel of acid in a Glasgow warehouse."

"That's horrible." Veronica sat back in her chair, appetite gone. Fear twisted inside her like a living thing.

"I was afraid Martha and Elaine would turn me in or take matters into their own hands after I confessed, but Mistress Elaine gave me a place here. She saw the good in me even if I showed her the bad first." Robin peered at Veronica from under her lashes, her chin on her chest. "Do you think differently of me? Now you know?"

"No. Robin, look at me." Veronica met Robin's gaze. "You're my friend. You've been kind to me since I got here—well, after you stopped being afraid of me."

Robin chuckled. "You have to admit you can be very intimidating."

Veronica smiled. "You mean stuck up? Acting like I was better than anyone else here?"

Robin snorted. "You weren't so bad. Ashley was far worse and still is."

"Do you think Millie is afraid of meeting my family? Afraid it's too soon?"

"I think Millie is like all of us with a past we'd like to forget. I can't leave here, at least not until Miss Pomroy has taken care of things."

Veronica shuddered as she remembered Jaya's warning when she signed her contract and imagined the way Jaya would take care of things.

Robin pushed up the long sleeve of her chef coat. Track marks and small scars stood out under the bright kitchen lights. "But even then, I'll be worried I'll run into someone who remembers me from before. Someone who'll remember me as a young girl, working on dirty street corners and in back alleys trying to feed my habit. I can't speak for Millie, but maybe she needs to know you won't be swayed by your family's opinion, you won't change your mind no matter what they think of her."

Veronica stood up and walked to Robin and gave her a quick hug. "Thanks for breakfast. And the advice."

Chapter Sixteen

VERONICA ROLLED BACK the door to the barn. Luna's tack was on the rack by the crossties. White lines of dried sweat edged the saddle; stark evidence of how hard Elaine had pushed Luna on their ride. Several grooming brushes were scattered along the bench. She picked them up and replaced them in the grooming box and tidied the area around the crossties. She heard murmurings coming from Luna's stall. She walked softly until she reached her stall. Elaine was standing next to Luna, her forehead resting on the horse's shoulder. Her clothes were mud-splattered, her hair wild and tangled about her shoulders.

Turn around. Don't intrude. Let her work it out. She's hurting. Damn. I'd want someone to ask, to listen.

"Come to see how the mighty have fallen?" Elaine kept her back turned to Veronica.

"No. I came to see if a friend needed to talk. I'm sorry about Roxy." Veronica took a step into the stall.

Elaine turned to her. "I don't need your sympathy. And since when am I your friend?" She glared at Veronica.

"Wasn't offering sympathy." Veronica glared back. "And fine, but you sure look like you could use a friend."

Elaine snorted. "You would be the first person to ever express that opinion."

"Well, you don't make it easy, but you're still less intimidating than my former roommate, Tiny, so whatever." Veronica tilted her head at Elaine and smiled.

"Come on, even the hardest ass needs to soften up sometimes."

Elaine laughed then, a genuine laugh. "Are you offering to soften my ass up?"

Veronica rubbed the back of her neck with her hand. "No. We've established that is not happening, but I'm happy to listen, if you want." She met Elaine's gaze. "I truly am sorry about Roxy leaving."

Elaine shifted her gaze to the floor. "As am I." She clenched her fists. "I can't believe she…"

Veronica waited.

Elaine lifted her face to Veronica. "You have anything to drink in this barn?"

"Millie showed me the emergency supplies the first day I was here. Come on."

Elaine latched Luna's stall door and followed her down the aisle.

Veronica opened the door to the office, tugged open the bottom file cabinet drawer, extracted a bottle of Talisker and two squat glasses. Elaine threw herself on the sofa and draped her arm over her forehead. Veronica had to stifle a giggle at her theatrics as she poured two glasses of the whisky.

"Here." She offered one to Elaine.

With an aggrieved sigh Elaine pushed herself to a sitting position and took the glass from Veronica. Her fingers were white where she gripped the tumbler as she tipped the glass back and took a large sip. Veronica studied the large irregular scar covering the back of her hand, the edges pink in contrast to the shiny white scar tissue. The scar flowed over her wrist and disappeared under the sleeve of her shirt.

Hell of a fire. That is some burn. Veronica sat on the opposite end of the battered sofa and tucked a leg under her as she turned to study Elaine.

Elaine pursed her lips. "I should have seen it coming. Roxy leaving." She lowered her chin to her chest. "Do you know what she said?" Elaine took another sip of her whisky. "She said I wasn't committed. Said I couldn't commit to a chair let alone a person. Bitch."

Veronica took a sip of her whisky, savoring the smooth sweetness and slight burn as she swallowed.

"She said..." Elaine took another big swallow of her whisky and emptied her glass. With an imperious nod of her head she indicated Veronica should refill it.

Veronica scrambled from the couch, grabbed the bottle off the desk, and refilled Elaine's glass.

"Leave the bottle."

Veronica placed the bottle on the floor next to Elaine's muddy boots.

Elaine tilted the glass back and chugged it.

A waste of good whisky, but I'm not buying so whatever. Veronica balanced her drink on the arm of the couch.

Elaine picked up the bottle and refilled her glass. "She told me she never said anything about wanting to wear my collar or be exclusive." She turned and faced Veronica. "She laughed when I asked her to stay, to wear my collar." Elaine shook her head and blew out a ragged breath, her fury palpable in the small room. "Of all the... Do you know how many women have asked to pledge to me? To be mine alone?"

"Err, a lot?" Veronica took a small sip of her drink.

"So many I've lost track." Elaine took another large swallow of her drink. Her face was red now, her eyes glassy, the whisky hitting her hard. "And do you know why I never agreed?"

Veronica stared at Elaine. "No."

"Roxy. I thought she felt the way I did. That she wanted what we had together. I thought she wanted it, to be as free, as was I." Her sad bitter tone was back now. "I've never wanted to be exclusive. I love the feeling of a new conquest or an old one revisited. Damn Martha and Lucia and Myfanwy, damn them and their happy little threesome. I never thought anyone could be happy in an exclusive arrangement. Until I saw them. Every damn day, so damn happy." Elaine twisted and glared at Veronica, a snarl on her face. "Are you and Millie committed to each other?"

Veronica frowned at Elaine's fierce expression. "We haven't discussed it. But I think so."

Elaine grabbed her hand. "Don't take her for granted. Don't take anything for granted." She finished her glass of whisky. She let go of Veronica's hand and stood. She swayed as she straightened.

Veronica rose and put a hand on Elaine's shoulder to steady her. "Let me walk you back to the house."

Elaine pursed her lips and shook off Veronica's hand. "No need. I'm perfectly capable of making my way to the house." She bent over and picked up the half-empty Talikser bottle, took a step, and stumbled.

Veronica caught her before she fell. She ignored Elaine's moue of disappointment as she took the bottle from her hand and placed it on the desk. She slung Elaine's arm over her neck and grasped her wrist to keep it there. "What is it with everyone here drinking themselves silly when they're upset? Why?"

Elaine wrapped her arm around Veronica's waist and pressed into her. "Good whisky. It's like mother's milk here." She giggled and slid her hand down and squeezed Veronica's ass. "Is this what friends do? I don't think I've ever been this kind of friend with someone."

Veronica could not stop her eye roll as she moved Elaine's hand from her ass to her hip. "No. None of that. Or I'll leave you where you fall. Did you eat anything today?"

"Nope. Did you?" Elaine patted Veronica's belly and giggled again. "You're very nice."

Veronica snorted and let Elaine lean on her as they navigated the office door and then the yard to the kitchen.

"MYFANWY!" VERONICA JOGGED across the gravel yard to catch up to Myfanwy.

Myfanwy rested one hand on her hip. A small basket dangled from the other. "I don't have time to chat. I'm on my way to gather the herbs I need for dinner."

"I'll go with you and help."

Myfanwy held out the basket she was carrying to Veronica. They walked in silence for a few moments. Myfanwy touched Veronica's hand, drawing her attention. "I'm guessing you didn't randomly decide you needed to help me gather herbs?"

Veronica avoided Myfanwy's eyes. "No. I wanted to ask you about Millie."

Myfanwy stopped and stared at Veronica, her gaze piercing. "She's my best friend. I won't betray her confidence. If there's something you want to know, ask her."

She made to take the basket back and Veronica held it out of her reach. The sudden flare of anger on Myfanwy's face made her remember the photo she had seen of her. "I know. I don't want you to betray her. But you know her better than anyone. I need your advice."

Myfanwy huffed out a breath, opened her mouth as if to say something, and then shut it. She turned and walked toward the herb garden and greenhouse, and Veronica followed.

Myfanwy picked up a pair of scissors from the potting bench. "So?" She walked along the garden pavers until she reached a sprawling rosemary plant. She bent and clipped a few dark green sprigs, and the bright scent of the herb filled the air.

Veronica held the basket out and she deposited the bundle of herbs on the cloth inside. "I saw a photo of a pregnant woman in Millie's apartment."

Myfanwy moved along the row and stopped in front of a savory plant. She plucked a few dead leaves off and then snipped four short branches. "And what is your question?" Her voice still held some of the frost from earlier.

"Who was she?" Veronica wiped a sweaty hand on her pants.

Myfanwy pushed her hair back with her hand. "Did you ask Millie?"

Veronica flushed. "I'm afraid to. Whenever I ask her anything about her past she stonewalls. Please tell me. I'm desperate to know."

Myfanwy's expression softened. "You love her." A statement, not a question, a firm acknowledgement of Veronica's feeling for Millie.

"I do. More than I've ever loved anyone."

"The woman in the photo, Maia..." Myfanwy's voice was quiet, and Veronica moved closer to hear her. "She and Millie were together for eight years. They had a baby." Myfanwy's voice grew hoarse. "A boy, Nathanial. Maia's family kicked her out when she started dating Millie. They found out about the baby and hired a private investigator. She dug around in Millie's past. She'd never told Maia about it. Maia left her. Millie was cut from the Black Ferns. Maia's family was able to convince a judge Millie was a risk to the child's welfare." Myfanwy's voice wobbled. "They took the child from Maia even though she had broken up with Millie. Maia was so..." Myfanwy turned her face to the sky and swallowed visibly. She brought her gaze back to Veronica's face, her eyes wet with tears. "Maia ended her life."

Veronica's stomach tightened, and she swallowed around the bile in her throat. She sat down hard on the ground and leaned her head on her knees. "My poor Millie." Her heart ached thinking about the pain Millie had suffered, losing her partner and child.

Myfanwy lowered herself to her knees. She reached out and grabbed Veronica's hand so hard it hurt. "Don't break her heart, don't break your own."

"HI, DAD." VERONICA thumbed her phone to speaker.

"Hi, baby mine." Her dad's voice filled her room. "How are you? When're you getting here for Violet's wedding?"

"I don't know. I'm going to look at tickets later today and I'll let you know."

"Have you been practicing?" Her mom's voice made her smile.

"Yes, Mom. Has Larry?"

"He'll be ready."

"Hey, um, I might bring someone with me." Veronica twisted the hem of her shirt in her hands.

"Oh?" Her mom's voice was loud like she had moved closer to the phone.

"Yes. Millie."

"Okay." Her mom's voice was neutral. "Where did you meet her?"

"How long have you been seeing her? Will you need us to make up the guest room? Or will she stay in your room?" Her dad failed to hide the hope in his voice.

"Easy, Dad. For a while, and if I can convince her to come with me, she'll stay in my room. She works with me, Mom."

"Why haven't you mentioned her before? And why doesn't she want to come with you?" Her mother's voice was sharp.

"I don't know, Mom. I should've. She's worried about meeting you."

"Why?" Her dad's voice was soft in contrast to her mother's strident voice.

"She's like me, uh, she's been to—prison too. She's worried you'll judge her." *Might as well get it out there. Never hidden anything from them before. Why start now?*

"Why would she think that? What have you told her she'd think that of us?" The pain in her mom's voice undid Veronica.

Veronica swallowed on a dry throat. "I told her how great you guys are, Mom, how you stood by me. But she's wary. She had a horrible experience with an ex's family."

"How horrible?"

"She lost her partner and their baby. The woman's family got a judge to take their baby away from them because Millie was convicted of manslaughter."

"Manslaughter? What happened? Was she driving drunk?" Her father's voice, full of censure, had Veronica scrambling to explain.

"No, Dad, no. Her mom's boyfriend was beating her mother and Millie stepped in to protect her."

"Do we need to talk to her? Maybe Skype with both of you?" Her mother's voice was softer now. "What do you need us to do?"

"I don't know. I asked her to the wedding, and she turned me down. She's special, Mom. More than Dee ever was." Veronica swiped at the few tears she wasn't able to swallow.

"If you care about her, don't give up, baby. Talk to her again. We'll do whatever you need us to do." Her dad's voice was steady and reassuring.

"Thanks. Love you guys."

"Love you too, baby mine. Let us know what she says." Her father disconnected the call, and Veronica lay back on the bed and closed her eyes. *Now to talk to Millie. She has to go with me. Has to believe in me. Us. Please let her believe in us.*

Chapter Seventeen

"I CAN'T LET you do this." Veronica paused with one hand on the railing.

"Sure you can. You want to look good for your sister's wedding, don't you?" Millie led the way up the red carpeted stairs. At the top of the stairs they turned left. Veronica flushed thinking about what went on behind the elegant dark wood doors and wondered what secrets lay inside the rooms lining each side of the long halls of Rowan House.

Millie opened the door and Veronica stepped into a warm and bright room. The walls were covered in dark wood paneling. Two large windows provided the light. Two leather club chairs were arranged to either side of a butler's table. A low stool was centered in the middle of the room. A petite woman dressed in a crisp white shirt and blood-red skirt stood with her back to the window. Her wavy black hair streaked with gray brushed the tops of her shoulders, a pair of reading glasses rested on top of her head, and a measuring tape hung around her neck.

Millie crossed the room and clasped the woman's hand in both of hers. "Signora Rossi, so good to see you again."

"And you as well." The woman leaned in and kissed Millie on both cheeks. Her voice was warm honey laced with a hint of seduction. "And didn't we decide you would call me Aurora?"

A flare of distrust ignited in Veronica's chest at the way they greeted each other. She clung to memories of Millie's attentions and squelched her jealousy.

Aurora turned and raked her gaze over Veronica. "Who have you brought me?"

Millie grinned and held out her hand palm up. "Veronica Fletcher, meet Signora Aurora Rossi."

Veronica held out her hand. "Pleased to meet you, Signora Rossi."

Aurora took Veronica's offered hand and held it tightly as her gaze traveled over Veronica's body. "My pleasure. Call me Aurora." She dropped Veronica's hand. "Turn for me, please."

"Um, what?" Veronica gripped the seams of her jeans. Under Aurora's gaze Veronica had the sensation of being naked.

"Arms relaxed at your side, turn in a slow circle. I want to see your shape." She murmured to herself in Italian as Veronica turned as she had directed.

"And this is a wedding, *si*?" Aurora's carefully sculpted eyebrows drew together.

"Yes." Veronica chewed her lip.

"Evening or afternoon? And do you know what colors the bridesmaids and the groomsmen are wearing?"

"It's at six in the evening. I haven't asked about the colors. Is it important?"

Aurora arched an eyebrow at Veronica. "*Si*, very important."

"It said formal wear on the invitation. Is that enough? I could call my sister." Veronica glanced at the mantel clock. "Later. It's too early now."

Signora Rossi held up her hand palm out. "No. Knowing it is formal is enough, we will work with that. What part do you have in the wedding?"

"I'm singing when they recess after their vows are said."

"Millie, get the notebook out of my bag. Be my scribe." Millie grinned and walked over to a burgundy leather case leaning against one of the chairs. Aurora fixed her gaze on Veronica's face. "Now strip. I need to measure you."

The brisk businesslike tone of her voice had Veronica tugging at the hem of her shirt to comply. "Everything?"

Aurora tilted her head at Veronica, a sly smile on her face. "As much as I would enjoy you completely naked, that is not what we are here for today. Leave on your underthings."

Veronica flushed and glanced at Millie, pleased to see the consternation on her face at Aurora's open flirting with Veronica. She folded her clothes and placed them on the couch.

"Stand with your arms out to your side." Aurora moved her reading glasses down and pulled the tape measure from her neck before wrapping it around Veronica's neck. She called out the measurements to Millie as she worked her way down Veronica's body. "Open your legs, please, I need your inside seam."

Veronica complied and kept her gaze fixed on the ceiling as Aurora kneeled and pressed the cool cloth of the tape against the inside of her thigh.

"Get dressed and then I will show you the samples of fabric I brought." Aurora pushed her reading glasses up to the top of her head. Her back to Veronica, she tugged a binder from the bag and began to flip through it.

Veronica dressed quickly, aware of Millie's gaze as it followed her movements.

"Here. What do you think of this?" Aurora indicated a swatch of charcoal sharkskin fabric and placed a dark-gray linen swatch next to it. "I see the suit in charcoal, a tapered fit to show off your shoulders and trim waist. The waistcoat will be this gray with a very pale blue shirt and a dark tie." Aurora flipped a few pages in her binder. She tapped a dark red manicured nail against a sketch of a suit. "This. What do you think?"

Veronica studied the elegant cut of the jacket and the waistcoat and tried to imagine herself draped in it. "It's fantastic—" She swallowed. "—but I'm sure it's out of my price range."

Millie rested her hand on Veronica's shoulder and squeezed gently. "It's my present to you."

Veronica gazed up at Millie. "It's too much."

"No." Millie's eyes glittered. "It's not, *mo ghràdh*. If anything, it's not enough."

She loves me. So much. This is her apology, her way of saying she's sorry she's not going with me. An olive branch, a peace offering. "Okay. Thank you." She turned to Aurora. "It's perfect, and I trust you."

"Excellent. Two weeks. I'll be back and we'll do the fitting." She placed the samples and notebook into her bag.

"Let me escort you to your car, Aurora." Millie turned from Veronica.

"No need. I know the way. And I promised to visit with Lucia. She has some ideas for Martha's wardrobe." Aurora tilted her head toward Veronica and smiled a wicked smile. "Lovely to meet you. I look forward to your fitting." She closed the door behind her as she swept from the room.

Veronica scrubbed her hand over her face. "Millie, I can't let you pay for this."

Millie clasped Veronica's hands and tugged her into a kiss. "Please. I want to do this." She placed small kisses along Veronica's neck, punctuating her words. "Please let me do this for you."

Veronica tilted her head back, giving Millie better access to her neck. "You know I can't say no when you do that."

"So say yes." Millie brushed her lips over Veronica's skin, her breath warm on her throat before she trailed her tongue along her collarbone.

Veronica groaned. "Yes."

Millie hugged her close, wrapped her arms around her, and sighed. "Thank you. It makes me happy to do things for you. I trust you won't mind if I come to the fitting?"

Veronica laughed. "The way Aurora looked at me you better come to the fitting to protect my virtue."

Millie laughed with her. "She's harmless. Unless you say yes, she'll behave."

Veronica snuggled into Millie's arms. "You're the only one I say yes to."

Millie rested her chin on the top of Veronica's head. "Good to know, *mo ghràdh*."

"I mean it. I'm committed to you. Us. Are you? We haven't talked about it." Veronica rubbed her hands up and down Millie's spine.

Millie moved her hands to Veronica's shoulders and leaned back and studied Veronica's face. "I only want to be with you, Veronica. You know how I feel about you, don't you?"

Veronica studied Millie's expression. "I know you love me, but…"

Millie frowned. "But?"

"Why won't you come with me?"

Millie pulled back and turned away. "Is it a test? If I don't come with you, it means I don't love you?"

"No. But my family is important to me. I want them to meet you. They want to meet you."

"You've told your family about us?" Millie kept her back turned.

"Of course. Why wouldn't I?" Veronica rested her hands on her hips.

Millie turned back to Veronica, her eyes dark. "Have you told them everything?"

"What do you mean *everything*?" Veronica stepped closer, and Millie took a step back.

"About me. About my past."

"That you were incarcerated like I was. Yes."

"No. Not like you. You're innocent. I killed someone. No matter how much he deserved it. I wanted him dead." Millie scowled. "I'm a murderer. Have you told them that?"

Veronica winced at the bitterness in Millie's voice. "That won't make a..."

Millie's voice was loud as she cut her off. "You don't know. It makes a difference. It always makes a difference." She turned away from Veronica and bowed her head.

Veronica rested her hand on Millie's forearm. "I'm not her. My family is not them. I told them. All of it. Please come with me. I want the most important person in my life to meet the other important people in my life. Look at me." Millie lifted her head. Veronica leaned in, cupped her cheek, and kissed her mouth gently. "No one could ever, ever make me give you up, Millie. Don't give up on me. On us."

Millie rested her forehead on Veronica's brow. "Never."

Chapter Eighteen

VERONICA ARRIVED LATE to staff meal and had to make do with sitting across from Millie instead of next to her. The scent of biryani and cardamom rice made her mouth water. A pile of fresh naan sat on a plate next to the large platter of biryani surrounded by small dishes of lemon pickle and raita.

The seat at the head of the table was vacant. *Is Roxy already gone? Damn I didn't get to say goodbye.* A wave of sadness washed over her. *She was so funny. Sassy as hell.* She pushed back memories of other friends being moved without warning and unsaid goodbyes that still haunted her.

Benita and Tessa sat across the table to Millie's right. Tension mixed with a hint of melancholy rolled off both of them. Veronica avoided looking at the empty chair as she helped herself to the glorious food laid out before her. Millie nudged her foot under the table, and Veronica spilled a bit of the biryani she was serving herself and fought a flush as she peered at Millie from under her lashes.

Myfanwy pushed through the kitchen door. "Don't stuff yourselves. Robin made some kheer for pudding." She placed a plate loaded with delicate papadams on the table.

Benita groaned. "How can we stop when you keep bringing out such delicious food?" She helped herself to a papadam. The crisp bread crackled as she bit into it.

Ashley flounced in and made a show of sitting in Roxy's usual spot. She wiggled her ass in the chair as she glanced around the table. "So much nicer in here. One less old slag to take up space."

Myfanwy scowled at Ashley. "You can sit in her seat, but you'll never be half the woman she is." She spun on her heel and shoved open the kitchen door. Veronica winced when it struck the wall behind it and rattled the frame.

Benita mumbled under her breath in Portuguese and glared at Ashley. She tipped her chin at her. "What the hell is wrong with you? You think you're so much better than the rest of us?"

"Hmm. Let's see." Her gaze settled on Tessa. "I'm not some wannabe librarian, turning tricks for signed first edition books." She shifted her gaze to Benita. "Or a former street whore who got lucky." Ashley ran her finger over the rim of her wineglass. She glanced at Veronica. "Or drug dealer."

"Shut your mouth, Ashley." Millie's voice was low and deadly.

"Or a murderer." Ashley's lips curled in a nasty smile.

Millie lowered her chin to her chest, avoiding everyone's eyes, and pushed back from the table. She left the dining room without saying a word, ignoring Veronica's plea to stay.

"Good riddance to bad rubbish."

Veronica stood up so fast her bench tipped and rocked. "I don't give a good fuck what you say about me, but if you know what is good for you, you will shut your fucking mouth and get the fuck out of here."

Ashley's mouth curved in a lethal smile. "Make me." The evil glint in her eyes made Veronica wary. "Come on. Or hasn't she given you any tips?"

"What?" Veronica curled her hands into fists, her nails biting into her palms.

"Millie knows all about making me. Or didn't she share that with you?" Ashley made a show of picking up her wineglass.

Veronica glanced between Tessa and Benita, who suddenly were very interested in the patterns on their plates.

Veronica shrugged off Ashley's insinuation. "Fuck that. And fuck you." Veronica kicked the bench aside and strode to the head of the table toward Ashley. Her vision narrowed, anger beat through her body like a drum, and her only thought was how much she was going to enjoy beating the smile from Ashley's simpering face.

She ignored the sound of the door opening behind her and Martha's voice, not caring about anything other than exacting justice from the woman who had hurt Millie with her harsh words. Veronica reached her hand out and grabbed the back of Ashley's chair and shoved it. Ashley squealed, and in one sharp motion she threw the contents of her glass toward her. Veronica twisted out of the way. The wine splashed Martha's face, and the blood-red liquid ran down the front of her white shirt.

Veronica stared. Martha strode toward Ashley and stopped short of her chair. Tessa offered a napkin to Martha. She took it from her and wiped her face before she tossed the red-stained cloth to the floor.

"She threatened me." Ashley's voice wobbled. She waved her hand in Veronica's direction. "I was trying to protect myself."

Martha lowered her brows. "The only thing you were trying to do is cause trouble. Again." Martha inclined her head toward the intercom on the wall. "The system works both ways. I heard every word you said." She jerked her hand toward the door. "Come with me."

Ashley paled and placed the wineglass on the table with a trembling hand. "I'm sorry. I…"

"Now." Martha's voice was low and even. The subtle menace in it made the hair on the back of Veronica's neck stand up. "You might want to wave goodbye on your way out. You will not have the pleasure of seeing any of these fine women again."

Ashley pushed her chair back and rose. She tilted her head back, nose in the air, and followed Martha out of the room.

VERONICA TUGGED HER boots on and hurried from the mudroom. Millie's apartment was dark, but a bay was open in the garage below it and a pool of dim light lit the gravel apron. Veronica stopped at the door and let her eyes adjust to the light. Millie was sitting on a high stool at the workbench, her back to Veronica.

"You didn't stay for dessert. I know you like kheer."

Millie shrugged. "Lost my appetite."

Veronica walked over to her and looped an arm around Millie's waist. She sighed and leaned her head against Veronica's shoulder. Veronica kissed her temple. "It never gets easier, does it?"

"No. And it's true."

Veronica hugged her close. "It doesn't make me think any differently of you, Millie. Not one bit."

"Aye, but it makes me think differently of myself. You're not like me. You're innocent. Some guilty fucker is out there having a good time and you lost your whole future. And people like Ashley can make your life hell because of it."

"She said something after you left. I need to ask you." Veronica's stomach roiled. "She implied you had been with her. Is it true?"

Millie shifted and disengaged herself from Veronica's arms. "I was. Once. A few years ago." Her face took on a wary expression.

"You didn't tell me." Veronica crossed her arms over her chest and rocked back on her heels.

"You didn't ask. Does it make a difference?"

Veronica studied the garage floor. "No. But when she said it, I wanted to vomit. I can't stand the thought of anyone else touching you."

Millie reached out and cupped Veronica's face. "No one has ever done to me what you do. We all have pasts. I can't change mine. I am reminded every time something like this happens. I did murder him. I wanted him dead."

"With good reason. If you hadn't stopped him, he might have killed you both."

Millie sighed and her hand moved to Veronica's shoulder. "If you looked up 'spiteful bitch' in the dictionary Ashley's face would look back at you."

Veronica leaned back and touched Millie's chin. "She won't be a problem anymore anyway."

"Why? What happened after I left? You didn't do anything to her, did you? You can't lose your job."

"Relax, babe, she screwed herself. She threw a glass of wine at me. I ducked, and it hit Martha. In the face."

Millie raised both brows. "What? What was Martha doing there?"

Veronica smirked. "I think a certain sous chef switched the intercom to broadcast mode."

Millie's laugh was loud and long. "Now I wish I'd stayed."

Veronica laughed with her. "It was epic. I wish I had a picture of her face when she realized what she had done. And when Martha told her to say goodbye."

Millie's face sobered and she stopped laughing. "I bet."

Veronica closed her mouth. "She wouldn't—I mean she won't do anything. She won't harm Ashley, will she?" Her stomach clenched at the thought. "I mean in the moment I wanted to kick her ass, but I wouldn't want…"

Millie pressed her mouth into a thin line. "Not all of us are murderers."

"No." Veronica placed her hand on Millie's hand. "That's not what I meant."

"Isn't it? It's the first thing you thought of when I said Martha would take care of her." Millie's voice was hollow. "Once anyone knows about me, it's the first thing they think of."

Veronica lifted Millie's chin. She kissed her on the cheek and the corner of her mouth and then brushed her mouth before capturing it with her own. "Not true. It wasn't the first thing I thought of."

Millie sighed and Veronica deepened the kiss. She broke the kiss. "What's past is past. I mean it, Millie, but will you explain what you meant?"

Millie trailed one finger over the back of Veronica's hand. "Martha's serious, and without a recommendation from her, Ashley won't be able to work anywhere else in the network."

Veronica frowned. "Network?"

"Mistress Lucia came to us after the Mistress of the Onyx passed. She and Martha and Elaine formed a consortium of houses. The former workers of the Onyx banded together and purchased Madame's villa in Lake

Como. Their new Mistress rebranded the house as the Phoenix. One of our former workers wanted to move closer to her family so she runs a house in Oslo, and then there is Rowan House."

"Three houses. I had no idea how big an operation this is."

"It grew after Mistress Lucia came. She's as brilliant at business as Martha is at investing."

Veronica pushed aside the small thread of jealousy at Millie's reverent tone when she spoke of Mistress Lucia. "How do they keep up with all of it?"

Millie traced her finger over the back of Veronica's hand. "The owners and two elected representatives of the workers from each house meet once a year in Stockholm and share information, best practices, customer lists, and the like. It was Mistress Lucia's idea, along with profit sharing for the staff, and other changes to improve conditions for the workers, to make it more equitable and safer. Ashley won't be able to work at any of the other houses, and if I know Martha, she won't be able to work anywhere on the circuit."

"There's a circuit?" Veronica could not keep the surprise from her voice.

"For people who like what we do here, they make it a point to visit the different houses." Millie smirked. "I told Mistress Lucia we should give out stickers for our guests. You know, like folks have on the back of their caravans when they've been to all the parks."

Veronica giggled. "What would they say?"

"Haven't worked out that bit yet." Millie stood and stretched. "Do you think there's any pudding left?"

MILLIE'S GRANDMOTHER PASSED on a bright fall day. Benita covered the stable for Veronica. Myfanwy had driven them to the home where they had worked together to pack up Millie's grandmother's room while Millie met with the funeral director. No one spoke on the ride back to Rowan House. At the base of the steps to Millie's apartment Myfanwy kissed Millie's cheek. She leaned close to Veronica and whispered, "Take care of her. Call if you need me."

Veronica walked ahead of Millie and opened the door to the apartment. Millie walked past her. She lowered herself to the couch and pulled her gran's suitcase filled with her effects from the nursing home close to her chest. No tears, no sobs, just a distant stare and silence. Veronica turned on the light and sat next to Millie. She said nothing knowing no words would ever be enough.

MILLIE'S POSTURE WAS rigid as the clergyman from the nursing home said the short eulogy at the graveside. Veronica noticed a short, razor-thin woman who had Millie's auburn hair and strong jaw. *Got to be her mother. Why the hell is she here?* Wearing heels, a short black skirt more suitable for a bar than a funeral, and large designer sunglasses over her eyes, she stood out against the backdrop of the conservatively dressed women from Rowan House. Her mouth was set in a hard line, and she checked the time on her watch as she shuffled her feet.

The sun glinted off the jet-black coffin as the priest concluded the service. Veronica rubbed her pinkie over the back of Millie's hand. Millie clutched Veronica's hand like a drowning woman as her gran's coffin was lowered into the grave. Once it was lowered, Millie moved forward like a sleepwalker, swept a large handful of earth into her hand, and tossed it into the grave, the red earth rattling against the lid. The priest nodded once in Millie's direction and left the graveside.

Every member of the staff of Rowan House filed past, each tossing a single yellow rose into the grave before they bent to scoop up a handful of earth and scatter it over the coffin. Heads bowed, voices quiet, they filed past to offer words of condolence to Millie, whose expression never changed as she silently clasped their hands. Myfanwy was the last, Martha's arm around her shoulder and Lucia's arm around her waist as she walked forward and tossed a large bouquet of yellow roses into the grave. The three women each hugged Millie in turn before turning to leave.

Veronica stood off to the side and a step behind Millie. The last person to walk up to the grave was the woman in the black skirt. She took her sunglasses off and placed them in her purse. "Millicent."

Millie shifted her gaze to the cloudless sky. Veronica noticed a tremor in her hands.

"Mother." Millie's words were clipped. Her eyes held the sheen of tears, the first she had shed for her gran.

"So lovely to see you, Millicent. And on such an auspicious occasion." She glared at Millie and Veronica. She used the edge of her foot to push some dirt in the grave. Millie's shoulders slumped. Veronica stepped closer and rested her hand on the small of Millie's waist.

Her mother's lips thinned before she spoke. "Still as loquacious as ever, I see. Well, don't let me keep you from the festivities. Ta." Her back to the grave, she stepped closer to Millie. "Oh, and I look forward to seeing you in court."

Millie took a half step back from her mother, her hands clenched into fists.

Her mother rested a fist on her hip. "What are you waiting for? Or is it only drunks you attack? Knowing they can't fight back." She raked her gaze over Millie. "I still can't believe I let her talk me out of an abortion."

Veronica could sense Millie's rage boiling, her thin veneer of control beginning to shatter under her mother's taunting. She slipped her hand under Millie's suit jacket and grabbed her belt. She wrapped her fingers tightly around the smooth leather. If Millie decided she'd had enough of her mother's taunts, Veronica knew she'd only be able to slow her down not stop her if she acted.

"Why don't you go on ahead now? I don't know what your game is, but this is not the time, nor the place." In Veronica's peripheral vision she saw Martha, Lucia, and Myfanwy turn toward them. Robyn stepped up next to Millie on her other side. She placed her small hand on Millie's forearm and clasped it tight, her trembling fingers white against the black of Millie's suit coat.

Millie's mother sneered at Veronica. "And why should I listen to some random black bit..?"

Before she could finish her sentence and start the fight she wanted to provoke, Veronica spoke over her. She released her hold on Millie's belt and stepped in front of her, shielding her from her mother. "Look, I don't know you, and I don't want to, but know this. If you ever, ever step to Millie again, you will have to go through me. Get the hell out of here." Veronica calculated how much trouble she would be in if she slapped her.

Martha's firm grip on Veronica's shoulder settled her. "I believe, as my friend has expressed quite clearly, it would be in your best interest to leave. Now." Martha's tone was deadly.

Millie's mother took a step back. "Fine. My solicitor will be in touch, Millicent." She drew out Millie's name in a mocking way.

As she backed up, her heel caught in the loose soil around the edge of the grave, and she tumbled over backward and landed on the coffin. Veronica stared, too stunned to move.

The grave attendants, who had stoically watched the drama unfold, pointed at the grave. "Did you see that?"

"Well, don't stand there, Matthew, we need to help her out." They dropped their shovels and ran forward to offer a hand. One of the men climbed into the grave and, with a well-placed hand on her ass, assisted Millie's mother out of the grave. Dirt clung to her suit, and she had lost a heel. Veronica chewed her lip to keep from laughing as the man in the grave climbed out, clutching a dirty black pump in his hand. He passed the shoe to the other man who wiped it on his pants before he lifted his hat and offered the shoe to Millie's mother. She snatched the shoe from his hand, shoved her foot into it, and stalked off, head high, trying to salvage what was left of her dignity.

Millie stared at her mother's retreating back. "I think Gran pulled her in."

Veronica bit her lip, trying hard not to laugh, unsure of Millie's state of mind. And then Millie's hand was on her shoulder and her laugh, loud, raucous, and hearty, rang out. She bent at the waist and wiped tears from her face as she laughed.

Veronica joined her as all the women of Rowan House surrounded her, their laughter and tears blending as the men waiting to fill the grave held it together for a moment, and then joined in.

Chapter Nineteen

"LET'S DO IT again." Veronica clutched the sheet music in front of her chest and scrubbed a hand over her scalp. "I can't screw this up."

Millie strummed the guitar softly. "As many times as you want, *mo ghràdh.*"

"I can't believe she picked this song. I love Skin Skinny and Skunk Anansie." Veronica placed the sheet music aside. "Do you think you could drop it down a bit? I don't feel solid on the high notes."

Millie nodded. "It sounded like you were straining." She moved her fingers over the strings of the guitar and picked out a few notes. "Like this?"

"Yeah, I think I can do that." Millie played "You Saved Me" as Veronica sang. Millie's eyes never left her face as she played while Veronica sang the words she knew by heart, and in a moment, she was singing them to Millie: every word, every sentiment, every note.

As much as they meshed making love, this, this was more intimate, creating something together. It was beautiful and ethereal. Veronica was breathless when she finished. Millie played the final notes and Veronica bit her lip. *Ask her, ask again, keep asking until she says yes. Take nothing for granted.*

"You did, you know." Millie clutched the guitar to her chest. "You did save me."

Veronica took the guitar from Millie's hands and placed it on its stand. She stood between Millie's knees and cupped Millie's face in her hands. "No, love, you saved me. You trust me, right?"

"With my life." Millie gripped Veronica's hips with her broad hands and rubbed her thumbs over the crests of Veronica's hipbones.

"I understand why you're afraid to meet my folks. Even if you don't go with me, I'll come back. I love you and nothing will ever change that." She pinned her in place with her gaze and rubbed her thumb over Millie's lower lip. "Please come with me. Please. They'll love you as much as I do."

"How can you be so sure?"

"Because I trust them. I trust them as much as I trust you." She kissed her then, letting her body say what she couldn't say with words, pouring every bit of her love into the kiss.

Millie groaned into her mouth and the sound set Veronica on fire. She broke their kiss a moment and pulled back to peer into Millie's eyes. "Yes? Please say yes?"

"Yes."

"What changed?" Veronica studied Millie's serious expression.

"I did. You were brave enough to stand up to my mother. The least I can do is be brave enough to meet your family.

"You don't feel forced into it, do you?" Veronica chewed her lip. "It's okay if you want to wait. We have time."

"I don't feel forced. I'll go with you. But you have to promise you'll do something for me." Millie stood and clasped both of Veronica's hands in hers.

"What?"

"You have to come to another wedding with me."

"Who else is getting married?"

"We are. If you'll have me."

Veronica threaded her fingers through Millie's hair and tugged her head back. She traced her finger over her lips. "I think this is extortion."

Millie grinned. "Just good old-fashioned Scottish negotiation. Besides, I want to see you in the suit I had made for you."

"Were you planning on asking me when you commissioned the suit?"

"It might have crossed my mind." Millie smirked. She stood and grabbed Veronica's ass and lifted.

Veronica wrapped her legs around Millie's waist, kissed her on the mouth, and then trailed her lips over her jaw. She made her way to her ear and whispered. "Yes. Yes to all of it."

MARTHA SAT IN the chair behind the desk. Millie and Veronica were in the chairs across from the wide walnut desk.

"We know it's a lot, but we both need to be off for this." Millie sat back in her chair.

Martha fixed her gaze on Veronica. "I'm willing to let you both be off for the wedding, but Veronica, I will need you to work an extra two weeks beyond the end of your contract."

Veronica reached out and clasped Millie's hand. "I wanted to talk to you about that too."

Martha raised an eyebrow. "Yes?"

"I want to extend my contract. Sign up now for next year."

Martha smiled, and Veronica understood exactly how a rabbit must feel when chased by a wolf.

"Excellent. I'll draw the paperwork up."

"And..." Veronica kept her gaze fixed on Martha's face. "We will need some time off next year in the fall as well."

Lucia and Myfanwy rose from where they had been lounging on the fainting couch. They stood behind Martha, each with a hand on her shoulder.

"Whatever for?" The hint of a smile played around Lucia's mouth, and Myfanwy covered her mouth with her hand.

"Wedding." Veronica pressed on. "Our wedding."

Lucia smiled as Martha dug into her jacket pocket and produced a roll of banknotes and passed it to Lucia.

Veronica frowned. "You bet on me?"

Martha raised an eyebrow. "I thought you would get married this year, Lucia said next year, and Myfanwy excused herself from betting."

Lucia leaned forward and placed the bundle of bills on the desk. "An early wedding present from me. Consider it a donation to the festivities."

"KNEEL, FACE TO the mattress." The light from the bedside lamp lit Millie's skin with a soft glow. Veronica smoothed her hands over her back. She worked swiftly, wrapping the coils of soft rope around her wrists and securing her to the bed rails. The graceful stretch of Millie's arms and the tension in her body sent a current of desire whipping through Veronica.

Millie moved and complied with Veronica's directions as Veronica looped the ropes she had prepared over Millie's ankles and bound her to the sides of the bed. She double-checked the knots.

"I love the way you look spread wide for me." She touched her fingers to the wet heat between Millie's legs and then licked them. "Mmm. Already so wet for me." She reached under her and flicked Millie's nipple, eliciting a yip. She pinched and rolled her nipple harder, and Millie arched into her touch. "You like that?"

"Yes, *Ceannard.* So much. More, please."

Veronica kneeled behind her on the bed, pressing her breasts against Millie's firm ass. She draped her hands over her back and splayed her fingers out over Millie's breasts. She cupped and squeezed the fullness in her hands. She licked her fingers, and squeezed and pulled Millie's nipples into hard peaks as she rocked against her. She scattered sharp bites over Millie's back, driven by her dirty groans and whimpers.

Veronica bit hard, rolling her taut muscles, relishing the feel of Millie's skin between her teeth, stopping short of breaking her skin. She interspersed her bruising bites with soft sucking kisses, soothing her with her tongue and savoring Millie's hisses and moans. Her face was turned to the side with her eyes closed.

Veronica picked up one of the nipple clips from the nightstand, reached under Millie, and applied it. She tightened the clamp slowly on her nipple as she watched her face. Millie grimaced and Veronica stilled. "Too much, babe?"

"Give me a minute." Millie panted and her face relaxed. "I'm good."

Veronica tapped her chin. "Look at me."

Millie opened her eyes and met Veronica's gaze.

"Remember your words. If you need me to stop say 'red.' If you need me to slow down or back off say 'yellow,' okay?"

"Aye. Yellow. Got it, *Ceannard*."

Veronica picked up the second clamp and applied it to her other nipple. When the clamps were in place she scraped her fingernails over the tips of her swollen nipples. Millie arched back into her and bucked her hips. "So good. Please don't stop, *Ceannard*. More."

Veronica shifted on the bed and kneeled between Millie's legs. She teased a finger over the dimple at the base of her spine and down the crease in her ass. Millie trembled under her. "In time, babe, patience." She touched her fingers to the folds between Millie's legs and gathered the wetness there. She lay against her, reached under her, and took a breast in each hand as she rubbed the slickness over Millie's nipples and rubbed her thick clit against Millie's ass. "I love how you feel under me."

Her clit slid over the firm muscles of Millie's ass as she wiggled under her. Millie's sweet sounds pushed her over the edge, and she came against her ass, gasping her release in Millie's ear.

Millie thrashed under her. "Now. Please, *Ceannard*. I need it. Now. Please."

Veronica cupped her. She was hot and swollen and desire dripped down her thighs. Veronica brushed her fingers over her entrance and teased her lips apart. "Mmm, so wet. For me."

"All for you."

"What do you need, babe? Do you need me to fuck you?"

Millie's blush spread from her collarbones, and she turned her face into the bed. Her voice was muffled. "Oh please. Yes please, *Ceannard*. Don't make me wait. Please fuck me. I want you so much."

Veronica kept up her teasing touches, slipping her middle finger in deep, knowing Millie needed more. "In time, babe."

With a snarl Millie arched off the bed. "Fuck me. Now. I need it."

"Feisty today, aren't you?" Veronica stilled and drew her hand away. "Behave, babe. I'll make it good for you." She kissed her cheek and left the bed.

Millie strained against the ropes around her wrists and ankles. She turned her head, her eyes tracking Veronica's movements. "No. Please. Don't leave me like this, *Ceannard*. Please. I'll be good. I'll do whatever you want. Please."

Veronica leaned down close to the bed. "You'll do what I want anyway." She looked into Millie's eyes. "Won't you?"

"Always, *Ceannard*. Please."

Veronica cupped her cheek, and Millie turned her face to kiss her palm. "Anything, *Ceannard*, always," she whispered.

Veronica opened the nightstand door. She pulled out a thick toy and harness. Millie's hooded eyes were glazed. "You'd let me fuck you with this? Fuck you until you scream my name and beg me to let you come? Would you do that?"

Millie shuddered and gasped. "Yes. Please."

"Ask properly." Veronica pinched Millie's ear.

"Please, *Ceannard*. Please fuck me. Now. Please. Until I scream. Please."

The desperate expression on Millie's face and tone of her voice made Veronica ache with her own need.

"Watch me." Veronica buckled the toy in place. She palmed and slowly stroked its length, watching Millie's face as she went slack jawed. "You want this?"

"Oh, yes. Please." Millie licked her lips. "Please."

"Show me. Move your ass. Show me how much you want me to fuck you."

Veronica mounted the bed behind Millie. Millie gyrated and moved her hips, silently begging Veronica to fill her.

Veronica watched until she was desperate to possess her. "Stop."

Millie stilled, panting, her body heaving.

Veronica pressed her fingers inside, opening her. The tip of the phallus at her entrance, she grabbed her hips and sank slowly into Millie. The pressure and vibration on her clit was delicious.

Millie groaned beneath her, a deep, guttural, animal sound.

Veronica pulled out to the tip and sank in again. Millie whimpered. "For all that's good in the world, please fuck me, *Ceannard*, please don't make me wait. I want to scream for you."

Veronica inhaled sharply and fucked her, sinking deep on the in stroke, pulling out almost to the tip each time, pounding into Millie, pouring out everything she had into her. The pressure on her clit drove her to seek her own completion, and she came over the base of the toy.

"Please. Oh Please. Now. *Ceannard*. Please!" Millie's voice was loud. "Harder, please. Let me. Let me come for you."

Sweat stung Veronica's eyes. She let go of Millie's hips, draped herself over Millie's back, and clasped a nipple clip in each hand. "Now, babe, now, scream for me." She tugged the clamps loose and hammered into Millie.

Millie screamed as she came, soaking Veronica's thighs, and slumped on the bed. Veronica collapsed on her back, pumped her hips twice, and came again. Veronica rocked gently against Millie, fucking her with slow shallow thrusts. "Again, babe, again, for me." She bit the back of Millie's neck and held on as a ripple of pleasure shook Millie's frame.

She eased the toy from her body, unbuckled the harness, and placed it aside. She got up and untied Millie, moving swiftly. Millie rolled to her back as soon as she was free. Her eyes were closed, her face a mask of relaxed pleasure.

Veronica kissed her, and Millie wrapped her arms around Veronica to pull her down on top of her. She shivered, and Veronica reached down and pulled the patchwork quilt over them. She snuggled into Millie's neck. "You are the most magnificent woman. I didn't hurt you, did I? I got lost in you. I lost control."

Millie kissed her forehead. "It was perfect. I love how you know what I need. You get me."

Veronica raised herself up on her elbow to cupped Millie's face. "I want to do everything with you." She sat up and leaned against the headboard as she opened the bedside table and drew out a plain wooden box. She passed it to Millie and slid down next to her to watch her face as she opened it.

Millie opened the lid. A wide pair of hand-tooled dark-brown leather cuffs rested on the deep-blue velvet lining the inside of the box. She glanced up at Veronica, passed the box back to her, pushed herself to sitting and held out her arms, palm up. "Put them on me, please. I want to wear your cuffs."

Veronica placed the first cuff on, buckled it into place, and placed a kiss on Millie's palm before she repeated the procedure with the other side. She unclipped the straps holding one of the stainless-steel rings close to the leather. "These are made to hold the rings close so you can wear them without the rings getting caught on things." She settled her hands on Millie's shoulders. "It's okay if you want to take them off when you're working."

"I'll want to wear them all the time." Millie cupped the back of Veronica's neck and kissed her hard. "They are perfect, *mo ghràdh*."

Veronica tweaked Millie's nipple, and she gasped and let go of Veronica's neck. Veronica rubbed the pad of her thumb over the tip of Millie's nipple. "How sore are your nipples?" The shudder running through Millie's body told her everything she needed to know.

"Not too, *Ceannard*."

"Lay back. Palms on your stomach."

Millie lay back, resting her hands on her stomach. The gleaming leather of the cuffs against her freckled skin made Veronica hard. "I like the way they look against your skin. The way you look waiting for me. But I think"—she drew a thin chain from the bedside drawer—"this will make it even better." She clipped the chain to one cuff. Millie's skin pebbled where the chain lay. "And these will make it perfect." She held up the set of clamps she had used earlier. With practiced movements she pulled Millie's nipples into hard points and applied the clips. She ran the chain through the loops and then clipped it to the other cuff. She sat on her heels and assessed her work. Millie lay panting, her hands bound by the cuffs and the chains connecting the nipple clamps to her hands. She tested the tension and slack in the chain and made an adjustment, tightening the chain so if Millie moved her hands down the clips would pull free.

Veronica raked her nails over Millie's stomach. "Spread your legs for me."

Millie opened her legs. Veronica lay between them and inhaled the sharp sweet smell of Millie. She licked softly over her clit, grazing it with her tongue. Millie gasped. Veronica mouthed her core, toying with her, sucking her labia before she thrust her tongue deep. Millie's hips twitched and Veronica used her thumbs to hold her open, taking what she wanted. "This is mine." She licked a long line from her center to her clit. "You are mine." She sucked her clit, laving it with her tongue, pulling it between her lips, and slowly letting it out. The chains rattled as Millie's breathing increased. Veronica lifted her gaze.

Millie was clenching and unclenching her hands. "So good. More, *Ceannard*, please. Let me come in your mouth. Let me come for you." Millie's voice was soft.

Veronica teased her tongue over her clit, making her jump. "You may come as you wish." She bent to her task. She took Millie's clit in her mouth, circling it with her tongue, sucking and teasing the hard pearl between her lips.

Millie rocked into her, the chains ringing, and then she went rigid and jerked her hands down to grab Veronica's head and hold her in place.

"Yours." Millie shouted as she came with a gush that filled Veronica's mouth and ran down her chin.

Chapter Twenty

VERONICA GAZED AT the steel and glass arches of the roof of the Glasgow airport. Six short months ago she had found her way out of customs and into the waiting black car that had carried her to the ferry to Skye and then to Rowan House. She shivered. Dread bubbled up, knotting her gut. Veronica thought about all the subtle and not so subtle racism she'd experienced over her life. It was a low frequency hum, affecting everything and every moment. Veronica slumped in her seat as she thought of all the ways she moderated the way she spoke, and looked, and acted growing up; how she had doubled down on it after her release.

She hadn't had to do any of that since she had arrived at Rowan House. And now they were headed back to a place where a wrong look or tone could have her face down on the sidewalk with cuffs on her wrists and a knee in her back. Sadness and anger battled for first place in her thoughts. *Will she understand? Will she get it? She's faced some shit over her butch appearance and being queer, but does she have any idea how much worse it can be? How assholes will react when we go out as a couple? She's not ignorant. She'll be okay. She wouldn't have said yes if she didn't mean it.*

She glanced over at Millie. Her face pulled into a grimace as she checked her phone messages. "Problem?" Veronica's voice squeaked. She swallowed around her apprehension.

"No. Another ridiculous email from that woman who shall remain nameless's solicitors." Millie turned her phone off and stuffed it into her pocket.

Veronica rubbed her hand over Millie's back in small circles. "I'm sorry, babe."

"Not your fault. And if she had any sense at all, she'd let this go. Before I call in some favors." The low tone of menace in Millie's voice shocked Veronica.

"What kind of favors?" Veronica's failed attempt to hide her fear was evident from the exasperated expression on Millie's face.

"Nothing violent. You've watched too many movies." Millie lowered her voice. "I've driven many people to Rowan House over the years. Powerful people who like me and trust me to keep their private trysts private. People who have the ability to make my mother's life a living hell if she doesn't stop trying to get her claws on my gran's money. Money for the scholarship Gran wanted to create in her name at Cardiff. I'm not going to let her take that from Gran." The set of Millie's chin and the resolve in her voice reminded Veronica of why this woman and no other would do for her.

THE FIRST-CLASS seats were roomy enough for Veronica to stretch out and sleep, but her thoughts circled around to what lay ahead. Her family had been great on the phone about Millie's past, but she had neglected to mention Millie was white. She sorted over her family's history and came up short with anyone ever even dating a white person, let alone being engaged to one. *No need to tell them we're engaged. Not right away. Let them get used to the idea of Millie first.*

She glanced over at Millie, her face peaceful as she slept. She had a fresh haircut, the edges of her fade sharp, and Veronica longed to reach out and touch the pink skin above her ear. Not wanting to wake her, she satisfied herself with simply enjoying the view. The deep laugh lines around Millie's eyes and the corners of her mouth and the strong angle of her jaw were visible in the low light of the cabin. Her long legs were stretched out and she had her arms clasped over her chest, holding on to the blanket. The subtle curve and dip of the muscles in her forearms had Veronica shifting in her seat as a low heat simmered in her belly. With no chance to do anything about it, she sighed in frustration and looked out of the window into the midnight blue surrounding the plane. *Damn it. They'll be okay. They'd never make me choose.*

She turned her head and took in Millie's sleeping form and knew who held the keys to her heart and life. She turned back to the window and peered out as their plane rushed toward a future she knew included Millie no matter what.

VERONICA'S HANDS WERE damp where they gripped the steering wheel. Millie had grown quieter the closer they got to Veronica's home. As she made the familiar turn on to her parents' street, she glanced over at Millie. Her expression was as blank as it had been when she came home from the nursing home the day her gran had passed. Her hands were clasped in front of her, white across the knuckles. Veronica pulled the car over to the curb.

Millie turned to peer out of the window. "Are we here?"

"No." Veronica reached over and smoothed her hand over Millie's forearm. Her muscles were whipcord tight under her shirt. "I wanted to talk a minute."

Millie sighed and lowered her chin to her chest. "Okay."

"No matter what happens, I'm not letting go of you. Nothing my parents or anyone else could say would ever make me change my mind about you." She touched Millie's cheek, drawing her gaze, and leaned over and pressed a kiss to her mouth. "Nothing."

Millie kissed her back, and Veronica sensed the tension bleed out of her.

"If you kiss me like that again, *mo ghràdh,* we'll be late to your parents' house."

Veronica settled herself in her seat and pulled the car out onto the street. Two blocks later she pulled into her parents' driveway.

She opened her door and stepped out, breathing in the scent of soft pines and a fire burning in the fireplace.

Millie stepped out of the car and inclined her head toward the car. "Should I get our bags?"

"No. Let's go in first. We can get them later." Veronica had been so worried about Millie she had squelched her excitement to be home. She made herself walk up the sidewalk but only got halfway before her father and mother burst out of the door and ran toward her.

Her father scooped her up in a hug so fierce her back cracked. "Easy, Pop, you'll break a rib." Her dad squeezed her once more before he let her go. Her mother elbowed him aside and wrapped her arms around her, rocking and hugging her. Veronica looked over her mother's back and saw Millie with one hand on the roof of the car, the other stuffed into her jacket pocket.

Veronica's mother finally let go of her. Veronica walked back and looped her arm through Millie's and led her to her parents. She saw surprise sweep over both their faces before their manners kicked in. Her father offered Millie his hand, and Millie took it. "Very nice to meet you, Millie."

Millie shook his hand and made eye contact. "You as well, sir." Her father released Millie's hand.

Veronica's mother stepped close, and she shook her head. "No. You are going to call us Vincent and Cora." She raked her gaze over Millie, cocked her head to the side, and met Millie's gaze. "You're taller than I imagined."

"I get that a lot." Her arm tensed beneath Veronica's grip.

"Ronnie, help your father with the bags." Cora took Millie by the hand and pulled her arm from Veronica's grasp. "Ronnie tells me you've been practicing together. Her cousin Frank will be joining you..."

Her mother ushered Millie into the house. Millie shot a look at Veronica over her shoulder and grinned. Veronica glanced at her dad. "Is it okay, Pop?"

Her father shrugged. "You know your mother isn't going to be okay until she hears Millie play. She wants everything to be perfect."

Veronica quirked her mouth at her dad. "That's not what I meant, and you know it."

Her dad kept his gaze fixed on Veronica's eyes. He rested his hand on the trunk of the car. "If you care for this woman, we care for her. Now pop the trunk and help me get your luggage into the house before your mother makes Millie play for her dinner."

"VIOLET, THIS IS Millie. Millie, Violet." Veronica rolled the hem of her sweater between her fingers. "She's going to accompany me for the recessional. On the guitar, I mean." Veronica flushed. "And to the reception."

Violet clasped Millie's hand in both of hers. "It's so nice to meet you." She glared at Veronica. "Finally."

Millie tilted her head at Veronica. "It's not her fault we're late." She leaned closer to Violet. "Your mother has had us practicing for hours." She dropped her voice to a whisper. "If you know what's good for you, don't ask her 'how's it going?'"

Violet laughed. "She has gone full-on 'mother of the bride' mode.

Violet let go of Millie's hand and hugged Veronica close. "You didn't tell me you were bringing home Prince Harry's twin." She whispered into Veronica's ear.

Veronica poked her sister hard in the ribs and broke their hug. "Violet!" She frowned at her sister.

Violet stepped back and smiled, never taking her eyes from her sister's face. "Millie, would you give us a moment?"

"Uh, sure." Millie tilted her head and raised her eyebrow. She glanced at Veronica.

"I think my dad could use some help." Veronica tilted her head toward the garage.

Millie stuffed her hands in her pockets and walked toward the house.

Veronica waited until Millie had closed the door behind her. "What the hell, Violet? Because she's white? Or because she's butch?"

Violet grabbed Veronica's hand. "Sissy, I don't care about any of that. Come on, I was kidding."

Veronica's anger melted at her sister's use of her family name. "I'm sorry."

Violet squeezed her hand. "You're worried about Aunt Jean, aren't you?"

"And everybody else, damn it."

"Well, they are going to say stuff—to you and to her. And you know Walter won't not say anything. You better be ready."

"I know." Veronica hated the defeated tone in her voice.

"And Millie is solid in who she is, right?"

Veronica nodded. "Yeah. I mean we both are."

"So, fuck them." Violet tugged Veronica into a hug. "You're my Sissy, and I want you at my wedding, and they can all go to hell if they don't like your girlfriend."

"Fiancée." Veronica watched her sister's face.

"For real? Sissy, that's wonderful." She grabbed Veronica and squeezed her hard. "When? Have you told Mom and Dad?"

"No. I wanted to tell you first."

"Who asked who?"

"She asked me, and I don't know when to tell Mom and Dad. Mom is crazy right now."

"Well, you better tell them soon. Mom will be pissed you didn't tell her as soon as you said yes."

Veronica hugged her back. "When did you get to be so wise?"

Chapter Twenty-One

PEOPLE SAT SHOULDER to shoulder, stuffed into pews anywhere they could find a seat. Veronica peered out at them and wiped her forehead with the handkerchief she had nabbed from her father. She jumped when Millie touched her shoulder.

"You okay, *mo ghràdh*?" Millie's voice was soothing.

"I don't know. I haven't seen most of these people since my cousin's baptism. And you know how that went."

"Well, we didn't fly all the way here so you could hide from them." Millie squeezed her shoulder. Veronica turned to her, and Millie straightened Veronica's tie. "Now. Let's go meet your people. It's rude to come in after the bride. Your mother has our seats marked off so we can get out and get to our instruments for the recession."

They left the safety of the vestry and made their way down the side aisle. A silence fell over each row they passed, replaced by a soft murmuring as soon as they had gotten out of hearing range. They arrived at their designated pew and her favorite cousin, Jordan, waved at her. She slid into the polished wood pew and scooted down to give Millie space to sit. They took their seats as the groom and the minister arrived at the altar.

Her cousin's posture was stiff. "I saw your name on the program," she whispered.

"Is Jimmy here?" Veronica craned her neck to see if Jordan's twin had arrived.

A wave of sadness passed over Janie's face. "He's not coming."

Veronica opened her mouth to ask why, but the strains of the wedding march filled the church, and everyone rose as her sister and her parents made their way down the aisle. Veronica swiped at a stray tear when her sister read her vows. Millie reached over and clasped her hand and laced their fingers together.

As the priest concluded the ceremony, Millie and Veronica left the pew quietly and met her cousin Frank at the back of the church. Frank and Millie picked up their guitars and sat on tall stools behind Veronica.

Veronica's hands trembled when she thumbed on the microphone, and then Frank and Millie began to play. Veronica sang as her sister made her way down the aisle. Her sister grinned and winked at Veronica as she walked past.

THE RECEPTION DINNER was an elegant affair. Her sister and her new husband sat at the head table surrounded by their parents. Veronica and Millie were at the cousins' table which still felt like the kids' table to Veronica. She listened to their banter as they all shared stories of what was going on in their lives. It was like being home for a holiday meal. Only Jordan seemed to not enjoy herself. Veronica caught her staring at Millie more than once.

Millie sat quietly by her side. Veronica let her thoughts drift away from the conversation and Jordan's confusing behavior and indulged herself in imagining taking Millie back to their room and divesting her of the handsome suit she wore one piece at a time. A subtle nudge on her shoe brought her back to the present.

"Earth to Ronnie. What have you been up to? Besides mountain climbing?" Walter, her favorite cousin, waggled his eyebrows and tilted his head toward Millie. "Does Meghan Markle know?" He cackled at his own joke. The rest of the table snickered, and Veronica took a breath. *Okay. I can do this. This is like when we were kids.*

Millie's voice cut into her thoughts. "We thought we'd keep it on the DL. Let her down easy, you know."

Walter's cackle grew louder. "All right, Ronnie, she's all right. Damn, I feel like I'm on that *Outlander* show. Your accent is sexy as hell. Say something else."

Millie leaned back in her chair, gazed into Walter's eyes, and spoke in a sultry tone. "*Taigh nam gasta ort.*"

Veronica laughed.

Walter grinned at Millie and tugged at his tie. "What does that mean?"

"Fuck off." Millie deadpanned.

Walter howled with laughter, and Veronica's other cousins laughed along with him. Jordan stood, tossed her napkin in her seat, and left the table. Veronica watched as she hurried out of the ballroom with her clutch under her arm.

"You got me. You're funny. Ronnie, don't let this one get away." Walter patted Millie's forearm. "Are there more like you at home?"

COMFORTABLE MILLIE COULD hold her own at the table, Veronica went in search of the bathroom. She pushed through the door and stopped. Jordan was sitting on a low couch. Her head was bowed, and she clutched her purse tightly.

Veronica crossed the floor and touched her shoulder. Jordan flinched. Veronica pulled her hand away. "Sorry." She leaned down to gaze into her cousin's face. "Are you okay? Did you drink too much?"

"No." Her mouth set in a firm line. "No. I..." She inclined her head and held Veronica's gaze. "Sit with me."

Veronica sat and rested her damp palms on her knees. *This is it. This is when she tells me she can't accept me and Millie.* She moved her hands and dug her fingers into the soft cushion under her hips.

"I need to tell you something, and I don't know how."

"The best way is to just say it. It's me, Jordan. You can tell me anything. You always did when you were little."

"I know who left the weed in your car." Jordan's voice was hoarse.

Veronica shook her head to clear it, sure she had heard wrong. "What?"

"It was Jimmy. And me."

A wave of nausea coursed through Veronica. "What? Why?" She stood up and began to pace the small space, anger flooding her body. "Why didn't you say anything? What the hell, Jordan?"

"We bought it for a party. Mama found it in Jimmy's backpack. We freaked and said we were holding it for you. She told us to give it back or she'd kick us out. We left it in your car when you gave us a ride to school. And then..." Jordan's breath hitched. "We never thought it would stick. You were so clean. We never imagined...." A sob shook her shoulders. "We were so afraid of what mama would do to us. We didn't know what to do. It wasn't supposed to happen like that. I'm sorry. So sorry."

Fourteen. They were fourteen. Same age as Millie. They panicked. Broken taillight. Flap of a butterfly's wing. Veronica fought the wave of sadness and betrayal that threatened to overwhelm her. "I don't know what you want me to say."

She left Jordan and pushed through the door leading to the toilet stalls, her lips pressed together to keep from spewing her dinner on the floor.

VERONICA SPLASHED HER face with cold water and dried it on a rough brown paper towel. She caught sight of herself in the mirror. *So much. So much they took from me. Dee. My fellowship. My career. Fuck. Would it have lasted with Dee? Would I have been happy in a vanilla relationship? I wouldn't have Millie now. I wouldn't have ever known how much working with horses feeds my soul.*

The sounds of the DJ and a pounding beat rattled the walls of the bathroom. Veronica rinsed her mouth again before she wiped her face dry. With a fake smile plastered on her face, she pushed through the door and conversation stopped. Aunt Jean and Jordan were sitting on the small sofa in the anteroom. Her aunt was holding a lighter in one hand and a pack of cigarettes in the other.

"Ah there she is, our family freak. Where did you leave the great white hope?" Her aunt's voice dripped acid. She left the couch and stepped in front of Veronica, using her considerable bulk to block the door.

Jordan grabbed her mother's arm. "Mama. Let it go. Please." Her voice was shrill, panic clear in the tone of her voice.

Tell her. Tell her what her kids did to you. Tell her you know she turned in her own niece. That her kids lied to her. She won't believe it. Doesn't matter now, does it? Be cool. Don't ruin their lives. They were kids.

Her aunt looked down her nose at Veronica. "You're in the wrong bathroom."

"Mama, don't." Jordan lifted her gaze to Veronica's eyes. Her voice quavered.

Pain. Fear. Regret. Why ruin their lives? For what? Why waste my time? Fuck.

Aunt Jean raised her voice. Her breath smelt of wine and cigarettes. "It says quite clearly 'ladies' room."

Veronica shook her head and blew out a breath. "Not sure why you're in here then, Aunt Jean, cause you are not now, nor have you ever been, a lady." She smiled at her cousin, touched two fingers to her heart in a salute, and left her aunt sputtering in the bathroom.

Chapter Twenty-Two

MILLIE'S HEARTY LAUGH and her cousin Walter's high-pitched giggle greeted her when she got back to the table. They had their jackets off, their ties were loose, and their sleeves were rolled up. Their heads almost touched as they talked.

"Hey, babe," Veronica called over the music.

Millie tilted her head, an easy smile on her lips, and raked her gaze over Veronica. "I was about to come looking for you. Walter requested some songs for us."

Veronica rolled her eyes at her cousin. "Walter, what did you do?"

Walter tipped his chair back on two legs and slung his arm around Millie. "Making sure you treat your woman right."

The familiar strains of Etta James's "Sunday Kind of Love" blared through the speakers. Millie rose from her chair, grabbed Veronica's hand, and led her out to the dance floor. Couples crowded the floor, swaying against one another.

Millie leaned close. "Do you want to lead, *Ceannard*?" Her breath tickled Veronica's ear.

Veronica slipped her arm around Millie's waist and held her hand as Millie rested her hand on Veronica's shoulder. *This. This wouldn't have happened. I wouldn't have her. I would have missed the love of my life.* They swayed to the music, Millie following Veronica smoothly around the floor as they danced. Veronica held Millie's gaze. *Love. She loves me. Loves me for all I am.* Veronica clutched Millie to her and kissed her hard, ignoring the catcalls and whistles from the cousins' table.

The song switched to Beyoncé's "Single Ladies." Millie slipped out of her arms and Walter joined them. Veronica laughed as the two of them danced and lip-synced the song perfectly. Veronica joined them, never taking her eyes from Millie's face.

THEY PUSHED THROUGH the door to Veronica's room. Millie tossed the bedraggled bouquet she had wrested from the bridesmaid scrum onto Veronica's desk. Veronica kicked the door closed as she flipped the switch and lit the bedside lamp. They tumbled onto the bed. Veronica tugged Millie's shirt loose from her trousers and smoothed her hands over the skin of her low back before she raked it with her short nails.

Millie mouthed her neck while unbuttoning her shirt. Veronica lifted her chin and moaned.

"Ssh, *Ceannard*, they'll hear you."

Shirts and jackets were tossed aside, belts clinked as they were unbuckled, shoes thudded on the floor, and then they were naked. Millie pressed a thigh between Veronica's legs as she kissed her. Her lips slow and gentle, she resisted Veronica's attempt to speed up their tryst.

"Slow, *Ceannard*, that's what you always tell me." Millie wrapped her fingers around Veronica's wrists and pushed her arms over her head before she gathered both wrists in one hand. She kissed Veronica's neck and then her mouth as she held her in place. Millie pulled back and pressed tiny kisses along Veronica's jaw. "Lie back, *Ceannard*, and let me. Please."

Veronica knotted her hands together, and Millie kissed her way down her body. She stopped to trace her tongue over her hipbone and then lower to the crease of her thighs and then her mouth was on Veronica. Hot, wet, and wicked, Millie's tongue traced a path from her clit to her slick center. Veronica gasped as Millie thrust her tongue deep and then up to circle her clit, lazily. Gentle pressure and then a single thick finger curled inside to rub her sweet spot. Veronica lifted her hips, seeking more. "Oh don't. Don't tease. Please, Millie."

Millie hummed against her, the vibrations sending a new wave of want through Veronica. "Please, Millie. More." She covered her mouth with her hand to stifle her loud groans.

Millie slipped her finger out and then slid two back in. She licked leisurely, timing it with her strokes, and Veronica panted and rolled her hips into Millie's mouth, chasing the sensations she craved. Millie gripped her hips and held her still, taking her time.

"Oh. I'm so close. Please don't stop." Veronica whispered. "Please."

Millie held her there, on the edge of coming, until Veronica was delirious with pleasure. Chest heaving, she gripped Millie's head and held her in place as she ground out her pleasure. Millie licked and sucked until Veronica pushed her away, too sensitive to continue.

Millie collapsed next to her on the bed. "You're not so good at following directions." She flicked Veronica's nipple, and Veronica arched up off the bed and shuddered through an aftershock.

Millie kissed the side of her neck and snuggled close.

Veronica groaned. "Give me a minute. I need to catch my breath."

Millie took Veronica's hand and placed it between her legs. Her thighs were slick and her clit hard under Veronica's fingers. "Won't take much, *Ceannard*."

Veronica jacked Millie's clit once, twice, and then Millie was clutching her arm as she came without a sound.

Veronica rolled on top of Millie and plunged her fingers deep. Millie wrapped her legs around Veronica and opened herself as Veronica fucked her. "Give it to me, babe, give me everything."

"Take it, *Ceannard*, take all of it." Millie whispered as she cupped the back of Veronica's neck and stared into her eyes and came again.

VERONICA SWIGGED THE last of her coffee. "I'm sorry we can't stay longer, Mom."

Millie carried their suitcases through the kitchen and out of the front door to the car.

"Me too." Her mother pressed a quick kiss to her cheek. "You keep us posted on how things are going. And if we need to reserve the hall for next year." Her mother tipped her head toward the door. "She suits you, Veronica, more than Dee ever did."

"She does, doesn't she?" Veronica turned to watch Millie as she loaded their bags into the car. "Thanks, Mom, for everything."

Her mom hugged her hard and stepped back.

Millie came back through the door to the kitchen. She took Veronica's mother's hand in both of hers. "Thank you for your hospitality, Cora. And the tips." She winked at Veronica's mom.

Veronica glanced from her mom's face to Millie's. "What tips?"

Millie smirked and let go of Veronica's mother's hands. Her mom patted Veronica's arm. "You need to go now, Ronnie. You'll miss your flight."

She caught her mother's wink at Millie as she mimed holding a telephone and silently mouthed, "Call me." Veronica huffed out a breath to hide her smile.

Epilogue

ONE YEAR LATER

"Hold still. I'm never going to get this thing tied." Walter frowned at Veronica. "She's not going to run off. Why are you fidgeting?"

"We're going to be late."

"We won't be if you hold still." Walter yanked on the ends of her bow tie. "There."

"Are we ready?" The minister peered at them over her glasses. "You have the ring?"

Walter patted his vest pocket. "Right here."

It's happening. It's really happening. Veronica smoothed her hand down the front of her suit and pressed a trembling hand against her stomach. *Get it together. Vomiting is not an option.*

"Follow me. Just like we rehearsed." The minister opened the door and Veronica and Walter fell into step behind her as she led them from the vestry.

Veronica gazed out over the pews. Dr. Kerr and Jaya Pomroy were in the second row right behind Veronica's mom and dad. Her sister Violet and her husband held hands in the front row. She made eye contact with Veronica and raised her hand and waved. Benita, Tessa, and June had all made the trip from Skye, along with Martha, Myfanwy, and Lucia. As the first notes of the wedding march sounded, she looked to the back of the church. Millie walked down the aisle, escorted by Myfanwy.

Veronica curled her fingers into her palm to keep them from shaking. Millie stepped up on the altar. Veronica turned to face her and held her hand out palm up. Millie placed her hand in hers, and they turned as one to face their future.

About the Author

Brenda Murphy writes short stories and novels. She is a member of Romance Writers of America and the Golden Crown Literary Society. When she is not loitering at her local library and writing, she wrangles one dog and an unrepentant parrot. She writes about life, books, photography, and writing on her blog, writingwhiledistracted.com.

I hope you enjoyed reading this book as much as I enjoyed writing it. For information on book signings, appearances, work in progress snippets, previews and sneak-peaks, sign up for my email list at:

Website: www.brendalmurphy.com

Facebook: www.facebook.com/Writing-While-Distracted

Twitter: @bmurphysideshow

Other books by this author

Dominique and Other Stories
One

The Rowan House series
Sum of the Whole
Both Ends of the Whip
Knotted Legacy

Coming Soon from Brenda Murphy

Double Six

Excerpt

"Are you sure this is what we need?" Elaine lowered the hairbrush and shifted her gaze to Martha's face reflected in the dressing table mirror.

Martha quirked her mouth. "We've been over this. Just give her a chance. You can't keep up with our client requests."

Elaine tossed the brush on the top of the dressing table. "Because you and Lucia don't help." She swept her titian hair back and up into a high ponytail.

Martha handed her an elastic. "We're not having this argument again. Lucia and I are finished with that side of the business. We can't keep putting people off or they'll find other houses to visit."

Elaine knotted a hunter green ribbon in her hair. "Oh please. Like they could find anyone like me. Or what we offer here." She shoved away from the vanity and turned to face her sister. "Fine. We'll see how she handles herself. But the timing sucks."

Martha placed her hands on her sister's shoulders. "We had to work with the dates she gave us. Lucia thinks she'd be a good fit. We've had our trip planned for a long time. We trust you to make a good decision."

Alone. Again. "I'm not worried about making a wrong decision. Who'll sub for her? Benita and Fallon are on holiday. No one else likes heavy pain play."

Martha grinned wickedly at Elaine. "Maybe you could give it a go?"

Elaine rolled her eyes at her sister. "The switch gene is not in me. Go on, go on your holiday. I'll figure it out." *Somehow. Damn, I miss Roxy.*

Also Available from NineStar Press

Connect with NineStar Press

www.ninestarpress.com

www.facebook.com/ninestarpress

www.facebook.com/groups/NineStarNiche

www.twitter.com/ninestarpress

www.tumblr.com/blog/ninestarpress